WINTER KISSES AT ROSEFORD CAFÉ

FAY KEENAN

Boldwood

First published in Great Britain in 2022 by Boldwood Books Ltd.

Copyright © Fay Keenan, 2022
Cover Design by Alice Moore Design
Cover Photography: Shutterstock

A CIP catalogue record for this book is available from the British Library.

Paperback ISBN 978-1-80280-563-5

Large Print ISBN 978-1-80280-559-8

Hardback ISBN 978-1-80280-558-1

Ebook ISBN 978-1-80280-556-7

Kindle ISBN 978-1-80280-557-4

Audio CD ISBN 978-1-80280-564-2

MP3 CD ISBN 978-1-80280-561-1

Digital audio download ISBN 978-1-80280-555-0

Boldwood Books Ltd
23 Bowerdean Street
London SW6 3TN
www.boldwoodbooks.com

For Cory.

1

'Mummy, Mummy!' The shrill, excited voice of Lucy Cameron's eight-year-old daughter, Megan, rang across the living room as she peered through the window that faced onto Roseford's usually quiet main street.

'Come on, darling,' Lucy replied, frantically trying to tie her own hair back in a ponytail, pack Megan's small school bag with her lunch and her reading book and scribble a shopping list. Megan got so easily distracted; even the sight of the chatty, combative group of sparrows who congregated regularly on the pavement outside the house was enough to put her off finding her shoes.

'But come and see! There's a massive lorry outside and it's got Santa painted on it.'

Lucy hurried to the window. 'They can't just stop there!' she said in exasperation. 'How's anyone supposed to get past?' *How am I going to get out of my parking space?* she thought. Since the houses in Roseford, the beautiful historic village where Lucy lived, were all listed buildings, very few residents had the luxury of off-road parking. In addition, being able to park outside your own house was becoming more of a rare privilege since the British Heritage Fund had taken over Roseford Hall, a charming seventeenth-century manor house just off the main square.

Lucy glanced at her watch. If she was going to get Megan to school and then get back in time to open her café, she had to get a shift on. Since Roseford's primary school had closed two years ago, Megan was at the one in the next village, and it was a good ten-minute drive away.

'Come on, munchkin.' Lucy assumed her best no-nonsense tone. 'Get your coat from the hall. Your shoes should be there, too.'

'They're not, Mummy!' Megan's little voice came from the hallway.

Lucy sighed. Systems were her survival mechanism, and even a minute's disruption when time was tight could derail things. 'Check in the cupboard under the stairs,' she said wearily, wondering, for a moment, if in a tiredness-infused flash of inattention she'd shoved them in there with the vacuum cleaner.

'Found them!' Megan said. She came scampering back through from the hall, and plonked herself down on the rug by the fireplace to do up the Velcro fastenings on her black patent school shoes. As she stuck one foot out in front of her while she fastened the other one, Lucy noticed there was a hole forming on the sole. Great. Megan went through shoes like no other child in her class. It looked like she'd need a trip to Taunton over the Christmas holidays for a new pair. Hopefully, the shoes would hold out for the last few weeks of the autumn term.

Just as they were zipping up their coats and heading out of the door, Lucy's phone pinged with a message. Glancing down at the screen as she pulled the door closed, Lucy saw it was from her friend Serena.

So... have you seen them yet? Tell me EVERYTHING when you do!

Lucy, despite her school run stress, smiled. Serena was a huge fan of, as she put it, 'cheesy happily-ever-after movies', and had been incandescent with excitement when the story had broken online about Roseford's new temporary residents. Lucy, despite her own history, and knowing that *happily-ever-after* wasn't exactly the way most things in life went, wasn't averse to a festive movie or three herself, and she and Serena had spent many happy evenings with Megan between them on the sofa watching the latest Hallmark Channel offerings on cold winter nights.

Lucy looked at the time and picked up the pace. She hated being late and was embarrassed at the thought of Megan having to go into her classroom after everyone else. Striding over to her car, she settled Megan into her car seat and then glanced out at the road. The lorry that Megan had spotted out of the window was still in situ, taking up most of the road.

Roseford boasted a picturesque village square, but unfortunately, with history came inconvenience. The road was narrow, barely wide enough to fit two modern cars through in places until it opened up into the square. There was no way she was going to be able to get out of her parking space and past the lorry.

Sighing in irritation, she walked round her car and out into the road, where the lorry had stopped. Heading towards its cab, she saw that the driver was on his phone. Pointedly, seeing him catch sight of her, she glanced at her watch. He gave a quick nod, finished his conversation and then wound down the window.

'Can I help you?' he asked.

Lucy gave a quick, encouraging smile. 'Can you move the lorry, please? I've got to get my daughter to school, and I can't get out of my parking space.'

'Sorry, love,' the driver responded. 'I need to get clearance before I can go anywhere. Shouldn't be long, though.'

'Can't you just pull forward a few feet?' Lucy persisted. 'I really do need to get my daughter to school.'

The driver looked in front of him, and it was then that Lucy realised that he was just one of a convoy of vans, lorries and other assorted vehicles who were forming a queue, snaking back from the turning to Roseford Hall and right past her house.

'The gates are still locked,' the driver continued. 'Sorry, though. Wish I could help.'

'Isn't there someone you could call?' Lucy's patience was starting to wear even thinner. 'I really do need to get out.'

'I've just been on the phone,' the driver said, his own tone exasperated. 'They're trying to locate the groundskeeper to get the gates open. I'm afraid I can't really do any more than that, love. I've been on the road since four o'clock this morning, so I'm just as keen to get moving as you are.'

Trying not to bristle at the unasked-for 'endearment', Lucy forced another smile. 'Fair enough.' She turned away, and as she did so, the deep rumble of the engines of the lorries in front sent a smell of diesel through the air.

'Looks like the gates are open,' the driver called to Lucy's retreating back. She raised a hand in acknowledgement, and then glanced at her watch. She had five minutes before the school gates closed and she'd have to send Megan in through the school's reception. Knowing that it would probably take just as long for the convoy to move off the main road, she gave a sigh of resignation, opened her car door and got in.

'Are we going now, Mummy?' Megan asked.

'Any minute now, sweetheart,' Lucy replied, clenching her hands on the steering wheel. She'd never been that good at responding to circumstances beyond her control, and knowing that there was nothing else she could do but wait was little comfort.

Why did this bloody film crew have to descend on Roseford anyway? Until a couple of years ago, no one had heard of the place. There'd been a few big UK drama productions that had 'borrowed' the High Street for exterior shots over the years, but nothing like this. Those crews had been so small that they'd stayed in rooms above the local pub, the Treloar Arms, and, despite the inevitable set dressing and inconvenience, they'd tried their best not to disrupt the lives of the residents of the village.

This production, though, was something else entirely. It was guaranteed to turn everyone's lives upside down. And having her life turned upside down was absolutely the last thing Lucy needed, having only just started to feel as though she was back in control.

Lucy breathed a sigh of relief, brought back out of her brooding, when she saw the lorry start to move. She slapped on her indicator and pulled out between that and the next truck behind it, and began the slow crawl round the bend and up the High Street towards the main road, and Megan's school in the next village. If this first morning was anything to go by, having even more strangers in Roseford was going to be a real challenge.

2

'So? Have you seen him yet?'

Serena's voice cut into Lucy's thoughts as she tried to focus on the mid-morning orders that were rapidly filling the tables in Roseford Café. Although Roseford Hall was closed to the public from November to January, plenty of people still liked to come to the village and wander around the historic square, and this, more often than not, was good news for the café. Lucy had bought the café and the adjoining house, with a little help from her mother, three years ago when Megan had started school. There was also a regular trickle of customers who came for the winter writers' and artists' retreats at Halstead House, at the other end of Roseford. Halstead House had opened its doors the year after Roseford Hall and so far had been busy all year, according to Stella Simpson, who co-ran the retreats with her partner, Chris Charlton. So, even though the winter months could be leaner than the summer, Lucy still made enough to keep the café afloat. The local book club took a table every month on a Saturday afternoon, and she had a good group of village regulars who liked to come in and exchange news and gossip over a slice of cake and a latte.

'Who?' Lucy asked, double-checking the trays of sandwiches, warming vegetable soup and drinks she'd put together. The café specialised in light meals, hearty soups and mouth-watering cakes, making it the perfect stopgap when you were exploring Roseford and its history. If people wanted a bigger lunch, they could always go to the local pub, the Treloar Arms, a few doors down. It also meant that she could do a lot of preparation in advance, which cut down on her stress considerably.

'Oh, don't be dense,' Serena replied. 'Him. The teen idol. The bloke from *High School Dreams* that you had the most thumping crush on all through your GCSEs and A Levels. The swoonsome guy who probably made you a little more susceptible to you-know-who than you should have been!'

'No.' Lucy flipped her order pad shut briskly. 'I haven't. Why? Should I have done?'

'What? You mean you don't know?' Serena's eyes widened in surprise. 'Look, I know your life mostly revolves around getting Megan to school and cutting the perfect sandwich triangles these days, but even you, with your determination to stay off social media, must know that Finn Sanderson is the lead in this cheesy Christmas movie they're shooting at Roseford Hall.'

Lucy's heart gave a huge thump and she nearly dropped the tray she'd picked up. 'What?'

Serena laughed and assumed a mock-American accent. 'I kid you not. Finn Sanderson, erstwhile teen idol and washed-up singing sensation, is looking to revitalise his career by starring in FilmFlix's new romantic movie, *A Countess for*

Christmas, shooting in the picturesque English village of Roseford this winter.'

'Aren't Christmas movies usually all filmed in the summer?' Lucy said, looking for reasons as to why what Serena was saying couldn't *possibly* be true. 'I mean, they're all snow machines and cosy sweaters when it's twenty-five degrees outside, aren't they?'

'Well, ordinarily, yes,' admitted Serena. 'But for whatever reason, and don't ask me why, this one's shooting now, for release next year.' She shrugged. 'But anyway, Finn Sanderson's coming here, to our very own Roseford. How cool is that?'

'It would be cool if I was still a teenager,' Lucy said. 'But since the cast are very unlikely to have anything to do with us plebs in the village, what difference does it make?'

Despite her nonchalant tone, Lucy's heart rate still hadn't returned to normal. 'He's probably being put up at some five-star hotel miles from here anyway. Getting brought in by a stretch limo thirty feet long. We won't see him.'

'Well, we won't with an attitude like that!' Serena said. She regarded her friend shrewdly. 'You can't say you're not a *tiny* bit excited? It's the first big film role he's had since *High School Dreams* ended. And...' She trailed off tantalisingly.

'And what?' Lucy picked up the tray again.

'It's the first time Finn Sanderson and Montana de Santo have acted onscreen together since the show ended! Imagine! They've got a romantic Christmas movie to rekindle all of that chemistry that we both swooned over when we were younger. FinnTana in the flesh! Now tell me you're not interested.'

Lucy laughed at the reminder of the smashed name for the romantic pairing of Finn Sanderson and Montana de Santo that was the shorthand way to refer to them at the height of their fame. 'All right, all right. If I admit I'm a little bit, er, *intrigued*, will you let me get on and serve Mr and Mrs Robertson their elevenses?' She walked past Serena and out into the main area of the café.

'You're not getting off that easily,' Serena called after her. 'I bet you'll have binoculars trained on the Hall every chance you get. After all, from your back garden you can virtually see in through the front door!'

'I'll leave that to you,' Lucy replied. 'Text me later if you want to come over this evening for a glass of wine in front of *Bridgerton*.'

'Sounds good, unless I get a better offer,' Serena replied. 'But I doubt Charlie's got any plans to take me anywhere more exotic than the pub.'

'Same old Charlie, then.' Lucy shook her head. 'I don't know why you put up with it.'

'It's not like there are many other marketable options,' Serena replied. 'Although, now the film crew's moved in, perhaps I'll find myself a gorgeous movie star to warm my nights, and my bed!'

'I'm quite happy with a hot water bottle warming my bed,' Lucy laughed. 'But you go for it. I can live vicariously through you.'

Serena sighed. 'One day, you're going to realise that there's more to life than serving scones to tourists and avoiding the school run mothers. I hope I'm still alive to see it!'

'I'm quite happy with things the way they are, thank you,' Lucy said primly, carefully placing a pot of tea and a couple of the aforementioned scones on a plate on the next tray. But as Serena sauntered out of the café and back to her temporary office at her mum's house a couple of roads away, Lucy couldn't help the frisson of excitement that shot through her at the thought of Finn Sanderson being in the same village as her. Surely, even though she was a respectable, mature, sensible grown-up, she was allowed a little moment to relive her schoolgirl fantasies? Maybe even a few more moments to scroll through Twitter to relive the best 'FinnTana' moments from yesteryear? Then, shushing those thoughts, she busied herself with the next orders. After all, a real heart-throb Hollywood star was hardly likely to drop his standards far enough to visit a quiet little café like this, even if he was filming a hundred yards away, was he?

3

The lunchtime rush was just revving up when Lucy glanced up from cleaning the table by the window that looked out onto the main street to see a harassed-looking woman walking in through the front door of the café. She had an earpiece dangling on a wire on her shoulder, and was talking animatedly into a mobile, chattering in a language that Lucy vaguely understood to be English, but littered with a whole manner of technical terms that seemed like they belonged in another world.

'Yeah, yeah, that sounds good. Get the dolly set up on the tracks and then make sure it's in position ready to do the first cover shots of the house after lunch.'

She approached the counter, and Lucy hurried to see what it was she wanted.

'Hi,' she said brightly as the woman glanced at her. 'What can I get you?'

The woman gestured impatiently to the phone, and Lucy, slightly put out, waited for her to finish her conversation. She scanned the café for any customers who needed her immediate attention, but they all seemed perfectly content.

Eventually, after a minute or two, the woman ended her call.

'So, there's been a bit of a cock-up at Roseford Hall,' she said, without preamble. 'I've got a skeleton crew with more due later this afternoon, not to mention the talent, and nothing to feed them. Can you help?'

'Depends,' Lucy replied. 'How many people are you talking?'

'Fifty, give or take. Can you whip something up? There doesn't seem to be an Uber Eats service out this far. The nearest takeaway is five miles away and doesn't open until five o'clock and I've got a ravenous crew.'

'What about the pub?' Lucy asked. The Treloar Arms was better equipped to deal with that number of covers, and Dave the landlord would appreciate the business in the winter.

'They're up to their neck already, and their sous chef's out sick,' Nicole replied. 'So can you do it?'

'Well, fifty might be pushing it at this notice, but I'll see what I can do,' Lucy said. 'There's Southgate's Stores a couple of doors down as well. They might be able to fill in where I can't.'

'How long will it take you to whip up a few sarnies?' the woman asked, eyeing Lucy keenly.

'Give me an hour,' Lucy replied. 'I've got a couple of vats of vegetable soup on the go if you want them, too.'

'Great,' the woman replied. 'I'll send someone down in a van to collect and settle up with you. Can you get an invoice sorted as well?'

'I'll do my best.' Lucy gave her brightest smile. 'Any food allergies? Preferences?'

The woman rolled her eyes. 'Probably, but at this point, I'm past caring. Can you do a few veggie options and fling a bit of gluten-free bread in, if you have it, to cover all options?'

'Sure,' Lucy said. 'I'm Lucy, by the way.'

'Nicole.' The woman thrust a hand forward. 'Look, I'm sorry to spring this on you, but I didn't know the caterers had let us down until I got the call half an hour ago, and now I've got to add that to my list of crap to sort out before the main cast gets here. All hell will break loose if there's nothing to feed them when they arrive.'

'Leave it with me,' Lucy replied, sounding a lot more confident than she felt. She wasn't completely sure there was enough left in the kitchen to cater adequately for fifty people, but she wasn't about to turn down Nicole's business. After all, in the winter, you couldn't look a gift horse in the mouth.

'Great. I'll send someone down with a van in an hour. Thank you, Lucy.'

'You're welcome.' As Nicole strode out of the café, Lucy let out a long breath. Fifty lunches in an hour? Well, why not? Thankfully, the soup was simmering in two catering tureens in the kitchen, and she had enough bread to put together a few options, provided things didn't get too busy out front. Feeling slightly naughty for doing so, but knowing she'd have to motor if she was going to get everything done before the van arrived, she flipped the sign on the front door to 'closed' and got to work.

* * *

A little over an hour later, Lucy stood back and surveyed her efforts. Fifty beautifully wrapped sandwiches were now stacked in a large bread crate, and she'd packed in the same number of cupcakes and flapjacks as well. The soup would be a bit trickier to transport, so she decided just to unplug the electric tureens, secure the lids and lend them to the crew up at Roseford Hall, hoping she'd get them back ready for the next day's business. Just as she was breathing a sigh of relief at a job well done under pressure, there was a loud rap at the front door. Lucy hurried to see who it was, only to see Nicole on the other side, looking even more harassed.

'Hi,' she said as Lucy opened the door again. 'Did you manage to get some stuff done for us?'

'Yes.' Lucy smiled, gesturing for Nicole to come in. 'It was a bit of a push, but I got there in the end.'

'Great.' Nicole paused. 'And the invoice?'

'Bugger,' Lucy replied. 'I haven't had time yet, but I can email it over if you give me the address.'

'Sure, sure,' Nicole replied. Her radio crackled, but she ignored it. 'I've brought Theo with a van. Would you like to come up with us to the unit and see what's happening?'

Lucy shook her head. 'I'd love to, but I need to stay open for lunch. This place is kind of a one-woman operation in the winter months.'

'Fair enough,' Nicole replied. She turned to the man who'd just joined her, who Lucy presumed was Theo. 'Can you point him in the right direction, and he'll get loaded up?'

'It's this way,' Lucy replied, leading Theo to the kitchen. In a few moments, he'd loaded the van with the soup and sandwiches, promising to have the soup kettles back to her by the end of the day.

'Goodness knows what we'll do for dinner tonight, but hopefully a new caterer'll be sorted out by then,' Nicole sighed. 'If there's one thing that makes a film set run smoothly, it's decent food.'

'Well, I hope this works for you.' Lucy smiled.

'I'm sure it will.' Nicole waved a hand as she left and Lucy watched the van pull swiftly away. Breathing a sigh of relief that she could now get back to the more usual business of the day, she flipped the sign back to 'Open' and waited for the lunchtime customers to come in. Well, she thought, at least she'd have something a bit different to tell her mum when she phoned her this evening. Her mum lived in Taunton with her new partner, and so was slightly removed from the excitement over the film crew, and its inconvenience. She also still worked full time so, with Lucy working flat out at the café, it was often tricky to see each other. They managed to speak on the phone most days, though, or exchange WhatsApp messages when things got too hectic. It seemed the film production was already starting to make its presence felt in Roseford, and Lucy wondered what chaos it would bring next.

4

Finn Sanderson looked out of the window of the black SUV that had met him at Bristol airport and wished for the thousandth time he'd pushed harder to drive himself. Having spent the past few years living the way he wanted to, splitting his time between his hometown on the outskirts of Vancouver and his apartment in New York, he'd got pretty used to going where he wanted, when he wanted. And while a few years ago he'd have loved the thought of a driver, he found the whole thing more than a bit awkward these days. But he'd signed the contract for this project, and so he had to go with it.

As the SUV counted down the miles and cruised through the English countryside towards the small West Country village that Finn would be calling home for the next six weeks or so, he spent his time alternating between reading the latest version of the script he'd been emailed and getting distracted by the changing scenery. He'd grown up among the huge forests and breathtaking landscapes of British Columbia, and while England didn't quite have the same scale, once the SUV got off the motorway, the quaint villages and towns full of history and heritage caught his eye time after time.

Nothing, however, could have prepared him for seeing the beautiful village of Roseford for the first time. As the SUV dropped down over the hump-backed bridge that led to the village, Finn's eye was drawn to the light sandstone-coloured buildings, the quaint streets leading off the main road and the large market square, decked with tubs of winter pansies all in deep, vibrant violets and yellows. The sun was shining in the bright blue sky above, casting the buildings into stronger relief, and Finn found himself taking in every detail.

'You're staying at the Treloar Arms,' his driver said, glancing back at Finn in the back seat. 'It's a bit tricky to park outside, but I'll do my best.'

Finn leaned forward to get a good look at the pub. 'Just drop me where you can. I don't mind a walk.'

Thankfully, there was a space outside, so Finn was able to jump out of the SUV and, as the driver grabbed his suitcase from the back, he gazed up at the building, taking in the mullioned windows and the sign outside the entrance proudly proclaiming 'Treloar Arms' with the heraldic crest underneath.

Wheeling his suitcase through the front door after thanking the driver, he headed to the bar to check in, immediately noticing the leather banquettes and armchairs that were scattered around the interior, the fire roaring in the grate of the huge fireplace, and the tantalising aromas of food being prepared for the customers who were seated at wooden tables through the bar area. Back in his teen drama days, he'd been banned from eating anything less wholesome than a quinoa salad, but a decade on, and with fewer roles that required him to take his top off, he was partial to a bit of hearty cooking. His mother, who was English, had introduced him to Yorkshire puddings and steak and kidney pies from a young age, and now he was in England, he intended to make the most of the winter offerings of filling, stomach-lining food; costumes permitting, of course.

The barman looked up from the pint he was pulling and gave Finn a brief smile. 'I'll be with you in a sec.'

'No problem,' Finn responded. He noticed, with a flash of amusement, that his accent caused a couple of the diners in the bar to look up from their plates and pints, before hurriedly looking away again. He guessed that, at this time of year, an unusual accent was something to gossip about.

'Hi, I'm Dave Morris, the landlord.' Pint pulled, the barman returned his attention to Finn. 'You checking in?'

'Yeah,' Finn replied. 'The room's under, er, Liberty Productions?'

Dave grinned. 'There're several booked under that name – can you be a bit more specific?'

'Sanderson?' Finn replied. He was tickled that Dave appeared not to recognise him, but the man was probably too old to have watched *High School Dreams* himself, and too young to have grown-up children who might have seen it back in the day.

'Ah, yes. Gotcha. Master suite, second floor, first on the right.' Dave turned away from him to grab an old-fashioned brass key from the key cupboard behind the bar, with a maroon Perspex tag on it. 'We're in the process of getting electronic key card locks,' he said turning back to Finn. 'For now, though, this should keep the masses out.' He passed Finn a piece of card with a key code on it for the door that separated the bar from the accommodation. 'Guard this with your life, though,' he said gravely.

Finn, unsure if he was being sent up, grinned. 'I will.'

'Can I get you a drink, mate, or would you like to get settled in?'

'Thanks, but I'll go and put this upstairs first,' Finn said.

'Okeydoke.' Dave gestured to the back of the bar. 'The accommodation's that way. If you get lost, Marie's up there cleaning. She'll show you the way.'

Finn thanked him, and then trundled his suitcase through the bar. Was he imagining it, or did one or two other people look up as he passed? He'd got used to being able to travel pretty much unnoticed again in the years since his television career had quietened down, his star fading not exactly into obscurity, but certainly dimming its light enough to allow for a relatively quiet existence. He knew, once word got properly out about this new project, he'd be kissing goodbye to that again. At the moment, polite curiosity was about as bad as it was likely to get, unless there were any hardcore fans living in Roseford, of course. But, a decade on, they'd all be grown up and past the screaming stage, he hoped.

As he headed up the stairs and then out onto the Axminster carpeted landing of the second floor, he passed a girl of about nineteen in the corridor, who was carrying a spray bottle and a cloth, obviously finishing off the rooms for the rest of the occupants. He smiled at her and said hello, and she smiled back somewhat nervously, scurrying into the nearest room at the first opportunity. That must be Marie, Finn thought.

Finn felt the jet lag catching up with him. The flight had been more than comfortable, but he suddenly was in serious need of either a cup of coffee or a nap, and as his fingers fumbled to get the brass key in the lock, he shook his head. Perhaps he'd get his head down for an hour or two before heading down to the bar. In the old days, he'd have been straight down there, knocking back a beer or three before making an evening of it, but his nights out were few and far between these days. Anyway, he doubted Roseford had much of a nightlife to speak of, apart from the pub.

The room was tastefully decorated with pale blue walls, a luxurious cream carpet and a huge queen-sized four-poster bed that was easily accommodated within its generous proportions. The front window gave him a wonderful view of the village square, and it was quiet enough, on the second floor, that he couldn't hear the noise from the bar beneath. *I've seen worse*, he thought, and for a sleepy village pub, it was surprisingly roomy.

As if on cue, Finn's phone pinged with a text. Seeing the name on the screen, Finn grinned, despite his tiredness.

Let me know when you get in, baby boy. First round's on me!

Finn shook his head. Trust Mateo Torres to already be raring to go. He dithered about whether to respond, but he really did feel shattered. Deciding he'd text Mateo when he woke up, he wandered over to the bed, and, unlacing his boots quickly, slumped down into the comfort of an Egyptian cotton-covered duvet and pillows. Within two minutes, he was sound asleep.

5

'Hello? Is that Lucy Cameron? Of Roseford Café?' The voice cut into Lucy's tired mind like a scalpel as she answered the call. She glanced at her alarm clock and was stunned to see it was 6 a.m.

'This is she,' Lucy replied, stifling a yawn. 'Who is this?'

'Lucy, it's Nicole from the film set. I'm sorry to call so early. Our caterers have let us down for a second day. Can you supply us with some lunch again?'

Lucy sat up a bit straighter in bed. 'Um. Okay. How many will it be for?'

'Around seventy. A few people came in last night. Can you do it?'

Seventy? And run the café? Lucy felt anxiety clenching in her stomach. She was single-handed as it was, apart from Rachel, who worked part time so that Lucy could have most weekends off. Could she really do all that food and keep the café open? But the winter was the trickiest time, and she'd never do seventy covers in a day in the place itself. Oh, why not?

'Of course,' Lucy replied. 'Same as yesterday? Soup and sandwiches?'

'That would be great,' Nicole said. 'I'll send the van down at about twelve o'clock, if you think you'll have them ready by then?'

Christ, she'd better get cracking. 'That's fine,' Lucy said, sounding calmer than she felt. Thankfully, Theo had returned the soup kettles at close of business last night, washed out and ready to be refilled, but with seventy covers, she'd definitely need to fill both of them again. Thinking rapidly, Lucy realised she'd better book Megan into the school's breakfast club, which opened at seven-thirty. At least that'd give her an extra hour to tackle the order. Ending the call, she jumped out of bed, and went to wake her little girl.

'Come on, little one,' Lucy said, shaking Megan gently awake. 'We're going to go to breakfast club this morning.'

Megan looked at her blearily. 'Will George be there?' she asked.

'I think so,' Lucy replied, although she didn't know either way. George was Megan's new best friend.

After a bowl of cereal, and having made a sandwich for Megan to take for her lunch, Lucy got Megan into the car and set out for school. Luckily, the road was clear this morning, and she made it to the school gates in good time to drop Megan at breakfast club. Kissing her daughter goodbye as she handed her over to the wonderful woman who ran the school's breakfast and after school clubs, she set her mind to the task at hand.

Luckily she kept a large supply of homemade soups in the freezer at the café, although she tried to make them fresh every day. That might help her for this urgent and large food order from the film set. Then it was just a matter of waiting for the bread to arrive, which it usually did around 8.30 a.m. She hoped she had enough sandwich fillings to go around, but then she suddenly had a brainwave. Slowing down, she drew up to the gate of the last cottage before Roseford village centre. There, as ever, was a small shed, just inside the cottage's driveway, which housed trays of free-range eggs and an honesty box. Grabbing a tray and stowing it carefully on the passenger seat, she also saw some jars of plum jam, and took a couple of those as well. They'd do for the batches of scones she was planning on whipping up to go with lunch.

'Right,' she said to herself. 'Come on, Lucy. Get your act together.'

Opening up the café a few minutes later, Lucy felt suddenly overwhelmed at the extra work. Could she *really* do all this, and get it done by twelve o'clock? Although, she reasoned, she'd managed fifty covers in about an hour yesterday, so perhaps it wasn't as impossible as her nerves were telling her. Mindful, now, of the possibility of food allergies and intolerances, it occurred to her that egg sarnies may not be the safest option.

As if reading her mind, Nicole had left her a voicemail, detailing the numbers of crew and cast whose food needed particular care. With relief, Lucy noticed that there were only two dairy intolerances, one coeliac and ten vegetarians on the order. Oh, and one vegan. This might just be doable.

Setting to work, she was momentarily distracted by her phone pinging with a message from Serena.

Guess what? I've got something to get excited about now! Finn's co-star in this cheesy film is arriving today!!! I can't wait to catch a glimpse of Montana de Santo in the flesh!! Xxx

Lucy smiled to herself. Serena had idolised Montana de Santo ever since *High School Dreams* had aired, loving her style, her savvy and her wonderful singing voice. The prospect of possibly seeing her, all these years later, in person, was obviously causing her best friend great excitement. She quickly texted Serena back and promised to keep her eyes open for Montana.

The response came back within seconds.

Pics or it didn't happen! I'm on work calls all day so I can't get out.

Lucy chuckled to herself. She'd try her best to get a snap for her friend. It was the least she could do. Serena spent most of her time in Bristol, where her job was, but she'd been based at her mum's place in Roseford more and more recently, because her job had allowed her to work from home a bit more. She'd often crash out in Lucy's spare room, rather than head back to Bristol or her mother's, and they'd spent many evenings with FilmFlix and a bottle of wine. This suited Lucy far better than going out on the town, with Megan to consider, and meant that the two women had stayed close over the years. In fact, Serena felt like the sister Lucy had never had, and she was a wonderful 'aunt' to Megan, too.

Rushing through the sandwich orders, she finished them just a whisker past eleven o'clock, and with the soup bubbling away, she was able to fully re-open the café just in time for the early lunchtime customers. It must have been the excitement of the morning, but Lucy felt really pleased with herself that she'd brought the order in on time, and as she served a coffee and a slice of carrot cake to a customer who'd come in almost the moment she'd opened back up, she breathed a sigh of relief.

At ten to twelve, Nicole entered the café, still looking harassed, but she did offer a smile to Lucy when she saw her.

'Thanks so much for this,' she said as she loaded up the two bread trays' worth of sandwiches that Lucy had prepared. 'That's the second time you've saved our bacon.'

'No problem,' Lucy replied. As Nicole slammed the back doors of the van and drove off, Lucy realised that she'd forgotten to load up the two soup kettles. Glancing at her phone, she noticed that Nicole's number was only in the call log as 'Private', so she couldn't call her back to alert her.

'Bugger!' Lucy swore. Apologising to a hovering customer, and locking up the café, she popped a 'back in 10 minutes' sign up on the door and hurriedly loaded the tureens into the back seat of her car, strapping them in carefully. Driving at a snail's pace, she trundled towards the iron gates of Roseford Hall, hoping she'd be able to deliver the soup and scuttle back for the lunchtime customers.

'I've got the rest of the lunch order,' Lucy said as the guy on the gate came over. 'Nicole forgot to take the soup.'

'Okay,' the guy replied. 'Give me a sec.' He radioed through to Nicole, who confirmed what Lucy had said. 'Can you drive it round?'

'Sure,' Lucy replied. Despite her worries about the time, and being back to open the café, she couldn't help feeling excited as she entered this strange new world, familiar because of Roseford Hall, but seeming so alien with all of the lorries and different people milling about.

Driving as slowly as she could, so as not to jolt and spill the soup, she navigated the gravel of the car park until she saw Nicole's van up ahead. Bringing her car to a stop, she hurried round to the back seat and hefted out one of the kettles. Christ, the thing was heavy, and although not warm to the touch, Lucy could feel the soup sloshing around as she gingerly walked it to the van.

'Nicole,' she called as she set it down on the open tailgate of the Transit. 'I've brought the soup.'

'Oh, you're a star!' Nicole emerged from round the front of the van. 'I can't believe I forgot it.' She called to a passing technician. 'Col, can you grab the other soup tureen from Lucy and find somewhere in the marquee to plug it in?'

Col nodded and hurried to the back of the van. As he took the soup away, Lucy, feeling suddenly out of place, turned back to her car.

'Got time for a look around?' Nicole asked. 'You're welcome to, if you want.'

Lucy glanced at her watch. 'I really should get back. The lunchtime rush'll be starting soon.'

'It won't take long,' Nicole urged. 'We haven't started shooting yet, we're just setting up, but it's an interesting thing to see.'

Despite the time, Lucy's curiosity was piqued by what already seemed to be a small village of trailers, lorries, marquees and other vehicles being created in the generous grounds of Roseford Hall, with cables running hither and thither, criss-crossing the ground, and various members of the crew setting up equipment, or talking on the site radios. A little way off in the distance were three more trailers, which, Nicole explained, were for the stars of the film, when they got here.

Lucy felt a fizz of excitement at the thought of having the stars from her teenage years so nearby, and couldn't help asking when they were going to arrive.

'Well, Finn got here yesterday afternoon, but he's not officially due to start until after lunch, and Montana's arriving on the evening flight, so she'll be starting tomorrow. Roger Painshaw, the other main actor, is commuting from his home about an hour away, but he's not needed until next week.'

Lucy was a little disappointed that she wasn't likely to see Finn Sanderson in the flesh today, but, she figured, it was probably for the best. Coming face to face with your teen idol would be nerve-racking at best, and embarrassing, too. She was sure to go all stammery and revert back to being the geeky fifteen-year-old who'd watched *High School Dreams* on repeat until her brother had deleted it from the DVR. She'd never really forgiven him for that, even after her mother had bought her the whole series on Blu-ray the next Christmas to replace it.

Of course, these days, with the abundance of streaming services, that wouldn't ever be a problem for her own daughter. Distracted from what Nicole had been saying by those thoughts, Lucy nearly tripped over a trailing black cable.

'Someone needs to put some warning tape on that,' Nicole said, and promptly radioed someone to do so.

'And this is where the camera unit hangs out,' Nicole said as they passed a large lorry, in the back of which an extraordinarily good-looking dark-haired guy dressed in tight blue jeans and a black leather jacket was handling one of the Steadicams, getting it ready to go on the hydraulic tailgate.

'Nicole,' he called as they passed. 'Has Ruby updated the afternoon's set-up yet? Or are we still working to this morning's version?'

'Better ask her, Mateo,' Nicole replied, her face, to Lucy's mind, looking a little tense as she replied. It was probably just the pressure of getting everything ready on schedule, but Lucy was sure she wasn't imagining it when Mateo's gaze lingered a little too long on them both. He looked to be of South American heritage, with warm brown eyes and thick, almost black hair, and a smile that Lucy immediately responded to. *A charmer*, she thought, *but a gorgeous one!*

'Catch you later,' Mateo called as they moved on.

'He's the best cameraman in the business,' Nicole said quietly, 'but he also knows it.'

'So it's not just the egos of the stars in front of the camera that need massaging.' Lucy grinned. 'Is, er, Finn the same?' She felt her face warming slightly at the question, which must have given her away as a fan.

Nicole grinned back. 'Oh, Finn's not like that at all,' she said as they moved on around the grounds. 'He's really easy-going. I worked with him back in the day, when I was just a runner, and he never let fame go to his head. He's just an all-Canadian boy at heart. That's why I agreed to do this film – I knew he'd be great to work with again.'

'And Montana?' Lucy asked, remembering what Serena had said about finding out as much as she could for their next catch-up. 'Is she the same?'

Nicole was about to reply when one of the runners came dashing up to her.

'Finn's PA's here,' she said breathlessly. 'And she says there's nothing suitable for him for lunch from the selection you've produced. Can we get a takeout?'

Lucy blinked, all of Nicole's words about Finn's easy-going nature seeming to ring false. She'd done such a range of sandwiches, surely there was *something* Finn could eat?

'Oh, I'm sure you can sort something,' Nicole replied, glancing hastily at Lucy. 'Just find out what his requirements are and charge it to the unit. Sorry about that,' she said to Lucy. 'Where were we?'

But, as the sun vanished behind a cloud, the enjoyment seemed to have gone from Lucy's experience of the set. 'I really should get back,' she said to Nicole, as they turned back to where Lucy had parked her car. She felt more than a little put out that Finn, or at least his assistant, apparently, had dismissed her efforts to cater so summarily. If not even a sandwich was up to scratch, she had to wonder exactly what this 'all-Canadian boy' considered to be up to par for his lunch.

6

Later that afternoon, Lucy was so fixated on wiping the tables after the lunchtime rush that she almost didn't notice the café's door opening. The gentle tinkle of the bell registered with her, but it had been an unusually busy day and she also had Megan's parents' evening to attend when she shut up shop at 3.30, so she hoped she'd be able to make a swift getaway.

As she placed the menu cards back on the table and turned back to the counter, she noticed a tall, broad-shouldered man standing next to it, swiftly removing his sunglasses now that he was out of the strong winter sunlight, which had suddenly put in an appearance. From the back, she could see long, long legs encased in mid-wash blue jeans and a battered brown leather jacket. When he turned slightly to glance at the menu board behind the counter, Lucy caught sight of a profile that, at one time, she'd have recognised in a split second. She'd had posters of it on her wall for about four years before she'd left home.

Her heart stopped.

It couldn't be *him*, could it?

Awe and remembered teenage fascination did battle with irritation as she took a moment to observe him before she moved back towards the counter. After the short shrift she'd got from his PA that morning, despite the years of adulation she'd given him from her side of the television, she battled not to feel cross. What was he doing here? And what on earth was she going to say to him?

'Um, hello,' she said, scuttling around to the other side of the counter, as if she was trying to use it as a barrier. 'Can I help you?'

God, up close, he was *heartbreaking*. From the carefully dishevelled brown hair, to the warm hazel eyes, to the chiselled cheekbones, down to the elegant neck and broad, broad shoulders, encased in a thick, pale cream jumper, even in casual clothes he exuded movie star charisma. And this was in his downtime. Apart from a few more lines around his eyes, he still looked every inch the heart-throb she remembered.

Lucy gulped, and realised with a start that she was staring. And, worse, she was still clutching the soggy dishcloth she'd been using to wipe the tables.

'Hi,' Finn said, and just with that one word, Lucy's stomach did a little flip. 'Can I, uh, get an Americano to go, please, ma'am?'

'Sure,' Lucy stammered. *Get a grip*, she thought in frustration. After all, what had she said to Serena not twenty-four hours previously? She wouldn't allow herself to act like the same smitten schoolgirl she'd been years ago. That wasn't her now. That much was obvious, from the way Finn Sanderson had just called her 'ma'am'.

Turning away from Finn, she tried to steady her heartbeat

and regulate her breathing. How many times had she dreamed of meeting Finn Sanderson when she was a teenager? And now, here he was, in the flesh. She had to get a hold of herself. Cursing as the hot water she was putting through the coffee machine splashed on her hand, she shook it dry impatiently.

'Are you okay?' Finn had obviously noticed her cock-up, and as she turned back to him briefly, having put the coffee cup safely down first, she managed a smile.

'I'm fine,' she stammered. 'It's, er, it's just been a long day.'

'You should really run that burn under cold water,' Finn continued. 'Or it'll hurt for hours.'

'Oh, it'll be okay,' Lucy said brightly. 'It's an occupational hazard. I've got used to it.' She popped the lid on the Americano and passed it to Finn, hastily removing her hands before they could touch his. She knew, if they had, she'd have made a most undignified noise. She tried to regain some sense of equilibrium by ringing up the coffee on the till.

'Well... thank you,' Finn said, giving her a smile that would have melted an iceberg at a hundred paces.

'You're gorgeous. I mean, you're welcome.' Lucy felt her face burning in mortification. Suddenly, her tongue felt far too big in her mouth and she swallowed hard on a very dry throat. 'Welcome. Very welcome. Always.' God, why wasn't the ground just opening up and swallowing her now?

Finn looked amused as he tapped his bank card against the contactless terminal on the counter. 'Thank you. I'll, er, see you around.'

'Yes, please do. I mean, please come again.' As he turned to leave, Lucy added, with a hint of desperation, 'I'm Lucy, by the way.'

Finn turned back and gave her another smile. 'I'm Finn. It's nice to meet you, Lucy.'

'Bye!' Lucy said, cursing the ridiculous levels of brightness in her tone.

As Finn left the café, Lucy thrust her hand under the small tap beneath the counter and left it there until her fingers went numb.

Stupid, stupid, stupid! she berated herself. All the times she'd fantasised about coming face to face with Finn Sanderson over the years, and when it had actually happened, she'd just acted like any other pathetic fangirl. What a class one, grade A idiot she'd been!

7

Finn Sanderson was used to people, usually women, falling over themselves in his presence, even if it hadn't happened quite so obviously in a long time. When he'd been the male lead in a smash hit TV show, a role that had catapulted him into living rooms right across America, and then made him a star across the world when it was syndicated to twenty-seven further countries, the adulation from fans had been both exhilarating and terrifying. He was, after all, just a guy from Vancouver who'd cherished dreams of acting, but never really done anything of note before his role as the 'all-American' boy next door in *High School Dreams*.

After the show ended, things took a year or two to calm down to the level where he wasn't mobbed every time he left his New York City apartment, but the rise of fan conventions a few years later, where legions of admirers got together to discuss and obsess over every last detail of the show that had run for a mere three seasons, meant that he was thrust, once more, into the limelight; albeit on smaller stages in large chain hotels where the conventions were generally held. Those, some sensible investments and the odd independent film project or a recurring role in a TV show here and there had been enough to keep him financially secure since *High School Dreams* had ended. He had kept his hand in, but he didn't need to work all the time, which suited him. It was his performance in a small stage production in a backstreet theatre off Broadway that had brought him to the attention of the director who'd wanted to cast him in *A Countess for Christmas*.

When the offer had come in, via his agent, for the starring role in FilmFlix's next Christmas project, he'd been torn; did he really want to put himself centre stage again? With exposure came pressures he'd happily lived without for years now, and with those pressures had come ways of anaesthetising them that he'd successfully walked away from, too. Too many of his contemporaries had fallen foul of drugs, booze or other destructions, and Finn, while he'd come close, had found therapy and rehab just in time.

But now, walking the quaint streets of this beautiful English village, he had to admit, there were some perks to taking the job. A couple of months of filming would mean he didn't have to work for the next year if he didn't want to, and a share of the revenue when it hit the streaming platform the following Christmas would keep reaping rewards. His mother, whose family had hailed from Roseford originally, had always talked about the joys of 'a real English Christmas', and it seemed, thanks to a quirk of the filming schedule, he might actually be getting to see one at last.

Of course, he reflected, Christmas movies were usually shot out of season. Actor friends of his who'd starred in them in previous years had always sweated their way through the summer heat in thick, cosy jumpers, waiting for the welcome relief of the snow machine to cool them down. When seasonal films were shot in cooler locations, as had been the vogue for several years (Eastern Europe doubling for some imaginary English-speaking independent nation), the weather still couldn't completely be relied upon, even if filming was pushed back to mid-autumn. Despite this anomaly, FilmFlix had enough faith in Finn and Montana's star quality to hold the release of the film over for twelve months, which meant that they could actually shoot a Christmas film in an English winter. The allure of 'FinnTana' was enough to ensure a huge audience on the streaming platform, and so they were determined to make it work.

And Finn was so glad they'd made that choice, looking at the charming village of Roseford now. On either side of the street, all of the buildings had miniature Christmas trees with white fairy lights attached to their walls, and nearly every shop and house was a riot of holly wreaths, gently tasteful Christmas lights (none of the garish colours and illuminated Santas here), and festive green and red colour schemes. Finn had done enough research on this place to know that it worked closely with the British Heritage Fund, who would, he imagined, have some strict rules on what could and couldn't be put on public display on the house and shop fronts.

As he wandered further through the village, sipping his Americano as he went, he saw that Southgate's Stores was doing good business, and there were still a few tourists mooching around, guidebooks in hand, crossing off things as they went. He was glad he had his sunglasses on; he didn't think he'd be mobbed by the people who chose to frequent

Roseford in the winter (most of them were retired, since it was a weekday and the school holidays didn't start for another few weeks), but he didn't want to risk it. He didn't mind talking to people, and posing for selfies, but there was something to be said for a little anonymity.

All the same, he did notice a woman in her early thirties do a double take when she saw him. She was pushing a buggy with a chatty toddler inside, and as they passed one another on the narrow pavement, Finn stepped out into the road to allow her through. She looked up at him and smiled politely and said thank you, her expression turning into one of incredulity when the penny dropped.

'You're welcome, ma'am,' Finn said, smiling back, but not stopping to prolong the moment. He was amused to hear her muttering, 'No... it couldn't be...' to her little boy as he passed out of earshot. Clearly word hadn't got all the way out yet that he'd arrived in Roseford, for which he was grateful. Once social media fired up again, and the FinnTana army got wind of it, there'd be no escape.

A little further on and Finn paused at the war memorial which stood proud in the village square. Scanning it, he saw, with heartbreaking regularity, the same surnames repeated on the engraving; fathers who'd fallen in the First World War, followed by their sons in the Second. He noted that there were two Treloars on the memorial; clearly the owners of Roseford Hall had also made their sacrifice. Further down, he felt the shock of recognition as he saw his mother's maiden name on the stones. She'd told him her grandfather had been among the dead of the Great War; here was his name, cast in bronze, for all time. He'd seen pictures when his mother had been researching her family history, and he knew that he himself bore a resemblance to the man whose name he was now looking at. Until this point, Finn, whilst an Anglophile, had never truly felt connected to his English heritage. Seeing the name on the war memorial seemed to bring it home to him, at last. Being able to spend some time in Roseford, where he had the family connection, was a big reason for saying yes to the job.

'Er, excuse me?' The polite, timid-sounding voice cut into his reverie. Turning around, he saw a couple of girls in their early teens, obviously students from the local comprehensive school, who'd just been dropped off by bus in the village square, smiling at him and clutching their phones nervously. 'Are you Finn Sanderson, by any chance?'

Here we go, Finn thought. Putting on his best game face, he smiled back at them. 'Yes,' he replied. 'I am.'

'We thought so!' The first girl jumped up and down excitedly. 'My mum used to love your show, what was it called, *High School*... um, something or other, when she was younger.'

'*Dreams*,' Finn said quickly. '*High School Dreams*.'

'Yeah, that's it,' she said. 'She's been showing it to me. It's pretty cool for an old show.'

Finn felt a flicker of amusement. He'd been playing seventeen when he was twenty-five years old at the start of that show, and now, thirteen years later, he supposed he could forgive the girl for calling it, literally, *old school*.

'Anyway,' she continued, 'would you mind if we got a selfie with you? Mum'll be well jel when she sees it. She used to have the biggest crush on you. Dad teases her about it all the time.'

Finn smiled. 'Sure.' He waited for them to get closer, and then ducked down to fit in the frame of the smart phone's lens. At nearly six feet five inches tall, it was a rare thing when he didn't have to stoop for a selfie. Plastering a bright smile on his face, and being mindful not to invade their personal space (although they were quite intent on invading his, he noticed, taking a slight step back), he allowed them to take their pictures.

'Thanks,' the girl said as she put the phone away again. 'I can't wait to get this up on Insta. My mum's gonna go nuts when she sees it.' She giggled. 'What are you doing here, anyway?'

'Oh, just passing the time,' Finn replied. He wasn't quite sure how much he should reveal, given the shoot was only just getting set up. He didn't want this lovely, quiet village to be inundated with old fans of *High School Dreams* on his account.

'Well, bye, then,' the other girl said, 'and thanks for the selfie.'

'You're welcome,' Finn replied, smiling at them.

They giggled and walked off in the direction of the estate of new houses that had been built on the outskirts of the village.

As they left, Finn's smile dropped instantly. The 'game face' was a little out of practise, he thought. He'd better get used to putting it on again. After all, once that selfie hit Instagram, everyone would know where he was. He felt a shiver of unease as he remembered what it had been like at the height of his fame. He couldn't leave his apartment, couldn't go out on a date, couldn't even go to the store for a pint of milk without some paparazzo following him with a long lens. Baseball caps and sunglasses were some protection, but even those were no defence once he was spotted. He hoped that enough time had passed for the publicity to be a little less intense for this new project, but given the advances social media had made in a decade, he worried that it was going to be far worse.

As the sun faded behind a cloud that looked like the presage of snow, Finn shivered, despite his jacket and warm jumper. He couldn't go back there again. This time, he had to protect himself.

8

'Sorry!' Serena mopped ineffectually at the arm of the sofa where she'd spat her mouthful of white wine when, that evening, Lucy gloomily recounted her mishap of a meeting with Finn Sanderson in the café. 'But I mean... really?'

Lucy nodded. 'Yup. Every single detail of what I have just told you is true.'

'And what did he say when you told him he was gorgeous?'

Grimacing, Lucy topped up both their glasses. 'He politely ignored my gaffe and gave me *that* smile. I mean, he must be so used to women falling over themselves in his presence, he didn't even blink.'

'Oh, poor Lucy,' Serena commiserated. 'I bet you never daydreamed about your first meeting with Finn Sanderson going like *that*.'

'You can say that again.' Lucy took a sip of her wine. 'I'm such a twat.'

'Hey,' Serena consoled her friend. 'Don't be so hard on

yourself. Like you said, he's bound to get things like that all the time. He won't have thought anything of it.'

'That's just the point.' Lucy rolled her eyes. 'In my head, when I'd imagined meeting him, I was always completely cool about it. Amusing, articulate, well dressed...'

'And of course, Finn would take one look at you, hear your witty banter and then fall in love with you immediately,' Serena said wryly. 'I thought you'd grown out of all that.'

'I have!' Lucy said indignantly. 'And I'm not stupid enough to believe in love at first sight, especially with a famous movie star who could have anyone he wants. I just wish I'd been *slightly* less of a klutz when I did meet him, so I could look back on the memory in my old age and feel a warm glow of pleasure, rather than the hot flames of embarrassment. Is that too much to ask?'

Serena reached forward and patted her hand. 'I'm sure he's used to it. I wouldn't lose any sleep over it, as my dad would say. And next time he comes in, you'll be better prepared.'

'I'd be surprised if there *was* a next time!' Lucy muttered.

'There might be,' Serena said. 'But for now, let's just get pissed and watch something on telly. I'm sure we can waste an evening revisiting Finn Sanderson's back catalogue. That's sure to make you feel better!'

Lucy contemplated chucking a pillow at her best mate, but figured she'd be the one cleaning more wine stains out of the sofa, so restrained herself just in time.

'Anyway,' Serena continued. 'I saw his co-star arriving earlier on today, when I was out for my lunchtime stroll, and from the way she was moaning at the gates of Roseford Hall, you're better off steering clear of the place while the crew's there.'

'Oh, yeah?' Lucy replied. 'Why was she moaning, then?'

'Well.' Serena leaned forward conspiratorially. 'Apparently, there are no more rooms at the Radisson in Bristol, where she's meant to be staying while she's doing her bit on the shoot, so she's got to stay at the Treloar Arms, and she wasn't happy about that.'

'Really?' Lucy replied. 'I had no idea the actors were staying at the pub, anyway. Dave kept that one quiet.'

'Probably had to sign an NDA or something,' Serena replied. 'Although the way news travels around here, it wouldn't be worth much. And it's not like they haven't had showbiz types staying there before for things. Remember when that Edwardian drama was shot down here before the Treloars handed over the house to the British Heritage Fund? We had half of RADA down here as extras!'

Lucy remembered it well. It had been fascinating to see the filming taking place, though, even if she'd had to stay out of sight while the cameras were rolling. And the karaoke in the pub had proved very popular with the lead actors, she recalled. One memorable evening, she'd found out just how badly one particular British theatre star sang.

'So we might get to see Montana de Santo drinking a pint at the Treloar Arms, as well as Finn Sanderson propping up the bar,' Serena continued. 'Talk about life imitating art – we were both all over FinnTana as a couple back in the day, weren't we?'

'Well, they did have great chemistry,' Lucy replied. 'It's cool that they're back together again for this film, after all these years.'

'Do you reckon they still, *you know*, for old times' sake?' Serena raised a wry eyebrow. 'I mean, they were close for a long time. Perhaps this project might bring them back together!'

Lucy laughed. 'You're as bad as one of those gossip websites. I'm sure they've both moved on since then.'

'And, of course, now he's met you...' Serena's laugh was infectious, and even though her hand still throbbed faintly from the burn, which was almost as hot as her face when she remembered what an idiot she'd made of herself, Lucy laughed too.

'I don't think Montana de Santo has anything to worry about there,' Lucy replied. All the same, she thought, a girl could dream. And after today's embarrassment, perhaps dreaming was the safest thing to do.

9

Early the next morning, Finn was up and in make-up, preparing for the first of a few scenes that would be shot outside, at the front of Roseford Hall.

He glanced at the script for that morning's scene, which wasn't anything too taxing, from his perspective. He was playing the caretaker of 'Harrington Hall', the place where the female lead discovers her royal heritage. This morning, his character, Jack Salmon, would meet Ashley Marchant, the female lead, on the steps of Harrington Hall and introduce himself. Sparks, presumably, would fly.

The sparks, he knew, were pretty much guaranteed. One of the reasons he'd agreed to do *A Countess for Christmas* was because his best friend and former co-star, Montana de Santo, was playing the role of Ashley. Their fizzy onscreen chemistry in *High School Dreams*, where they'd played star-crossed sweethearts Mal and Rebecca and stolen the show nearly every single episode with their 'will they, won't they' romance, had been one of the reasons FilmFlix had been keen to recruit them both. Nearly a decade after their last scene together, the nostalgia bug had bitten and the world needed more of 'Finn-Tana', as they'd been known by the fans.

Finn and Montana had once played their romance for real, but those times were long over. Their relationship had turned to friendship, and an enduring one at that. But, even though they hadn't been romantically involved for years, their old chemistry still attracted new fans. Even if *A Countess for Christmas* retrod a lot of familiar ground, Finn and Montana would guarantee it a good audience.

'Hey, you!' The voice broke into his perusal of the script. 'Want to borrow my reading glasses?'

Finn looked up and grinned. 'Hey, yourself. What time did you get in?'

'Oh, late yesterday evening.' Stopping briefly to kiss him, Montana breezed around the make-up trailer, checking out her reflection in one of the lit mirrors before flumping down in the chair next to Finn's. 'Didn't know which room you were in, so decided not to disturb you.'

'You're staying at the pub, too?' Finn replied. 'I thought you were booked into the Radisson?'

'I was supposed to be,' Montana rolled her eyes, 'but there was some mix-up. I don't know how you can stand the sound of the extractor fan in the kitchen all night. I'm hoping they'll get me back into the Radisson in a day or two.'

'I sleep pretty well these days,' Finn said evenly. Montana, while certainly no diva, was rather more particular about her accommodation than he was, and given that she was the *real* star of the movie, she obviously deserved a bigger hotel. He rather liked the quiet anonymity of staying at the Treloar Arms, though. It gave him the chance to really get to know

Roseford, and hopefully find out a bit more about his mother's family while he was there.

'I'm glad to hear it,' Montana said, a note of mischief in her voice. 'You ready for today?'

'Yup,' Finn replied. 'It'll be fun to be opposite you again.'

'I'm so glad you decided to do this.' Suddenly serious, Montana turned towards Finn, then, realising he had to keep looking into the mirror while Carol, the make-up artist, worked her magic, looked back at his reflection. 'I think it's the right time, you know. For a lot of things.'

Finn raised an eyebrow. 'Oh, yeah? Such as?'

Montana smiled back at him. 'You'll see.' She turned her chair to face him. 'I want to hug you so hard, but I guess it'll have to wait until after we've done this scene.'

'I'll hold you to that,' Finn replied gently. 'I've missed you, Montana.'

'I've missed you too,' Montana replied. There was a brief pause between them.

'How's Sam?' Finn asked as Montana sat back in the chair.

'Great, as far as I know,' Montana replied.

Finn raised an eyebrow. 'As far as you know?'

Montana sighed. 'We broke up about six weeks ago. It just wasn't working. We decided we needed different things.'

'I'm sorry. I know how happy you were.'

Montana shrugged. 'It'd been coming for a while. It was amicable in the end, thank God.'

'Why didn't you tell me?'

'I didn't want to worry you. You had enough on your plate as it was.'

Finn, seeking tacit permission from Carol, turned in his

chair and took one of Montana's hands in his. 'I'd have been there for you, Montana. I'll *always* be there for you.'

Montana smiled. 'I know. But sometimes it's just easier to deal on my own. And I'm fine. Honestly. I'm looking forward to making this movie with you. Let's focus on that and do the best we can.'

'Sounds like a plan,' Finn replied. The moment was broken a few seconds later by the third assistant director poking her head around the door of the make-up trailer.

'Montana, you're wanted in costume,' the third AD said as she caught sight of Montana in the chair next to Finn.

'Sure thing,' Montana replied. 'I'll be right there.' She stood, and Finn ducked away as Montana, unable to resist mischief making, kissed him on the cheek again. 'See you on set, Jack Salmon.'

Tutting, Carol wiped Montana's lipstick off Finn's cheek.

'Sorry,' Finn said. 'It's been a while since we've seen each other.'

'Well, maybe keep the passionate reunions until you've done the scene, if you can.'

Finn grinned. 'We will.' He looked in the mirror. Jack Salmon's costume was a tweed jacket, a sensible white shirt with a crimson cravat and a pair of cream cord trousers; a typically 'English' look, considering that the production wanted him to keep his Canadian accent. But, he reflected, Christmas movies rarely made any actual narrative sense; that was part of the fun. His hair, prone to spikiness without a good handful of product, was already starting to break free from the side parting that had been imposed upon it, and Carol gave it the once-over with a fine-toothed comb and a bit more wax to set it in place.

'There you go,' she said, once she'd finished. 'Try not to fiddle with it too much before you're needed on set.'

'I'll do my best.' Finn stood up from the chair, stooping slightly from the low ceiling of the trailer. 'Thank you, Carol.'

'A pleasure,' Carol replied. Right on cue, the third AD popped her head round the door again.

'We're ready on set, Finn,' she said.

'I'll be right there,' Finn replied. This was it. He'd done an interior scene yesterday evening, but this was the first time he and Montana would be onscreen together, and he needed to give it his all. It was, after all, what much of the audience would have been waiting for. Exiting the make-up trailer, he glanced up at the sky, which was an optimistic shade of blue, and felt that familiar sense of anticipation as the character he was playing began to unfold inside him. He looked the part of Jack Salmon on the outside; now it was time to bring him to life.

10

Later that day, Lucy was preparing herself for a longer evening than usual. The Roseford Christmas Countdown Night had been brought forward slightly to accommodate the film crew's schedule, as they'd requested that the street be closed off for a few days in the first week of December to allow them to film their own version of a festive village evening. Therefore, Lucy had been baking up a storm for sale in the café that night; people came from far and wide to wander the streets of the village, and, while access to Roseford Hall would be limited because of the film crew already being in situ, there was still plenty to see and do.

The door of the café opened, and the bell tinkled brightly as Stella Simpson, co-owner of Halstead House, the writers' and artists' retreat at the other end of Roseford, came through the door.

'Hi, Stella,' Lucy called from the kitchen, where, thankfully, she could still keep an eye on the activity in the café. 'I'll be with you in just a sec.' Sweating from the heat of the oven, she pulled out a tray of just cooked mince pies, all topped with delicately formed holly leaves rendered in pastry, and put them on the counter.

'No rush,' Stella replied. 'I'm on my way to see Simon at the Hall, and I just thought I'd take him a slice of your red velvet cake if you've got one or two to spare. And a couple of coffees, of course!'

'Sure thing,' Lucy replied, wiping her face and removing the smudge of flour from the tip of her nose where it had settled during her frantic baking session. Simon, the current Lord Treloar, lived in the parts of Roseford Hall that hadn't been taken over when the British Heritage Fund had acquired the Hall a few years back. Essentially he was now the site manager, and kept himself busy implementing the BHF's plans to keep the future of Roseford Hall secure. 'How's he doing with the intrusion from the film crew?'

'That's what I'm going to find out,' Stella said, sitting herself down at the table nearest the counter while she waited for Lucy to prepare her order. 'He's pretty used to people tramping all over the Hall, what with it being open to the public for nine months of the year, but I know he was hoping for a slightly quieter few months, just to catch up. The film's pretty much put paid to that, for several weeks at least.'

'But it must be exciting, as well,' Lucy said as she decanted two flat whites into Stella's proffered reusable coffee cups. 'I mean, we all loved *High School Dreams*, didn't we? It's cool to think of its stars being so close to us in Roseford.'

Stella wrinkled her nose. 'I don't remember much about it, to be honest. I was that annoying teenager who decried popular culture and refused to watch what everyone else was watching. I spent my evenings reading Proust and watching

Channel 4, I'm afraid.' She burst out laughing, and Lucy realised she must have an incredulous expression on her face. 'No, it's my own fault,' Stella continued. 'I was even more of a nerd back then than I am now. But if Simon can impart any gossip about what's happening on set, I'll be sure to let you know.' Stella shook her head. 'Although Simon's older than us... it might have passed him by altogether. Oh god,' she groaned. 'I can just imagine him going up to Finn or Montana de Santo and asking them, in all seriousness, what they do on set!'

'I can *so* see that happening!' Lucy giggled. She liked Simon a lot, and she'd known him since he was a gangly teenager and she was a scruffy eight-year-old. Somehow, though, he still radiated a lack of understanding of the modern world, as he always had. She supposed it was the title of Lord Treloar that did it, but often wondered if that was just the way he was. It would take a brave woman to take on Simon and his particular way of life, she thought.

'Here you go,' Lucy said, carefully placing the two slices of red velvet cake into a box and sealing down the lid. 'Enjoy.'

'Thanks, Lucy,' Stella replied. 'It's nice to have a bit of downtime before the last of the year's retreats begins next week. Chris, Gabe, Helena and I are really looking forward to a quiet Christmas after that.' Gabe was Stella's partner Chris's son, and Helena was the mother of Chris's late wife. The blended family had found each other when Stella had become Writer in Residence at Roseford Hall during the year it opened, and Chris and Stella had fallen in love. Now, they both ran the retreat, which was proving enormously popular.

'Sounds good,' Lucy replied. 'Have you got many bookings for next year?'

'Fully booked until next October,' Stella replied. 'But it's a relief, after everything it took to get Halstead House functioning. We might even have an outside chance of making a profit this year!' Stella and Chris had turned the crumbling Victorian wreck on the other side of Roseford into a picturesque retreat, after its future had been under threat for a number of years, and Lucy was glad they were now starting to make a decent living from it. It was another example of the wealth of creativity in Roseford, and she hoped their success would continue.

'Well, take care, and thanks for these.' Stella picked up the cake box and balanced the coffees on top. 'I hope the festive night goes well.'

'Pop in later if you get the chance,' Lucy said. 'I'll have a vat of mulled wine on the go, if you fancy some.'

'I will,' Stella replied.

It was then that Lucy realised that both of her electric soup kettles were still up at the film set, and she didn't have Nicole's mobile number to ask for them back. The voicemail she'd left about food preferences had come from a withheld number. She'd also forgotten to ask Nicole for her email so she could send her an invoice, so she couldn't contact her that way, either. That was annoying. Perhaps she could pop up there before she picked Megan up from after school club and get them back.

11

Finn collapsed onto the sofa in his trailer, head spinning from the lines he'd had to remember and the repetitive nature of filming. Although he was well accustomed to long days, it took a while to get back into the rhythm of a set. Luckily, he knew many of the crew from past projects, both smaller indie productions and bigger films, and they'd fallen into the accustomed patterns quickly. He was particularly pleased to see Mateo Torres again, the chief camera operator on this production. He and Mateo had both just been starting out during their days on *High School Dreams*, and he was one of the positive influences during that time in his life. It had been Mateo who'd offered to put Finn in touch with the people who'd eventually set the young actor back on an even keel, after some of the excesses of the high-pressured lifestyle of sixteen-hour filming days during endless weeks had threatened to derail him, and he'd be forever grateful. He trusted Mateo, and felt proud to call him a friend.

Deciding against grabbing a shower in his trailer, he ran a

brush through his hair to bring his natural style back and remove the traces of Jack Salmon for the night. Shrugging back into comfy jeans and a T-shirt, topped with a cosy knitted grey jersey, he hung his costume back up on the rail, ready to be collected by wardrobe later. He felt hungry after the long day's shooting, having skipped lunch to run some lines with the dialogue coach, and wondered if the catering wagon, which had eventually arrived, was still open for an early dinner. The evening was setting in, presaging a cool, crisp, clear night, and the half moon was shining over Roseford Hall, whose lights had already been turned off. The building looked almost ghostly in the evening air, and as Finn closed the door to his trailer and strode across to the large wrought-iron gates which led to the village centre, he could hear raised voices in that direction.

'No, I'm sorry, miss, you can't come in. This is private property for the duration of the shoot.'

'But I just want to get my soup kettles back for the Christmas Countdown Night. Nicole, the second assistant director, borrowed them when the caterers didn't turn up a few days ago, but I need them back so I can serve my mulled wine in them later. I own the café in the village, you see.'

Finn, recognising the voice as the woman who'd burned herself on his coffee when they'd met in the café, picked up his pace, wondering if he could help.

'If you could just call Nicole, I'm sure she can vouch for me,' the voice continued.

'I'm sorry, love, but she's knocked off for the day. You'll have to come back tomorrow.'

'But I need them for tonight!' The woman's voice sounded frustrated. As Finn drew closer to the gates, he saw that it was, indeed, Lucy, and she looked as exasperated as she sounded. Her cheeks, pink from both the cold and her irritation, emphasised her English rose complexion, and her blonde hair, tied back in a sensible ponytail, seemed paler in the moonlight.

'Is there a problem here?' Finn asked as he approached the security guard.

'Oh, hello, Mr Sanderson,' the guard replied. 'I was just explaining to this lady that I can't let her go roaming around the place looking for her kitchen equipment unsupervised. She'll have to wait until the morning.'

'And I was just explaining to this gentleman that I need my soup kettles for tonight!' Lucy sounded more upset than frustrated now, and Finn's heart went out to her. Perhaps he could help? He didn't like pulling rank on set; he regarded it as rude and unnecessary, but he could vouch for Lucy, and she didn't seem the type who'd be a security risk.

'It's all right, Geoff,' Finn said calmly. 'I can take her to see if we can find them.'

'I don't know,' Geoff said dubiously. 'No one's supposed to be on set without clearance.'

'I'll be responsible for her,' Finn said. Over Geoff's head, his eyes met Lucy's and he felt his mouth twitch in a smile. He saw her face flush slightly, and a brief smile grace her features, too.

'Well, if you're sure,' Geoff replied. He opened the gate and let Lucy through.

'We won't be long,' Finn called over his shoulder as he and Lucy fell into step.

'Thanks,' Lucy said, glancing up at Finn. She looked

suddenly shy, and Finn hoped she wasn't still suffering from being star-struck.

'It's no problem,' Finn replied. 'From what I heard, you made it possible for us all to eat lunch, so it's the least I can do.'

Lucy felt a flare of the irritation she'd experienced when one of the unit PAs had summarily dismissed her food on Finn's behalf, and she couldn't help muttering, 'I wasn't aware you actually tried any of it.'

Finn looked surprised. 'I did. I thought the roasted vegetable soup was out of this world.'

'Oh,' Lucy replied, wrong-footed. 'It's just that I heard what I'd supplied wasn't, er, "suitable" for your dietary requirements.'

Finn looked embarrassed. 'Oh, right. Well, I'm not sure who made that call, but I definitely enjoyed what you brought in. It was perfect for a cold winter's day.'

Not wanting to drop the PA in it with one of the stars of the film, Lucy let it go. She was secretly pleased that Finn had actually enjoyed the soup. 'Well, if you can help me find my tureens, I'll save you a glass of mulled wine at the festive night later!'

Smiling, Finn pointed in the direction of the catering wagon. 'That's probably your best bet,' he said. 'Shall we see if it's still open?'

They hurried towards the catering area, and Finn briskly pulled the door to the main van. Unfortunately, though, it was locked securely.

'Damn,' he muttered. So much for his bright idea. But then, he figured, it was unlikely to have been left open, even with the security on the unit.

Turning back to Lucy, who was hovering hopefully nearby, he shook his head. 'I'm sorry,' he said. 'I thought I'd solved the problem, but obviously not.' He grabbed his phone from his pocket. 'I'll call Nicole. I'm sure she can get hold of the keys from the caterers.'

'No, honestly, don't go to any trouble,' Lucy stammered, and Finn saw her face turning slightly pink again in the cold evening air. 'I can use a couple of saucepans. It's no bother.'

But Finn found that he really wanted to help Lucy; she'd helped the unit out of its catering crisis; it seemed only fair that he should return the favour.

'Hi, Nicole, it's Finn,' he said. The call had gone to voicemail, but Finn left a message.

'Thank you,' Lucy said as they walked back towards the main gate.

'You're welcome. When she calls me back, I'll make sure you get them. Hopefully in time for later.'

Lucy thanked him again, and there was a gentle pause between them, as if both were unsure where to go next.

'Well, I'd better get back to the café,' Lucy said, after a beat or two. 'I've got a lot to organise tonight.' She smiled at Finn, and he noticed how pretty she was when she wasn't worrying or flustered.

'I'd better get back to the pub, too,' Finn replied. 'I've got an early start in the morning. The director wants to catch the frost on the lawns of the house, and film a couple of sunrise scenes.'

'Sounds like fun,' Lucy said as they began walking back to the gate. 'If a bit cold this time of year!'

'I'm from Canada,' Finn laughed. 'Cold weather is in my

DNA! My co-star, Montana, might be less enthusiastic, though.'

'Oh, that's right,' Lucy laughed, too. 'She's a California girl, isn't she?'

'Yup.' Finn rolled his eyes. 'She didn't realise, when she signed up for this movie, that it was actually going to be shot in the winter.'

'That is unusual, though, right?' Lucy said. 'I mean, aren't most festive films shot in the summer?'

'Yup, but this one had to wait.' Finn glanced around him at the grounds of Roseford Hall, which still retained its majesty, even in the darkness. 'I'm glad, though. This place is so gorgeous, and the winter seems to accentuate that.'

'Well, I've seen quite a few winters, living here all my life, and I have to say that you're right.' Lucy gestured to the house as they moved back down the drive towards the gate.

'You like it here?' Finn replied.

Lucy smiled. 'It's a little quiet, but I wouldn't be anywhere else.'

Another pause descended between them, and Finn felt a slight prickle of envy at Lucy's obvious contentment. He'd never really felt at home anywhere, since leaving the small town near Vancouver where he'd grown up twenty years ago. New York had been where he'd lived for the past nine years, but could he truly call it home?

Just as they were approaching the gate, Simon Treloar, the current lord of the manor and custodian of Roseford Hall, came hurrying from the direction of the house.

'Lucy,' he called as he approached. 'I'm glad I caught you. I've got your soup kettles back at the house. One of the crew asked if I could store them somewhere safe and return them when I got the chance.'

'Simon, you're a lifesaver!' Lucy exclaimed. 'I desperately need them back for the Christmas Countdown Night, and it starts at six o'clock. Finn thought they might have been put in the catering truck, but I'm so glad they weren't.' She turned back to Finn. 'Thanks, though. It was really kind of you to ring Nicole.'

'No problem.' Finn smiled down at her, pleased that the issue had been resolved. 'Do you need a hand carrying them back?' He suddenly found he didn't want to say goodbye to Lucy just yet. 'I'm happy to help, since I'm going that way.'

'Oh, I don't want to put you out,' Lucy replied. 'I'm sure you've got better things to do.'

'It's fine, honestly,' Finn replied. 'Besides, I think there's a Christmas market scene in the movie. It'd be nice to see the real life one, before we sprinkle the place with fake snow and glitter!'

'I think the Parish Council vetoed the glitter,' Simon said dryly. He thrust a hand out to Finn. 'We haven't met yet. I'm Simon.'

'Not just Simon,' Lucy teased. 'Simon Treloar, Tenth Lord of Roseford, to give him his full title.'

'Nice to meet you,' Finn replied, shaking the proffered hand and introducing himself. 'I hope the movie's not causing you and your family too much inconvenience.'

'Not at all,' Simon replied. 'We're used to having people on site most of the year since the British Heritage Fund took over the house. My nieces are super excited to see all of the inner workings of the film, and it's really interesting to see how it all

works up close.' Simon looked thoughtfully at Finn. 'So, what
do you do in the production?'

Lucy's burst of laughter made Finn turn his head and grin
at her. Before he could answer, Lucy got there first.

'Simon, you're so daft! This is Finn Sanderson. *The* Finn
Sanderson?'

Simon looked blank. 'Nope. Sorry... you've lost me, Lucy.'
He turned apologetically to Finn. 'As Lucy will doubtless tell
you, I'm not particularly good at putting names to faces!'

Finn grinned at Simon. 'No harm done. I'm not sure you
were the target audience for the show I was in, back in the day,
anyway.'

'Finn was only in one of the biggest teen television shows
in the world a decade ago,' Lucy said, still smiling. 'Ask Sarah
about *High School Dreams*. She'll get it.'

Sarah was Simon's younger sister and had recently moved
out of Roseford Hall into one of the newly renovated cottages
on the estate with her two daughters.

'I'll do that,' Simon said, a trace of amusement in his tone.
'I'm sure she'll fill me in.'

Finn found that he instinctively liked Simon, and, far from
being offended by Simon's lack of recognition, he thought it
was sort of charming.

As they headed back to the house with Simon to pick up
Lucy's soup tureens, Finn suddenly began to sense what it
must feel like to be part of something other than the movie set.
It felt good to be able to help Lucy out, and perhaps, as
someone who'd lived here a long time, she could shed some
light on the history of the village. It couldn't hurt to integrate
himself a little more fully while he was here, could it?

12

Lucy couldn't quite believe she was in the same space as Finn Sanderson for a second time, and that he'd been so helpful. In the minutes that they'd been hunting for the missing soup kettles, she'd actually begun to relax around him, to forget how star-struck she was. She'd noticed the way he'd seemed slightly shy and that he'd been genuinely tickled by Simon's complete lack of recognition. Bless Simon, she thought, as the three of them headed to the house. Much like Hugh Bonneville's character in *Notting Hill* when he came face to face with Julia Roberts's character, Simon's scant knowledge of popular culture was both endearing and difficult to believe. But she knew, with Simon, it was all genuine. Finn hadn't seemed to mind, anyway.

'Thanks again, Simon,' she said as he unearthed the tureens from the staff kitchen at Roseford Hall. 'I can finally get that mulled wine on to warm up, now.'

'You're welcome.' Simon smiled. 'Will you be okay carrying them back?'

'Yeah, no worries,' Lucy replied. 'See you later for a glass?'

Simon grinned. 'Try and keep me away.'

As Simon departed back upstairs to his private quarters, Finn grabbed one of the soup kettles and passed it to Lucy. 'You okay?' he asked as she took it.

'Yup.' Lucy smiled, and he grabbed the other one. They looked heavy, but were actually fairly manageable when empty.

Walking briskly to the gates once more, Geoff, the security guard, spotted them from a few metres away and had the lock open in a trice. They both thanked him, and then headed back towards the café.

The village square was already starting to come to life for the Christmas Countdown Night, with stallholders setting up on the cobbled space, their colourful festive wares being produced from car boots and small vans. Lucy smiled and waved at Helen, an acquaintance who lived in the next village, as she set up the stall with her beautiful pieces of silver jewellery, which were already glittering under the fairy lights that had been hung on the buildings around the square. Further along the square was an artisan chocolate seller, and then someone selling pottery of various shapes and colours. The obligatory doughnut wagon was off to one side, and Lucy could already smell that pungent scent of sugar and warming oil. It was starting to snow, which was enough to cause a little fizz of excitement in the village, and the flakes danced in the air before trying to settle on the canopies of the stalls, and on top of the roofs of the buildings that bordered the square.

As they approached the café, conversation flowing easily between them, Lucy glanced around to see if anyone had noticed that Finn Sanderson was walking next to her, but most people seemed preoccupied with sorting out their own stalls and shops, and apart from the odd smile, no one gave them a second glance. Finn was dressed down and looked a little different away from the lights of a film set, so perhaps it wasn't that surprising. She'd have loved it if one of her old school mates had seen her with him, although the moment she thought that, she told herself off. Finn was a person, after all, not just a face on a screen, and he'd been very helpful this evening.

'Well, here we are,' Lucy said as she popped the tureen she was holding briefly down on the step of the café to slide her key in the lock. Pushing open the door, she nodded towards the table on her left. 'Just pop it down on there – I'm going to serve the mulled wine, alcoholic and non-alcoholic versions, as people come in the door.'

'So, what's this festive evening like?' Finn asked as Lucy started to arrange the tureens.

'Usually very jolly,' Lucy replied. 'And it's a good chance to catch up with everyone. There are some people I only usually see once a year, when they all come out to join in the evening.'

'Perhaps I'll head out a bit later,' Finn replied. 'Then I'll be able to compare it to our film version!'

'Why do I get the feeling the fake one will include a whole lot more sparkle and about a million candy canes?' Lucy asked wryly, then apologised. 'Sorry. I've watched a lot of Christmas movies over the years!'

Finn shook his head. 'Nah, you're probably right. It's definitely not going to be quite the same as the real thing.'

'But people need the fantasy,' Lucy said kindly. 'And that's what films like *A Countess for Christmas* gives them, isn't it? I should think there are lots of us who will want to step into that

world for a couple of hours, to leave normal life behind and
enjoy a little escapism.'

'I guess so,' Finn replied. 'Perhaps I've just had too much of
the illusion over the years. I get a little conflicted about selling
a dream that's completely unattainable.'

'Maybe you should look at it from the other side.' Lucy
fiddled with one of the small winter posies on the nearest
table. 'People choose to buy into those dreams, and it makes
them feel good. It doesn't mean festive films and romance
films are any less valid for that, just because they sell a fantasy.
I mean, *Star Wars* and *Game of Thrones* do the same thing.' She
paused. 'And you did sign up for it, after all.'

'I know,' Finn laughed. 'It's a bit rich to be dismissive of it,
isn't it?' He looked surprised. 'In fact, I can't believe I just
admitted my cynicism to, well, to an almost total stranger.'

'It's the smell of the mince pies,' Lucy said wryly. 'There's
truth serum in them along with the mixed spice!'

Finn's laughter grew a little less self-conscious this time,
and Lucy felt a warmth spreading through her at the sound.
He seemed relaxed in her company, and although it was still
weird, having him here in her café, she felt herself relax a little
more too.

'Well, I'd better leave you to it,' Finn said, after a moment
or two. 'Good luck for tonight. I hope it goes well.'

'It'll go a lot better now I can make the mulled wine,' Lucy
replied. 'Thanks again. And pop in later, if you like. I'll save
you a cup.'

'I'd like that.' Finn smiled down at her, and Lucy's heart
raced a little faster. He really was lovely-looking, especially
when he smiled. 'See you later.'

As Finn turned and left the café, Lucy couldn't help

hugging herself in excitement. She'd played things admirably cool, this evening, and she hadn't turned into a blithering mess in Finn's presence, like the first time she'd met him. Perhaps, she thought, it was because he'd seemed more like a normal bloke than a movie star this time around. She found that she liked this version of him, and she hoped she'd just seen the real Finn Sanderson. Hurrying to the kitchen to get the ingredients for the mulled wine, she wondered if he would pop back in later. She found herself hoping he would.

13

'Oh, how sweet.' Serena made a soppy face as Lucy filled her in on her time with Finn, half an hour later. 'You're the one who should be in the Christmas movie, with Finn acting as your knight in shining armour!'

'Right time, right place,' Lucy muttered, laying out the mince pies under one of the clear glass cloches on the café's counter. 'And anyway, Simon was the one who really came to the rescue, bless him.' She smiled fondly. 'He knew where the soup tureens were, after all. Finn just provided the muscle.'

'And got you through the gate,' Serena reminded Lucy. 'Or you'd never have found them, Simon or no Simon. Besides,' she paused mischievously, 'compared to Finn, Simon's not exactly fantasy material!'

'Oh, I don't know,' Lucy mused. 'He's always been kind of attractive, in that harmless, bookish way.'

'Yeah, but he's not what actual daydreams are made of, is he?' Serena grinned. 'Not like Finn.'

Lucy's face burned. 'Shut up. Daydreams are daydreams for a reason. Meeting him was... different.'

'Oh, yeah?' Serena said. 'You mean this time you didn't spill coffee all over yourself and call him gorgeous to his face?'

'Well, no, I didn't,' Lucy said. 'But we talked. And I kind of felt as though I was talking to an actual person, you know, not the movie star. It was nice.'

Serena gave her a nudge. 'I bet.'

Glancing at the clock in the tearoom, Lucy came quickly back to earth. 'I'd better go and get Megan from after school club,' she said. 'Are you okay to keep an eye on this place until I get back?'

'Sure,' Serena replied. 'What time do you want to open the door?'

'About six o'clock,' Lucy replied. 'But I'll be back long before then. Help yourself to a glass of mulled wine if you want.'

'I might just do that,' Serena said. 'And if a film star comes knocking, should I let him in?'

'I'd be surprised if he did,' Lucy replied. 'I'm sure he was just being polite when he said he might come by later. But sure, let him in if he does.'

'I'll keep an eye out for Montana, too,' Serena said.

'You have my permission to ply her with mulled wine if she drops in,' Lucy laughed. 'See you in a bit.'

As she drove the short distance to Megan's school, Lucy reflected on how lucky she was to have Serena to rely on. Lucy's one regret for Serena was that she hadn't yet found anyone to settle down in a longer-term relationship with; her last one had ended when the other party went travelling, and although she'd had a few dates with the pub-loving Charlie since, Lucy couldn't help thinking that Serena hadn't quite given Charlie her heart. Perhaps a new year would be a fresh start for them both? Without realising it, Lucy's thoughts had drifted, albeit unintentionally, to Finn and the rapport they seemed to have formed in the short time they'd spent together. Hastily, she shushed those thoughts. Finn was only going to be in Roseford for a few weeks at most. He wasn't the answer to any sort of questions.

* * *

A short time later, when Lucy returned to the café, she could see that Serena had added a characteristic sparkle to proceedings. She'd dimmed the lights in the main dining area, and threaded the fairy lights that Lucy hadn't got around to putting up across the window that looked out onto the main street. Christmas music played softy on the Bluetooth speaker that Lucy had put behind the counter, and the enticing smells of freshly baked mince pies and mulled wine made Lucy's mouth water.

'You're an angel!' Lucy said, hugging her friend. 'I'd completely forgotten I'd bought those lights. They look great in the window.'

'All part of the service!' Serena said, picking up a still warm mince pie from under the cloche on the counter and passing it to Megan, who grinned and stuffed it greedily into her mouth.

'It's snowing harder now!' Megan said through a mouthful of the crumbly pastry. 'Do you think it's going to settle, Serena?'

'Who knows?' Serena smiled down at Megan. 'But I

promise I'll make a snowman with you if it does. Well,' she said, turning back to Lucy, 'shall we get these doors open?'

'Absolutely,' Lucy said.

She and Serena wandered over to the front door and Serena dropped the latch and flipped the sign to open.

They both gazed out at the main road, which was starting to get a little busier with people. Lucy spotted and waved at a few locals but was also pleased to see quite a few new faces, presumably including members of the film crew, who had come out to enjoy the evening. She thought again about how lucky she was to live in Roseford, which looked even more picturesque with a light dusting of snow, like a smattering of icing sugar on a mince pie. The snow was coming down a little more heavily now and she wondered if Serena's offer to make a snowman with Megan would actually come to fruition tomorrow morning.

Roseford was beautiful in any season but in the winter with its light stone-coloured buildings, cobbled village square and festive, Victorian-themed decorations and real Christmas trees, it really did look like something out of an old-fashioned Christmas card. When the choir started to sing a few moments later, this image was complete and from the looks on the faces of the people who were heading up and down the street, they appreciated it too.

There was something special about the Christmas Countdown Night. Whatever festive spirit Lucy might have been lacking so early in the season was rapidly starting to creep over her.

As a local couple came in and gratefully received paper cups of mulled wine from one of the rescued soup kettles, Lucy smiled and made polite conversation with them. They decided to take two slices of Lucy's divine red velvet cake with them to have once they got home and Lucy popped them into a cake box and one of her brown bags with the café's logo on the front for them to take. Wishing them goodbye, she headed back to the mulled wine and readied herself to welcome any more visitors who would like a complimentary drink.

A short time later, as she looked up from ladling out another serving of mulled wine to another customer, Lucy's heart gave a little leap when she saw a figure heading up the High Street towards the café, head and shoulders and a little bit more above most of the people who were shopping. She would have recognised him anywhere, but it still gave her a little thrill of shock and recognition to see him in Roseford, looking so relaxed and at home. Of course, that could have been part of his 'act', his public face. After all, a famous film star wouldn't want to get posted on Instagram looking anything other than happy and content, but Lucy hoped what she saw on Finn's face was actually real, and an effect of being here.

'OMG!' Serena hissed from by her side. 'Is that who I think it is with Finn?' Lucy and Serena moved a little closer to the bay window of the café, leaving their customers to their own devices as they were both momentarily distracted by Finn and the small, dark-haired, extremely pretty woman who was walking by his side.

'I think so,' Lucy murmured. 'Either that or she's a very convincing body double.' For a second, Lucy and Serena stood speechless at the sight of their teen icons strolling in animated conversation down the main road.

'Why is it that when you add a movie star or two to any scene, it automatically feels as though you've stepped into a

Christmas movie, even when we haven't?' Serena, her voice pitched slightly higher than usual, turned to Lucy and gave her a broad smile.

'Must be the time of year,' Lucy said.

'Well? Aren't you going to give him a wave and ask him to sample your wares?' Serena was still looking out of the window, but she turned briefly and gave Lucy a mischievous glance.

'I don't want to look desperate,' Lucy muttered. 'He was probably only being polite when he helped me out earlier.'

However, Serena's attention was further diverted now at the sight of Finn's co-star Montana de Santo as they both drew nearer.

'Oh god,' Serena breathed as Finn and Montana glanced at the café door. 'Montana is even more gorgeous in real life than she was all those years ago. Ten years on, I would at least have expected a few wrinkles and a couple of extra pounds, but she looks almost exactly the same.'

'That's a Hollywood lifestyle for you!' Lucy said, amused by her usually confident friend's suddenly star-struck behaviour. 'I bet it's all macrobiotic this and biorhythmic that and sixty hours a week in the gym just to maintain that seemingly effortless look.'

Serena regarded her levelly. 'If I didn't know better, I'd say you were jealous.' She gave Lucy a prod in the ribs. 'I mean, what's she got that you haven't got?'

Lucy rolled her eyes. 'I'm going to pretend you never said that.' With Serena by her side, still staring agog out of the bay window as Finn and Montana approached, she felt uncomfortably like the sixteen-year-old she had been trying to shrug off ever since she'd met Finn. Serena, with all the excitement of someone seeing her idols up close in real life, was now going through the same thing that Lucy had when Finn had come into the café for the first time.

Before she could prepare herself to welcome Finn and Montana, who definitely looked as though they were heading in the direction of the café, Lucy was snapped out of her excited staring by a hearty voice.

'Hi, Lucy!' Simon Treloar said as he ducked his head to come through the café's door. At six foot one, he wasn't as tall as Finn, but these old buildings were slightly hazardous to those of six feet and over. Many a customer had had some sense knocked into or out of them by the low oak beam above the doorway of the shop, and Lucy had wisely invested in some hazard tape to put across it. What it lost in olde worlde charm, it more than made up for in lowering the number of concussed customers.

'Oh, hi, Simon,' Lucy said hurriedly approaching her mulled wine kettles again. 'Would you like some of this to warm you up?'

'That would be lovely, but just the one.' Simon grinned at her. 'I've been offered so much booze on my way round this festive night, anyone would think my family's still in charge around here!'

Lucy looked at him sympathetically. 'You'll always be the lord of the manor to Roseford,' she said consolingly. She sensed that a part of Simon still regretted being the one who'd had to hand over Roseford Hall to the British Heritage Fund, despite the fact that the alternatives had been too awful to think about. Even though he and various members of his family still lived in the house and on the wider estate, the situation still obviously rankled a bit.

'Thank you so much for your help earlier,' she continued, handing him a cup. 'As you can see, the mulled wine is a real draw and I'm selling a few slices of cake as well.'

'I'm glad to have been able to help,' Simon replied, taking a sip from his paper cup. He wrinkled his nose briefly. 'Wow!' he said with a short laugh. 'This has got a whole lot more kick to it than any of the others I've tried tonight. What have you put in it?'

'Oh, you know,' Lucy replied. 'It's my grandmother's recipe and she never believed in stinting on the booze.' The recipe passed down in Lucy's family also included a hearty dose of cinnamon, mixed spice and cloves and was a guaranteed winter warmer. The non-alcoholic version was no less so for the lack of booze and over the years, Lucy had perfected her own recipe for the non-drinkers in the village.

'Well, I'd better stop at one cup or I really will struggle to find my way home,' Simon laughed. He turned to Megan, who was helping Serena wipe the tables as people ambled out of the café after their refreshing pit stop. 'And how are you, Megan? Did you have a good day at school?'

Megan cocked her head to one side and thought about it for a moment. 'Not bad.' She gave Simon a gap-toothed grin. 'But I prefer being here. I can eat all of the mince pies that don't get sold.'

Lucy laughed. 'That's what you think, young lady!' She gestured to the table nearest where the mulled wine tureens were. 'Don't forget, you've got your reading to do before tomorrow.'

'Okay,' Megan muttered. Even at eight years old, she'd mastered that teenage don't-hassle-me glare, and Lucy couldn't help but burst out laughing. 'Well, maybe we can slack off for one night.'

'Yay!' Megan did a little skip towards the door, and, not looking where she was going, crashed straight into two people who were on their way in. As she looked up to see who they were, Lucy couldn't help drawing in an involuntary breath when her daughter's icing sugar-covered fingers collided with the designer coat of a small, beautiful woman, who was standing next to a man who'd definitely needed to duck through the café's door.

14

'Hello, Finn,' Lucy squeaked, knocked for six at the sight of him. As she glanced at Serena, who'd dropped her dishcloth on the table she'd been wiping, she noticed how pale her friend suddenly looked. 'What can I get you?' Then, seeing the light dusting of icing sugar that had now transferred itself to Montana de Santo's winter coat from Megan's fingers when she'd bumped into them, she gasped.

'Oh god, I'm so sorry!' Lucy rushed from behind the mulled wine tureens to whisk Megan away before she could do any more damage.

Montana glanced up from Megan and gave Lucy a smile that was so bright, it rivalled the twinkly white Christmas lights in the café's bay window.

'Don't worry about it,' she said. 'A little sugar never hurt anybody, right?' Her voice was so exquisitely the same as it had been in *High School Dreams* that Lucy was brought up short again.

'Well, the least I can do is get you a mince pie on the house and a mulled wine to make up for it,' Lucy replied.

She'd been so preoccupied with getting her sticky daughter away from Montana that she had forgotten that Finn was there, too. As she looked up from Montana's smiling face to Finn's, she felt her cheeks start to flame and she cursed the fact that she clearly wasn't quite over her teenage crush. 'Hi, again,' she said. 'Would you like to try some of this mulled wine that wouldn't even be here if it hadn't been for your help?'

Finn grinned. 'I've been looking forward to it all evening,' he replied. Simon, who was finishing up his drink, turned to Finn and also smiled. 'I'd go a little easy on the alcoholic version if you've got anything heavy to do tomorrow,' he said. 'Lucy's grandmother's recipe has got quite a kick!'

'Uh, thanks for the warning, Simon,' Finn replied, 'but I think for tonight I'll just stick to the non-alcoholic option if that's okay.'

'Me too.' Montana smiled.

'Coming right up.' Lucy reached for her ladle once more. 'Serena, can you grab a couple of mince pies and put them on some plates?' Lucy was surprised to see her confident best friend still temporarily struck dumb by their famous visitors.

Roused out of her shock, Serena shook her head. 'Yeah, sure no problem,' she said eventually. She walked to the counter and retrieved a couple of the mince pies from underneath the glass cloche.

As Lucy watched her, Serena seemed to fumble with the mince pies and very nearly dropped the plate when she brought it over to where Finn, Montana and Lucy were standing.

'Here you go.' Lucy passed two cups of the non-alcoholic mulled wine to Finn and Montana. 'I hope you enjoy it.'

Finn took a sip and nodded as he swallowed. 'It tastes great. You'd never know it wasn't the real thing!' Then, rather unnecessarily, but rather wonderfully, too, he introduced Montana to Lucy.

'It's a pleasure to meet you,' Lucy said, shaking Montana's hand before Serena could give her a mince pie.

'Likewise,' Montana replied. Her deep chocolate-brown eyes swivelled from Lucy to Serena, who was hovering with the plate of mince pies. 'And you are?'

'Serena Johnson.' Serena looked a little taken aback to be asked, but she did manage to give Montana a bright if somewhat nervous smile.

Montana turned back to Finn. 'I do hope you're not planning on eating too many of those pies,' she teased, an arch note in her voice. 'You know what a stickler wardrobe are for us both keeping in shape through a shoot.'

Finn laughed. 'At least it's not the kind of movie where I need to take my shirt off! I'm sure I can afford to have one or two. And they are really good.'

Montana shook her head in light-hearted remonstration of him. 'Well, much as I'd love to hang around, I promised Mom I would buy her some authentic English Christmas tree decorations this year, so I'm going to look around and see if there's anything here I can send her that fits the bill. I'll see you back at the pub later?'

'Sure,' Finn replied. 'Have fun.'

Lucy, wanting to help Montana out by sending her in the right direction, couldn't resist the chance to mention the handmade craft shop that was two-thirds of the way down the main road.

'It's got some really lovely stuff in this time of year,' she said.

'If you like, I can show you the way,' Serena interjected.

To Lucy, Serena still sounded on edge and a little star-struck, but she figured that wasn't surprising, under the circumstances. Serena had always idolised Montana; any excuse to spend a little more time with her was clearly an opportunity too good to miss. Montana turned back towards Serena and smiled, but this time it wasn't the megawatt smile of the movie star; it looked more genuine, more *human*.

'That would be great,' she said, then turning back to Lucy, 'if you're sure Lucy can spare you for a few minutes?'

Lucy, who knew she'd never hear the end of it from Serena if she denied her the chance to walk a few paces with Montana, nodded. 'Of course. Take your time. I'm sure we can cope here if you want to spend a little bit of time looking at what's up there.'

Serena gave Lucy a quick, grateful smile. 'Thanks, babe,' she said, briskly untying her apron and hanging it over the nearest chair. 'I won't be long. I wouldn't want to leave you in the lurch on a night like this.'

Lucy put her arm around Megan. 'I'm sure we've got it covered for a few minutes at least.'

Montana, even when she reached up on tiptoes, was too short to land the kiss on Finn's cheek, and Lucy thought it was very sweet that he ducked his head to enable her to plant a quick peck on the side of his face before she headed out of the café again. They were clearly still close and enjoying spending time together and Lucy just knew that

that kind of chemistry could not be faked. With a slight pang of desolation that a reconciliation between the two ex-lovers seemed inevitable, she turned her attention back to Finn and asked him if he wanted a top-up of the non-alcoholic mulled wine.

'I'd love one,' he said as he gave her back his paper cup. 'We could do with some of this when we shoot our outdoor scenes.'

'Well, your director knows where I am if they want me to whip up a batch or two!' Lucy joked. Although she was sure there were far more exotic options now the official unit catering truck had arrived, at last.

Simon, who had been standing by the window all this time, popped his now empty mulled wine cup into the bin that Lucy had put out for the purpose and turned back to her. 'Well, I'd better get off now,' he said. 'Thanks for the pit stop, Lucy, and it's nice to see you again, Finn. I'm sure I'll see you around.'

'Take care, Simon, see you soon. Thanks for dropping in,' Lucy replied. As she had so often, Lucy couldn't help wondering why Simon hadn't been snapped up by some girl who wanted the romantic lifestyle of a stately home and a handsome lord, but then Simon had never been particularly good at putting himself out there, despite his eligibility on paper. Perhaps one day he'd find his soulmate, or at least someone who could manage the slightly unusual reality of his life at Roseford Hall.

Finn, meanwhile, was indeed tucking into the mince pies that Serena had brought over on the plate.

'Hey,' Lucy teased, 'I don't want to be held responsible for your costumes not fitting!'

Finn grinned back at her, his cheeks full of pastry and mincemeat.

'Don't worry,' he said once he'd swallowed his mouthful and taken another sip of the mulled wine, 'I promise I'll go on a long run tomorrow morning to work it all off.'

Lucy laughed. 'Glad to hear it.' And just like that, the easy rapport that they had established when they were looking for the soup kettles seemed to have returned. Lucy wondered if it was because Montana wasn't there any more, but she couldn't exactly say that Montana had been hostile; quite the opposite, in fact. She seemed really lovely and exactly what Serena and Lucy had imagined her to be all those years ago.

'So have you had a good look around tonight?' Lucy asked.

Finn nodded again and helped himself to another mince pie. 'It's all so... English. I don't mean that in a patronising way. Roseford is beautiful but it's also so understated. The same event in the US would have involved more noise, more candy, and about a hundred more stalls. This place couldn't be more different. I know Kathryn, our director, is going to be on the lookout for any finishing touches she can use when we film our own version of a festive fayre, but to be honest I kind of wish we could've just set the cameras up tonight instead. It would've come across as so much more real.'

'Yeah,' Lucy said, 'but you'd have needed a ton more snow and a whole lot more glitter for it to come across well on camera!'

'You sound like the film star, not me.' Finn smiled. 'Have you ever thought about going into the business?'

Lucy smiled and shook her head. 'Nope,' she said. 'I'm quite happy watching the people who make the films from the safety of my café window.'

The pause settled between them for a bit longer and Lucy noticed that Finn was sticking around, watching her serving customers that came in, and helping himself to another mince pie and the non-alcoholic mulled wine.

As the café's custom lulled again, Finn suddenly looked a little bit nervous. What did he have to be nervous about? she wondered.

'So will you get the chance to get out or are you stuck here for the whole of the evening?' he asked eventually, toying with the top of his now empty mulled wine cup.

'It depends how busy we get,' Lucy replied. 'And, of course, there's my daughter Megan to consider. It's a late night for her.'

Megan, who was waiting quietly by Lucy's side, gave Finn a smile. If he was surprised that Megan was Lucy's daughter, Finn didn't show it. 'Hey, Megan,' he said, leaning down so that he was more at her level. 'I'm Finn. It's nice to meet you.'

'I know who you are,' replied Megan immediately. 'My mum's got a T-shirt with your face on that she goes to bed in sometimes. It's a bit scruffy.'

Lucy's face started to flame. So much for relaxing in Finn's presence. 'It's quite an old T-shirt,' she said. 'I've had it since I was about sixteen.' She tried to distract herself by furiously stirring the mulled wine tureen in front of her. The cloud of steam that rose when she did so did not make her face any cooler.

Finn laughed. 'Honestly? I've heard a lot worse. You wouldn't believe some of the places my face has ended up!' Realising just how awful that sounded and especially in front of an eight-year-old, Finn groaned. 'Sorry,' he said. 'What I meant to say is, an old T-shirt is really not the worst of it.'

Lucy felt slightly better in the face of Finn's palpable

embarrassment. Even media-trained film stars could drop unwitting innuendos, it seemed.

'I'm glad to hear that,' Lucy laughed. 'Maybe, when little ears aren't listening, you could enlighten me.'

'I'd love to, if I didn't think you'd never speak to me again,' Finn replied. He turned back to the door as Montana and Serena returned. Montana was laden down with bags from various shops, and the two women looked as though they'd got on famously in their brief trip around the market.

'You should see what I've got my nieces,' Montana said without preamble as she came through the café's door. 'They'll die when they see how cute they are.'

Serena, who was following in Montana's wake, had a couple of packages of her own and her flushed cheeks, Lucy surmised, weren't entirely from the cold weather outside. Spending a little time with her idol seemed to have put a spring in Serena's step and Lucy was alternately pleased to see her so happy and also tickled that she would be able to tease her about it later.

However, Serena was not so distracted that she didn't have the wherewithal to shoot a speculative look at Lucy and Finn. Before Lucy could ask her how her shopping trip had gone, Serena spoke. 'Well, I reckon it must be your turn to get out and about and do some socialising and some shopping before everybody packs up and goes home. That snow is really starting to come down quite heavily.'

'I wish I could, but I should probably stay here,' Lucy said. 'Someone's got to keep an eye on this little munchkin so that she doesn't eat all of my profits!' She glanced down at Megan.

'I'm sure I can manage this place and throw a few pieces of cake at punters while you take a bit of time off,' Serena replied.

'Besides,' she continued, 'Montana found some incredible Christmas spice-flavoured fudge at the sweet shop that you just have to try. I reckon it would be the perfect present for your mum.'

Lucy looked doubtful. 'Mum isn't supposed to have too much sweet stuff any more,' she replied.

'What about you, Finn?' Montana interjected. 'We didn't get to see everything earlier. Why don't you go with Lucy and see what you can find?'

Was Lucy imagining it or did a significant look pass between Montana and Serena at the suggestion?

Finn looked a little uncomfortable, as if he and Lucy were being manoeuvred into something he wasn't sure how to handle, and Lucy felt embarrassed for him. She was sure that the last thing he would want to do was wander around a hokey Christmas market with her. If he did agree, he was probably only doing it to humour his friend and so that he didn't look bad in front of his fans.

'No, honestly, it's fine,' she repeated. 'I don't often get the chance to look round the Christmas market, so this year isn't going to be any different.'

'Oh, don't be such a stick in the mud! It'll do you good to get out and about for once,' Serena said briskly. 'I can take care of this place *and* Megan with one hand tied behind my back.' She raised an eyebrow at Lucy which clearly brokered no argument. 'So will you just bugger off with the handsome movie star and have a little wander around for a bit?'

'And you, Finn,' Montana said briskly. 'If you and I are going to spend the whole day filming outside on the street tomorrow, the least you can do is have a look and get to know the place.'

Finn smiled. 'I'm more than happy to,' he said gently. 'You don't have to twist my arm.'

Lucy, still doubtful that Finn was being anything other than gracious, felt unsure, but a warning glance from Serena not to protest any more had her untying her apron and passing it to Serena to hang up behind the counter. 'I won't be long,' she said to Megan, who, already excited at the prospect of Serena calling the shots, was diving for the leftover cake on the counter and waved her away.

'That Christmas cake and the rest of the red velvet will have to go by the end of the night,' Lucy said, 'so you can sell it half price if anyone wants a slice.'

'Got it,' Serena replied. She winked. 'I'll see you in a bit.' Turning back to Montana, she said, 'Can I get you a coffee?'

'That would be lovely,' Montana replied.

As Lucy left her own café with Finn by her side, she glanced back to see her best friend chatting to Montana de Santo, teen star and role model for them both for so many years, her young daughter Megan looking spellbound, and had to wonder if it was she who'd been thrust into the middle of a Christmas movie. After all, stuff like this only ever happened in fairy tales, didn't it?

15

'Wow!' Lucy gasped as she and Finn stepped out of the café and onto the main street of Roseford. 'The snow is really starting to come down. Megan was desperate to build a snowman with Serena. Looks like she might get her wish!' She pulled her jacket a little more tightly around herself. She was glad she'd grabbed it from the coat stand near the front door. Inside her left pocket was a pair of gloves and she hastily pulled them on.

Finn, who looked completely at home in the cold, smiled down at her. 'Mom always says that the Brits can never cope with a few flakes of snow. She's never stopped being amazed by the Vancouver winters and how life just seems to go on somehow, even when there's five feet of the stuff outside the front door.'

'She has a point.' Lucy smiled ruefully. 'Everything does tend to grind to a halt if we get heavy snow, or in fact any at all.'

Finn looked to the sky and furrowed his brow. 'Kathryn,

the director, isn't gonna like it if the weather stops shooting tomorrow. She's ordered a snow machine to cover the market square with the fake stuff, but I'm really not sure how well that's going to go if we end up with a lot of real thing on the ground instead.'

They were walking at a leisurely pace up the main street. Already Lucy could see that visitors to the festive night were starting to thin because of the deteriorating weather. 'We don't usually get much snow in the West Country,' she said. 'This is all bit of a novelty for us.'

She waved at Helen, the jewellery maker. 'We've still got plenty of coffee and mulled wine left if you fancy warming up in the café.' Helen was valiantly trying to sell some beautiful handmade silver pieces and stuck up a thumb, calling back that she might well pop in in a bit and take advantage of the offer.

'I'm sorry that you got pushed into coming out here with me,' Lucy said as they continued walking. 'It was kind of you to humour them.'

'I wasn't,' Finn replied, smiling down at her. 'If Montana hadn't suggested it, I was going to ask if I could see you for a coffee or a walk anyway.' He paused. 'I mean, if you'd like to. If you're not... seeing someone else? In a relationship?'

Lucy was increasingly aware of the slippery surface underfoot as the snow continued to fall, and her knees suddenly going incredibly weak did little to steady her. Was Finn Sanderson asking her out? 'Um, no. I'm not. In a relationship, that is. It's just me and Megan.'

Finn looked relieved. 'I'm sorry I asked so directly,' he said. 'But I've found that sometimes people aren't as straight with me as they could be. It's better to try to be honest.' He paused. 'So... um... will you? Go for a coffee? Or a walk?'

'Really?' she stammered. 'But why?' Her face, despite the chill in the air, felt hot again.

Finn stopped walking and turned to face Lucy. 'I, uh, I don't usually ask women out when I'm on a shoot, if that's what you're wondering. But... I'd like to spend a little more time with you, if you're interested in spending some time with me.'

Lucy shook her head. 'If anyone had told me that I'd be standing in the centre of Roseford with the snow falling and Finn Sanderson asking me out on a date, I would've laughed right in their faces!'

'Then don't think of it as Finn Sanderson asking you out on a date,' Finn replied. 'Maybe try to think of it as this guy who is new to the village who would really love it if you'd agree to have a drink with him sometime.'

Lucy laughed. 'You make it sound so simple.'

'Isn't it?' Finn asked. Looking adorably uncertain, he reached out and took one of Lucy's gloved hands in his. She was startled that she could feel the heat of his touch through her glove, and that his hands were still warm, even in the chilly air. 'I'd like to get to know you better, Lucy, if you'd like to get to know me, too.'

Lucy let out a slightly shaky breath which ghosted out in front of her. 'I'd like that too, Finn. I'd like that a lot.'

Finn, too, let out a long breath. 'I don't know why I was nervous about asking you,' he said. 'I guess I'm more out of practice at this than I thought!'

Lucy laughed. 'Tell me about it! The last time I had a proper date, Megan was still at pre-school!' She blushed. 'And if that doesn't make me sound like a saddo, I don't know what would.'

'It must be difficult, with a young daughter, to find time for much else,' Finn replied as they walked. 'Is Megan's dad around?'

Lucy smiled. 'Yes, to a point,' she said. 'He sees her as regularly as he can. He lives in the States most of the time now, so it's a bit more difficult. But our relationship is amicable.'

'So he's not going to come after me with a shotgun or anything?'

Lucy laughed. 'Not that I'm aware of, no. He's got a new partner now. Megan loves her to bits, and she even has a half-sister she gets on with.'

They wandered between the stalls, chatting easily, until Lucy glanced at her watch in surprise. They'd been out a little longer than she'd expected to be. Mindful of the icy pavements, they began to head back to the café. Lucy could see that many of the stallholders were also calling it a night due to the heavily falling snow. On the one hand, it was lovely to see snow falling in Roseford as it didn't happen very often; on the other, she felt disappointed for the main street of independent businesses and stallholders whose profits would've been curtailed by the poor weather.

As Finn and Lucy reached the door of the café, Lucy could see that Serena, always more able to persuade Megan around to her way of thinking, was sitting on the sofa at the back of the seating area with her, happily reading her school book aloud. At least that was one job Lucy wouldn't have to worry about when she got home, she thought.

'Well, this is me.' Lucy smiled up at Finn. 'That was a

lovely walk. I'm glad to have got some fresh air and not been stuck in the café all night.'

Finn smiled back. 'So, would you like to join me for a drink sometime this week?'

'That would be lovely. Megan's nativity play is tomorrow night but I'm free on Friday if that suits you?'

'That would be great. What time is good for you?'

'Let me just check that Mum is available to babysit. Why don't you pop into the café tomorrow afternoon and I'll let you know?'

'Okay,' Finn replied.

He hesitated for a moment and then, as if double-checking with himself that it would be all right, he leaned down and placed a brief kiss on her cheek.

Lucy felt the warmth of his lips on her face and it sent a shiver right through her. She hadn't been expecting a kiss, but it wasn't unwelcome. She found herself wondering what it would be like if he kissed her more passionately. Stopping those thoughts in their tracks – after all, they'd only just arranged to have a first date – she looked back at him.

'I'll see you soon.'

Before they could say any more, Montana came bustling back through the café door and out onto the street.

'You're still here?' Finn asked in surprise. 'I thought you'd have gone back to your room by now.'

Montana grinned. 'Serena co-opted me into helping her tidy, and she might have convinced me to have at least one of those wonderful mince pies too.' She smiled warmly at Lucy. 'It was lovely to meet you.'

Then, turning back to Finn and looping her arm through

his, she said, 'Come on, lover boy! We've got an early start tomorrow.'

'See you tomorrow,' Finn said as he was dragged briskly away back in the direction of the pub by Montana. As she watched them leave, Lucy couldn't help wondering what exactly the nature of their relationship was these days. They were clearly still close, and had once been even closer; every teen girl in the country had had FinnTana as their relationship goal at one time. Their onscreen chemistry was what would drive the success of *A Countess for Christmas*, but surely there wasn't anything else between them in real life these days, or why would Finn have asked her out?

Realising that going down that road was going to inevitably create a whole set of complications she wasn't sure how to handle, she resolved to try really hard not to overthink the situation. Finn had asked her out for a drink; he wouldn't have done that if he had any 'complications'. And as for her, with Megan and the café in the equation, it wasn't as if she could dump everything and run off with a film star, was it?

As she walked back into the café, Serena raised a speculative eyebrow at her.

'Nice walk?'

Determined not to give anything away, even to her best friend, Lucy replied, 'Fine, thanks.'

She looked around the café, which, apart from the dregs of the mulled wine in the soup kettles, looked clean and tidy.

'Has anyone ever told you you're an absolute marvel?' she said to Serena as she crossed the room and hugged her warmly. Lucy wasn't really a hugger except with Megan, and Serena was a little surprised.

'It went that well, did it?' Serena teased, returning the hug.

'I'll tell you about it when I know exactly what *it* was,' Lucy replied.

She leaned over to see how far Megan had got in her reading book. The little girl's head was drooping on the arm of the sofa that inhabited the far corner of the café.

'Come on, sweetheart,' she said gently. 'It's time to get you to bed, I think.'

Turning back to Serena, she said, 'Are you heading back to Bristol tonight? The weather has taken quite a turn out there.'

Serena shook her head. 'Nah. Mum's made up the spare room for me. I can work from here tomorrow. The weather's so bad, I don't think many people will make it in.'

A dreamy expression crossed Serena's features, an expression that Lucy hadn't seen on her friend's face for a long time.

'Everything okay with you?'

Serena smiled. 'Of course. It's been a nice night, that's all.'

'That's all?' Lucy laughed. 'We get to spend time with our teen idols and it's been *a nice night*?'

'Well, perhaps it's been a bit of a surreal one as well,' Serena conceded. 'I almost wish I was back in the office tomorrow just so I could tell everyone. No one would ever believe it!' She hugged Lucy again and then headed for the door. Before she left, she paused. 'Perhaps dreams do come true at Christmas time,' she said, the glow from the fairy lights around the bay window casting her face in a gentle haze.

'I think you and I are a little too old to believe in Christmas fantasies,' Lucy replied.

'Yeah, probably,' Serena agreed, 'but for tonight, perhaps we can.'

Content with that thought and still a little tingly from her encounter with Finn, Lucy gathered up Megan's things, made sure everything was switched off in the kitchen and in the front of the café and prepared to head home.

Just as she was switching off the main light by the front door, her phone buzzed with a message. Taking a moment to check, in case Serena couldn't get into her mum's house, her heart gave a little pitter-patter as she realised that it was Megan's father. Rob usually just phoned when they needed to talk, so she was surprised by the message. As she read it, her blood ran cold.

Just seen this on Twitter. Be careful, Lucy-Lou.

The message was attached to a grainy photograph, which could only have been taken a few minutes ago. The figures in the photo were indistinct, but anyone who knew Lucy like Rob did would have spotted her immediately, and Finn's face, while shadowed, was recognisable. In the half light shining from the café's open door, there stood Lucy, eyes closed, as Finn Sanderson kissed her cheek.

16

The next day was a busy one on set. At the end of it, Finn wanted nothing more than to return to his room in the pub and crash. He'd managed to sneak off and confirm his date with Lucy during a break, though, and they were all set to meet in the pub tomorrow night. The hanging around on set had taken its toll as much as the actual acting, and he now needed to get his head down. His good friend Mateo Torres had other ideas, however. Catching Finn on his way out of the gates of Roseford Hall, Mateo, who was staying in a bed and breakfast a couple of streets away, fell into step with him.

'Karaoke? Seriously?' Finn's mouth twitched in a smile as he looked at Mateo.

'Sure, why not?' Mateo grinned. 'I thought it'd be a good bonding exercise for the cast and crew, since we're shooting some of the ensemble scenes tomorrow. Why not spend the evening banging out some cheesy tunes for the locals?'

Finn shook his head. 'Not my scene, man. I haven't done

any real singing since *High School Dreams* ended. Not sure I'd know how any more.'

'Oh, come on,' Mateo chided, 'you'd knock any of us out of the park even if you are out of practice.' He raised an eyebrow at Finn. 'Don't tell me you're scared, Mr Mountie?'

Finn bristled slightly under the shorter man's scrutiny. 'Absolutely not. And don't call me that.'

'So come on, then,' Mateo continued. 'Prove it. Warm those pipes up on a bit of English karaoke.' His brown eyes, the same colour as liquid milk chocolate, that had been known to melt women at fifty paces, were now turned full beam on Finn.

'The English can lay claim to many things, but I don't think karaoke is one of them,' Finn replied, but he knew he was going to lose the debate. He'd worked with Mateo many times since they'd met, and he knew the cameraman was relentless in his pursuit of a good night out. If Finn didn't just acquiesce, he'd spend the evening being nagged by text about it.

'Besides,' Mateo was saying, 'it'll give us the chance to check out the, er, *charms* of Roseford. We've been so busy on set, I've barely had time to get to know the locals.'

'You're incorrigible,' Finn muttered, but grinned in resignation.

'You know it.' Mateo grinned back. 'So it's a date?'

'Sure. Okay.' Finn shook his head. 'But I'm not singing. You can get up there and embarrass yourself if you want to. I'll get the drinks.'

'We'll see,' Mateo replied. 'I have a feeling that, once the music starts, you'll be pulled straight back to your musical dramedy roots, and there'll be no wrestling you off the mic!'

Finn really did laugh then. 'My singing days are definitely over,' he said. He'd had far too much of all that, back in the day, complete with musical arrangements that stretched his lungs, and choreography that tried the patience of a young man who, at six foot four and a bit, was entirely too tall to be dancing around a stage. He'd never really gotten over the feeling of being the gangly ostrich in a flock of perfectly formed swans.

And despite his lightness of tone with Mateo, over the years, Finn had developed a bit of a phobia of singing in public. The further he'd got away from *High School Dreams*, the more the prospect of singing in front of people again frightened him. It was something he was more than happy to consign to the past. Or the shower.

The two friends agreed to meet later at the pub, and as Finn set off back to his room to learn his lines, he found himself thinking about Lucy again, and looking forward to their date tomorrow night.

As Finn climbed the stairs to his room, he received a text from Kathryn, the director, that reminded him about the early call in the morning. He wondered with a wry smile if she'd got wind of Mateo's plans for a wild night of amateur singing at the local pub. *That's what passes for a wild night, these days, is it?* he thought ruefully. He'd had his fair share of those in his mid-twenties, and was now more often to be found with a cup of coffee and a good book during his downtime. But, despite himself, he was starting to look forward to it. After all, chances were it would only be him, Mateo, and a couple of locals. How wild could it get?

At about seven-thirty that evening, Finn got his answer. He'd heard the babble of punters downstairs in the bar from his room above, slightly louder, it seemed, than on a normal night, and as his phone pinged with a message from Mateo, he headed down to the bar. Finn had given up alcohol some years back, but he still liked the atmosphere of a pub, and was getting quite accustomed to the taste of the many alcohol-free beers that were now on the market. One too many mornings waking up after late nights in dubious bars and clubs in whichever location he happened to be working in had put paid to his drinking, and a short stint at a wellness clinic in Arizona had taught him some better habits; better ways to manage the stress.

As he opened the door from the accommodation that led into the bar, Finn could see Mateo already chatting to the landlord.

'What can I get you?' Mateo asked as he approached.

'A pint of Guinness Zero, please,' Finn replied.

'Still on the wagon, then?' Mateo said. 'How long's it been?'

'Five years,' Finn said. 'You oughta try it.'

'You're joking, right?' Mateo gave a grin. 'If I knew I'd have to kiss goodbye to tequila for good, what would be the point in going on?'

Finn gave a theatrical shudder. 'That's one shot I can definitely live without.'

'Suit yourself,' Mateo replied. He turned back to the landlord and waved his card at the reader on the bar. 'So, what time does the karaoke start, Dave?'

'About eight o'clock,' Dave the barman replied. 'Why? You boys good singers? You'll have to do a lot to wrestle the mic from Big Barry Somers and his mates. They like a good sing-along once a month.'

'Well, I'm more your gifted amateur, but our boy Finn here is a pro.' Mateo flashed a mischievous grin over his shoulder at

Finn, who grimaced back. 'Surely you remember him on the TV?'

Dave regarded Finn solidly for a long moment, then shook his head. 'Nah,' he replied. 'Can't say as I do.'

Finn felt his face flush a little as Mateo clapped him on the shoulder. 'Finn here was quite the singer. He'd be more than happy to give Big Barry a run for his money.'

'Well, I'll look forward to it,' Dave replied.

Mateo led Finn to a table near where the karaoke machine had been set up, and settled back into the cushioned banquette seat.

'Jeez,' he said, taking a deep gulp of his pint. 'I'd forgotten just how complicated the camera set-ups were for a FilmFlix production. There's so much money on the line, Nicole can't afford any screw ups, and she's pushing us all to the limit already, to make sure Kathryn's happy.'

'Well, this is a big deal for her,' Finn said reasonably, bringing the pint of Guinness Zero to his lips. 'Her first Film-Flix production as second assistant director, and a Christmas movie as well. She's bound to be uptight.'

'Yeah, I guess,' Mateo replied. He had an odd, wistful expression on his face that Finn wasn't used to seeing. 'I wish I could do something to make it easier for her, that's all.' He shook his head. 'But she doesn't tend to listen to me much any more.'

Finn grinned at his friend. 'What, not since you and she hooked up on that documentary shoot, you mean? I thought you were both over that.'

'So did I,' Mateo replied. 'But she won't let me in on this job. And it would be so much easier if she did.'

'Hardly surprising,' Finn replied. 'I mean, you made no

secret of the fact that what happened before was just a stopover for you. I thought Nicole felt the same?'

Mateo shook his head. 'I thought that's all it was at the time. Ships that pass, you know. But... oh, I don't know... three years later, seeing her again... makes me wonder what I've missed.'

Finn feigned a shocked expression. 'Who are you and what have you done with Mateo Torres?'

Mateo punched him playfully on the arm. 'Says the man who hasn't got laid since he was playing a high schooler!'

'Not true,' Finn replied. 'I just don't feel the need to shout about every conquest.'

'Touché,' Mateo replied, but then his face assumed its serious expression again. 'I just hoped that a few weeks on location with Nicole might make her realise that I'm not the asshole she thought I was after our fling. I'd like to think this job'll give me time to change her mind.'

'Don't you think it'd be easier not to mix business with pleasure?' Finn asked. 'I mean, relationships on location aren't exactly renowned for their longevity. Perhaps it's better to get the job out of the way first, then talk to Nicole about how you feel.'

'Ah, but where's the fun in that, my friend?' Mateo gave a deep, rumbling laugh. 'Life wouldn't be half so interesting without the complications.'

'Oh, I don't know,' Finn replied. 'I like uncomplicated. It's a whole lot less stressful.'

'I'll take that from the guy who was America's sweetheart for three years,' Mateo said. 'Uncomplicated must seem appealing when you couldn't even leave your apartment without getting a long lens shoved up your ass.'

Finn nodded. 'You know it.'

They drank their beers in companionable silence and watched as the pub began to fill up. In the far corner, Finn could see a group of guys who'd just come in getting in some drinks and wondered if that was Big Barry Somers and his mates. They seemed an amicable lot, but made short work of their first batch of pints. Karaoke night was obviously the place to be, as the party atmosphere was starting to build now they'd arrived.

Finn's first impressions were confirmed, as within half an hour, he was glad he and Mateo had snagged a table. The pub was heaving, both with locals and people he recognised from the film set. For a hopeful moment, he wondered if Lucy would come out to sing karaoke, but then he remembered what she'd said about Megan's nativity play being tonight. Having a young daughter obviously meant that she couldn't just drop everything, he reasoned.

The first few singers got the crowd going, and when Barry and his friends approached the mic for their turn, Finn regarded them with polite interest. Barry, a tall, rotund, middle-aged man, turned out to have a strong Welsh baritone, and did a reasonable job of singing Tom Jones's 'Delilah', much to the appreciation of his mates and the rest of the crowd. Mateo turned to Finn and grinned. 'He's a tough act to follow,' he said, downing his pint as his name was called out next.

Mateo, true to his South American roots, had a great sense of timing and a husky, seductive voice, which he'd often used to great effect between takes to raise the spirits of his crew. He acquitted himself well singing 'Suspicious Minds' and earned a reasonable round of applause for the effort. Grinning in triumph, he returned to his place next to Finn.

'Still got it.' Mateo's eyes twinkled as he took a sip from the pint he'd ordered on the way back to his seat. 'Wonder if you have.'

'We're not going to find out,' Finn replied. 'I told you, my singing days are over.' Just the thought of standing up and singing was enough to send him into an anxiety spiral.

At that point, the landlord pulled the next name out of the hat. 'And the next lamb to the slaughter is... Finn Sanderson.' He glanced around, searching the pub. 'Come on... don't be shy, Finn!'

Finn turned to Mateo. 'You didn't...'

Mateo waggled his eyebrows. 'I know you wouldn't want to let the audience down. And the song seemed a good fit.'

Finn shook his head. 'I'm not going up there,' he said firmly.

The crowd was getting restless, looking around for Finn to take his place by the karaoke machine. A couple of the younger customers nudged and pointed in his direction as the penny dropped. Finn had tucked himself away in the darkest corner of the pub, but his famous name was now drawing attention.

'Go on!' Mateo hissed. 'What harm can it do?'

'No,' Finn repeated. 'You go and sing it if you want to.' He drained the rest of his pint. 'I'm out of here.'

Standing up quickly, he headed towards the exit. As he left, he heard Mateo speaking to the landlord. 'Sorry, he doesn't want to sing tonight after all.'

The cold night air hit Finn like a slap in the face after the warmth of the pub. Putting his hands into his jacket pockets, he took in several gulps of icy air, and tried to still his racing heart. It was only pub karaoke, after all. No one was asking him to do an arena tour, like he'd done back in the old days. Nevertheless, the fear rolled over him in waves as he struggled for breath. Mateo hadn't meant to upset him, he knew, but the thought of standing up in front of people was enough to make Finn tremble. There was no way he was ever doing that again. He heard Mateo calling to him from the pub doorway, his voice laced with concern, but he picked up his pace and slipped away, heart still racing.

As he headed further away from the pub, a figure slipped out of a doorway and began to tail him, eyes fixed on Finn's departing back.

17

'Not such a big movie star now, are you?' The voice was slurred, but still felt like a lash on Finn's back as he was walking away. He had been used to people, mainly men, courting confrontation back when he'd been a globally recognisable face, but it hadn't happened in so long that it took him by surprise, especially in a small place like Roseford.

Finn kept walking. 'Hey, mate,' the voice continued, 'I'm talking to you.'

Finn sighed and stopped. 'Can I help you?' he said, carefully composing his features into a look of what he hoped was placid neutrality.

'Why didn't you sing in there? We not good enough for you?' Alcohol marred his voice, and Finn knew he had to tread carefully.

'Not at all,' he said. 'I guess I just wasn't in the mood tonight.'

'Nah,' the guy replied. 'I don't think it's that.' He paused, and Finn could see the man's right hand clenching slightly. 'I think you think you're better than all of us. Why'n't you prove it now?'

Finn felt the threat of a fight starting to creep up his spine, and knew he had to get away.

'I don't think so,' he said calmly. 'I've gotta go.'

'Oh, don't go, mate.' The guy was persistent; he'd give him that. 'C'mon. Let's get a selfie.'

Finn straightened his back and looked the guy in the eye. 'Maybe some other time.'

'What? I'm not good enough to take a selfie with you? That it?' He lurched towards Finn, and Finn took a step away, not wanting to turn his back on his harasser. He'd encountered plenty of drunks in his time, and he knew when to push back and when to walk away. It would be all too easy to snap back and find himself the subject of a whole lot of headlines, for all the wrong reasons.

'Some other time,' Finn repeated, turning once more. But before he could put some distance between them, the guy had taken a swing. It was a lucky shot, and one, given his state of drunkenness, he never should have landed, but as the guy's fist connected with Finn's right eye, stars exploded in Finn's head and anger in his craw. Balling his own fists, and breathing heavily, he had to tense every sinew not to strike back. As he shook his head, trying to clear his vision, another punch landed, in his gut this time, and the wind was knocked out of him.

'Jake! What the hell are you doing?' A horrified female voice came from behind Finn as the guy prepared to take another swing. As the owner of the voice dashed to Finn's side, obviously completely unconcerned about getting caught in the crossfire, Jake, distracted by her cries, overbalanced and ended up falling on his face. Finn turned to see who she was, and he quickly realised it was Lucy. The adrenaline was still coursing through him, and as a result, he was a little more abrupt with her than he should have been.

'This guy a friend of yours?' he said, staring down at the man's prone but thankfully moving form.

'Not really,' Lucy said back, equally briskly. 'We were at school together. His temper's a lot shorter than he is.'

'That'd take some doing,' Finn muttered. The guy was barely five feet six standing, and now looked considerably shorter, sprawled in the gutter.

'Get up, Jake, you stupid twat,' Lucy said firmly. 'Go home and sleep it off.' She tried to heave the man up from where he was lying, but he merely groaned and buried his head in his arm.

Finn, realising that Lucy wasn't going to be able to shift the guy by herself, leaned down and grabbed Jake's other arm, hauling him to his feet. 'Come on,' he said as the reluctant Jake found his feet, 'let's get you home.'

'He lives in the newer bit of the village,' Lucy said. She paused. 'Look, can you wait with him for a minute? I'd just nipped out to get a pint of milk and Megan's in bed. I'll help you get him home, but I need to ask my neighbour to sit in the house while I do, just in case Megan wakes up.'

'Sure, sure,' Finn replied. Privately, he was inclined just to leave Jake in the gutter, but it was freezing outside and he didn't want the guy to get hypothermia on top of everything else.

'I won't be a sec.' Lucy hurried off back to her house, and within a few minutes she was back again. Jake still hadn't stirred, despite the fact that Finn was now basically holding him up. As Lucy got under Jake's other arm, between them, they started half dragging, half walking Jake towards where he needed to go. Puffing and panting as they went, by the time they'd got to the cul-de-sac where Jake's house was, they were both exhausted.

'Thanks, Luce,' Jake muttered, conveniently regaining consciousness as, eventually, they deposited him on the doorstep and then rang the bell. 'Mum's gonna skin me alive me for this.'

'As well she should,' Lucy said. She was breathing heavily, as was Finn, and despite the cold air, Finn felt hot and bothered, having supported more than half of Jake's weight the three-quarters of a mile to his door. Lucy had helped as best she could, but he didn't want her to struggle. He could feel his eye getting puffy, as well as an ache in his torso from the surprisingly well-placed punch, and wondered what the hell make-up were going to say in the morning.

Double-checking that Jake wasn't going to fall off the step where he'd sat down, waiting for the door to open, Lucy turned back to Finn. 'I think it's safe to leave him to his own devices now,' she said breathlessly, her face flushed from exertion and the cold.

'All right.' Finn smiled, and then winced at the pain. 'I'd better get back to my room, anyway.'

'Have you got anything to put on that eye?' Lucy asked. 'It looks really sore.'

'I'm sure Dave can sort out some ice for me,' Finn replied.

'I don't think it's such a good idea to go straight back into a crowded pub looking like that,' Lucy said. 'I mean, if you weren't caught on camera fighting Jake, there're bound to be a few people who'll be more than happy to take a picture of you with a black eye. Wouldn't exactly be the best thing for your reputation, would it?'

Finn considered her words. 'I wasn't fighting him,' he said at last. 'But he seemed pretty intent on fighting me.'

'Well, I only caught the tail end of it,' Lucy said as they walked, 'so I'll have to take your word for that.'

Finn sighed. 'Guilty until proven innocent, is that it?'

'Not at all,' Lucy said stoutly. 'Anyway, what's the best plan?' She stopped and Finn could immediately see that she was struggling with something. He waited.

'So, I have a bag of frozen peas at my place,' she said, after a long pause. 'Don't take this the wrong way, but it might be a good idea to get your eye sorted out before you brave the pub. Then you can sneak back in when it's quieter.'

Finn smiled at her. 'Aren't you worried about inviting a strange guy with a beat-up face over your threshold?'

Lucy laughed. 'You're not exactly a strange guy. We're going out for a drink tomorrow, remember?'

Finn found himself smiling back at her, despite the pain it caused in his cheeks. 'All right, then. But I promise I wasn't fighting Jake, for what it's worth.'

'I believe you,' Lucy said. They walked briskly back towards the centre of Roseford, their progress a lot quicker now they weren't lugging Jake between them. Lucy made a quick call on her mobile to let her neighbour, Bev, know that she was on her way home, too, and she'd be back very shortly so she could go. Finn felt relieved that there wasn't going to be anyone else at Lucy's place to ask probing questions about his black eye.

In a few minutes, Lucy slowed down and dug a door key out of her handbag as they reached the small terraced house next to the café. 'This is me. Come in and make yourself comfortable. Lounge is on the left. I'll get the peas.'

Finn, feeling grateful that Lucy had rescued him from running the gauntlet of the bar in the pub, followed behind her, and then veered off into the cosy living room as Lucy had directed. His eye was throbbing quite badly now, and he cursed Jake for deciding to pick a fight with him the night before his big scene with Montana. He knew from experience that make-up artists were miracle workers, but hoped Lucy's frozen peas would at least start to ease the swelling. He debated texting Montana to fill her in on what had happened, but she was probably learning lines for tomorrow, and he didn't want to bother her. Settling back into the cushions of Lucy's very comfortable sofa, he closed his eyes against the pain and hoped Lucy might be able to dig out some painkillers to go with the peas.

18

As she hurried through the hallway to her kitchen at the back of the cottage, Lucy puffed out a breath. Bloody Jake! He had a nose for trouble at the best of times, had done since school. What on earth had he been thinking, picking a fight with Finn, who was almost a foot taller and twice as broad? She was reminded of a run-in she'd once seen between a Highland Terrier and a Great Dane. The terrier, fur flying, had launched itself at the Dane's neck, who, after looking in bewilderment at it, had calmly grabbed hold of the red coat the Scottie had been wearing and rolled the little dog over, right into a juicy, fresh cowpat. Jake, for all of his noise and fury, would probably regret the confrontation in the morning, as he always did.

Retrieving the bag of peas from the under-counter freezer in her kitchen, she flipped the switch on the kettle and then headed back to the living room, where Finn had found the sofa. As she entered the room, she drew a sharp, involuntary breath at the slightly surreal sight of him, leaning back on the cushions, eyes closed, long legs spread out in front of him, knees bent and slightly apart. His right eye was rapidly turning purple, and she hurried to give him the peas to put on it.

'Here you are,' she said, loudly enough to alert him to her presence. His eyes flew open and he tried to sit up a bit.

'No, don't move,' she continued. 'You look comfy there.'

'Thanks,' Finn said quietly, taking the bag of peas from her and wincing as he placed them on his eye. Lucy tried not to feel a surge of electrifying excitement as their fingers touched.

'Can I get you some paracetamol as well?' Lucy asked. 'I didn't want to presume, but I've got plenty if you need them.'

'That would be great,' Finn said, eyes closed again.

'I'll go and grab some. Would you like a cup of tea, too?'

'Oh, that fine English solution to every problem!' Finn said wryly. 'My mom used to hand me a cuppa for everything from a grazed knee to a broken heart.'

'Well, it works,' said Lucy. 'Unless you'd like something stronger?'

'Uh, no, thank you,' Finn replied. 'The tea's fine.'

Lucy hurried off to get the tea and the painkillers, and while she was in the kitchen, she remembered a gel pack in the freezer that she'd bought to soothe Megan's knocks and bangs. She figured it would be just as good as the peas, which would be starting to warm up soon. Returning to the living room with two cups of tea, a glass of water and a packet of paracetamol, she passed the gel pack to Finn and then sat down in the armchair nearby.

'Thank you,' Finn said again, removing the peas from his eye to take a sip of the piping hot tea, before resetting the gel pack on the bruise.

A slightly strained silence descended between them as they both contemplated their mugs. Lucy, feeling as though she ought to try to put Jake's behaviour in context a little, finally broke it.

'So how did it start?' she asked.

Finn shook his head, and then winced at the action. 'That guy, Jake, he's not the first one to try to take me on. Some people just see a face they recognise and want to provoke, I guess.'

'So it kind of goes with the territory, does it?' Lucy glanced from her cup of tea back to Finn, who was looking her way. As her eyes locked, she gave a sympathetic smile. 'But what caused it this time?'

'I didn't want to join in with the karaoke at the pub,' Finn replied. His pulse started to race as he relived the anxiety of being put on the spot to sing, even in a casual setting like the pub. 'I find it... difficult to sing in public these days. He, er, saw that as an insult. Must have followed me from the bar. Decided to take matters into his own hands.'

'Doesn't it drive you nuts, being called out like that on every little decision?' Lucy asked.

Finn laughed, and Lucy felt her stomach do a little flip at the sound. 'You get used to it after a while.'

'Not exactly fair, though, is it? I mean, there you are, minding your own business and one of the locals starts on you.'

'I'm more concerned about what the make-up artist is going to say tomorrow, to be honest,' Finn replied. 'But then they've had to cover up some pretty bad things in the past.'

'Oh, yeah?' Lucy was trying to keep the conversation going, but she was also intrigued. 'Like what?'

'Oh, similar things,' Finn said vaguely. 'One of my co-stars on *High School Dreams* had a habit of seeing the wrong end of the night and getting covered in bruises at the worst moments.'

Lucy had a clear feeling she knew which co-star Finn was talking about. Far from Finn's character, who was a bit of an all-American goody two shoes, the other male lead had been well known as a bad boy, both on and off screen. Happily settled now with a wife and kids in America's Midwest, he'd turned it around, but Lucy could imagine his antics in the old days would have made any self-respecting make-up artist cringe.

Finn sat back again, having swallowed the painkillers with a gulp of water, and sighed. 'That guy had quite a punch, though.'

'Jake used to box, back when he was a teenager,' Lucy replied. 'Was convinced he was going to be the next Wladimir Klitschko. Didn't quite work out like that, though.'

'So what's his story?'

Lucy sighed. 'Same as pretty much anyone's around here. Jake left school, went to agricultural college but dropped out when his dad was taken into hospital. He had a series of low-paying jobs, but now he's in his mid-twenties, can't afford to buy a house in the village he grew up in. There's plenty of people with a similar story in Roseford, unfortunately.'

'And so the pub is his arena, now, instead of the boxing ring?' Finn replied. 'Like one of those guys who lives for the ball game at the end of the week.'

'Something like that,' Lucy replied. 'He'll sort himself out one day, but in the meantime it's a bit of a slog for his mum, and his sister Marie, who's younger than him, trying to keep him out of trouble.'

'I'm glad I didn't fight back, in that case,' Finn said, wincing as he prodded his bruised eye gingerly with a fingertip. 'Sounds like the guy's got enough to deal with.'

'Yes and no,' Lucy conceded. 'He does need to grow up, as well! I mean, lamping everyone he disagrees with is really going to get him into trouble one day. It's a good job you're so calm.' She paused, before adding, with a trace of devilry in her voice, 'For a famous film star and all that.'

Finn laughed, then drew in a sharp breath as the pain in his torso reminded him of Jake's other punch. 'I've had bigger guys than him trying to take me on, just because of who they think I am.'

'And who *are* you, Finn Sanderson?' Lucy's voice was teasing still, but she suddenly really wanted to know the answer.

Finn considered this for a moment. 'Just some guy who had a lucky break, I guess.'

'Although not quite so lucky tonight.' Lucy observed Finn flinch as he shifted slightly on the sofa. 'Are your ribs all right?'

Finn looked at her again. 'They will be. There's probably a bit of a bruise there as well, but the make-up artist won't be worried about that.'

'No need for any shirtless scenes in this movie, then?' Lucy asked, and then felt her cheeks burning when she realised what she'd said. 'Sorry. None of my business. And a bit unfair.' She had a sudden, vivid flashback to a poster she'd had on her bedroom wall as a sixteen-year-old that had all five main male cast members from the show dressed in board shorts and posing with surfboards. Finn's oiled torso had haunted her adolescent dreams irresistibly for a long time after that.

Finn laughed, and then grimaced. 'It's fine. Although I'm

kind of glad. I'm not the same person I was thirteen years ago! I, er, don't have to wax my chest any more, for one thing.'

'I'm trying not to think about that,' Lucy said, and then, before she could catch Finn's eye, put her flaming face in her hands. 'I am *so* sorry. I don't want to sound like all those other mad fangirls.'

Finn stayed quiet for a long moment before he answered. 'I get it, Lucy, really I do. This must feel surreal. But I'm just a guy, honestly. And I'm thankful you came and broke things up tonight when you did. That took guts.'

'Oh, Jake wouldn't have hurt me,' Lucy said. 'As I said, we go way back.'

'All the same,' Finn replied. 'I'm grateful.'

There was another pause. Finn shifted again on the sofa. Lucy could tell the painkillers hadn't quite kicked in yet.

'Can I get you a biscuit?' she said suddenly, to counteract what would soon be an awkward silence.

'I'm good, thanks,' Finn replied. 'But don't let me stop you.'

'I'm fine,' Lucy said. 'The pub'll be emptying out soon and you should be able to get back in without too many people noticing you.' She leaned forward in her chair. 'Let me take a look at that eye.'

As Finn took the gel pack away from his bruised eye, Lucy regarded him speculatively. 'It looks a bit less inflamed,' she said, 'although it's bloodshot still. Can I take a closer look?'

Finn smiled. 'Sure. Go for it.'

Gently, she put a hand on his cheek and turned his head slightly, so she could get a better view. 'If I were you, I'd sleep with an icepack on it tonight.'

'Great,' Finn groaned. 'I'm nervous enough as it is about the set-up tomorrow. Now I'll be sleep deprived as well.'

'Oh, the things you endure for your art!' Lucy grinned. It still felt strange, having a normal conversation with the bloke she'd had such a teen crush on, but joking with him felt oddly... *natural*, somehow.

Looking down at him, Lucy's heart did a little flip. Despite the black eye, he really did have such a lovely, open face. His gorgeous, hazel-coloured eyes were closed, but his long dark lashes fluttered as she spent a little longer than necessary examining his bruised right eye. His mouth was just as kiss-able up close as she'd imagined it to be, all those years ago, but she put a halt on thoughts like that instantly.

Suddenly, Finn's eyes flew open as one of Lucy's fingertips probed a little too firmly on his cheekbone. She felt him recoil under her touch.

'Sorry,' she stammered, taking a step back. 'I didn't mean to make it worse.'

'It's all right.' Finn smiled up at her, and then cleared his throat. 'I, er, really should be going. I've got an early start in the morning, and from what you've said, I'd better keep some ice on this eye.'

As Finn stood up, Lucy found herself gazing upwards at him, and wondering... wondering...

'Well, thank you for sacrificing your frozen peas,' Finn said, bringing her sharply back to earth. 'I, er guess they won't be much good for eating now.'

Lucy burst out laughing. 'In all of the daydreams I had about you as a teenager, frozen peas did not figure high on the agenda, but I'll take it!'

'I'm not sure I want to know what did,' Finn laughed as Lucy walked him to the door.

'Don't get me started.'

There was a pause before Finn stepped through the door that Lucy had opened. 'I guess I'll see you tomorrow,' he said, a little more softly. 'Goodnight, Lucy.'

'Goodnight, Finn,' Lucy replied.

She closed the door, watching him lope in his long-legged way down the High Street and back towards the pub. *What a night.* For a long moment, she allowed herself to wallow in the memory of touching Finn's face, and the incredible temptation she'd had to lean down and plant a gentle kiss on his mouth, and all that might have happened next...

A moan from upstairs tore her away from the fantasy, which was rapidly becoming decidedly less PG-rated, as Megan awoke and groggily called her name.

'Coming, darling,' Lucy called softly as she ambled up the stairs. It was then she realised that, in rescuing Finn from Jake's fists, she'd completely forgotten to grab the extra pint of milk from Southgate's Stores she'd snuck out for in the first place.

19

A little later that night, having managed to settle a dead-on-her-feet Megan back into bed, Lucy made another cup of tea with the last of the milk she had in the fridge and braced herself to look more closely at the photograph that Rob had sent her. She guessed she shouldn't be surprised; Rob was across social media more or less all the time as part of his job and, despite the fact that they weren't raising their daughter together, he was still involved with their lives and they had maintained a good friendship.

Rob and Lucy had split up shortly after Megan's birth and although, at the time, it had been devastating, things had all eventually worked out for the best. Lucy's mother had welcomed her home with open arms, and even moved out of the cottage in Roseford and into a house in Taunton so that Lucy could have her own space with her growing daughter. Rob had determinedly pursued his desire to become a film director and was now based largely in California, where he'd won awards and settled with his long-term partner, Tina.

They'd gone on to have a child of their own and Megan loved spending time with her blended family when she saw them. Lucy, with the money that Rob and his family had given her to support herself and Megan as a deposit, and a hefty mortgage, had eventually bought the café next door to her house, and had made the slightly run-down business into a successful enterprise. She'd knocked through the party wall between the two properties for convenience, which made working there even easier.

Rob and Tina, and their young daughter, were due to come over during the Christmas holidays to see Megan and stay with Rob's mother in Henley-on-Thames. He would take Megan with him and Lucy knew that Megan would have a wonderful time. Lucy's situation was somewhat unusual but, over the years, she and Rob had made it work. So she didn't feel angry that he had immediately texted the photograph to her; but she did want to speak to him to find out what the possible implications of having this photograph on social media might be. Sipping her tea, she dialled through to Rob, who would just be having his lunch.

'Hey, gorgeous,' he said, picking up the phone on the fourth ring. 'Thought I might be hearing from you soon. How are you doing?'

Lucy, despite her discomfiture at the photograph, smiled at Rob's pronounced transatlantic twang. 'Not bad,' she said. 'A bit less than good since you sent me that photograph.'

'I thought you'd like to know,' he said. 'So, what gives?'

'I don't know,' she replied. 'And that's the honest truth.'

'Are you seeing him?' There was the glug of what sounded like coffee pouring into a mug as Rob waited for her response.

'Not really,' Lucy replied. 'It's, er, complicated.'

'Well, if you are going to be seen in public with Finn Sanderson, you'll have to get used to these kind of photographs appearing, even in your safe haven of Roseford. Are you ready for that?'

Lucy shook her head, even though they were on a call and Rob wouldn't be able to see it. 'I just don't know. I was never really comfortable with the prospect of being the partner of a director, let alone a leading actor. This is all such new territory to me.'

'Well, I wish I could offer you more advice, but if there's one thing that I've learned over the years, it's that you will follow your instincts and your heart and there's nothing wrong with that. Just be careful. There's Megan in the equation too and I'd hate to see her exposed to any unwelcome publicity.'

Lucy, despite her amiable relationship with Rob, felt a prickle of irritation. 'As if I would let anyone put Megan in that position!'

Rob let out a long sigh on the other end of the line. 'I know you wouldn't,' he said. 'But as you've seen tonight, it's not always in your control. If you've got a smart phone, you can take a photograph these days. Anyone connected to the film will sign an NDA, of course, but that really doesn't stop a random guy with an iPhone trying to get a bit of cheap publicity. Be careful, Lucy-Lou. You can't really protect yourself against that.'

'I am being careful,' Lucy replied. 'We've only agreed to go out for a drink. I doubt anything will even come of it.'

'On the upside,' said Rob, 'I worked with Finn on an indie film a few years ago. He's about as decent as they come for someone who's worked in the industry for as long as he has.'

'You never told me that!' Lucy replied.

Rob laughed. 'I know what a fan of his you used to be,' he said. 'I didn't want to put you into his orbit.'

'Twat,' she replied with a laugh.

'Well, you did have that T-shirt with his face on when we were dating,' he said. 'That's quite a tough act to live up to.'

'You mostly managed,' Lucy said wryly.

'Just be careful, Lucy,' Rob replied. 'I've seen lots of these relationships go public and the intrusion can be too much to bear.'

'I will,' Lucy replied. 'And I do appreciate the heads-up.'

As they said goodbye, Lucy felt grateful that she had Rob in her corner. Things could have gone so differently when their relationship had ended. It wasn't that she hadn't been dreadfully hurt when they'd called it a day, but she knew he was a decent person, and that he had her best interests at heart, even from so many miles away.

Feeling suddenly tired, she decided to turn in. She was going to be on her feet most of tomorrow as usual at the café, and with Christmas rapidly approaching it was going to be another long day. Heading off to bed, she tried not to give that rogue photo any more thought.

20

The snow continued to fall steadily through the night, and when the morning came, Finn was not surprised to see a message on his phone from the director, cancelling the early call, but summoning him to a meeting at the site of the second unit at 8 a.m. Assuming that Montana had received the same message, Finn jumped in the shower, grabbed a light breakfast from the bar area downstairs in the pub and waited for his co-star to join him.

In very little time, Montana had come down to the dining room. She had her hair pulled back in a ponytail and was wearing an oversized hoody, a pair of skinny jeans and sturdy trainers. It was her typical 'off duty' look; there was no point in putting make-up on and dressing up if it was all going to be changed once she got to the unit.

'So it looks like the shoot in the centre of the village is off,' Finn said as Montana helped herself to coffee and a couple of pieces of fruit from the self-service continental buffet that Dave the landlord had put on for them.

'Guess so,' Montana murmured.

She was never great in the mornings and Finn knew better than to get into specifics before she'd had her first cup of coffee of the day. She hadn't even noticed that he was sporting a rather impressive shiner after his altercation with Jake, although Lucy's swift attention and a bag of ice from the bar before bed had done much to take it down overnight.

'Although I wouldn't put it past Kathryn to shovel the real snow away and make us do the same with fake stuff anyway!' Finn joked. But as soon as he said it, he knew the problem wasn't the snow so much as getting a hundred or so extras into Roseford when they would have trouble making it safely down the valley on the minor roads. Movie shoots could deal with a lot of things, but heavy and unexpected snowfall probably did mean rescheduling today's scenes, at least.

'So long as we don't need to learn new lines at short notice,' Montana said. She was starting to revive now she'd had a couple of gulps of coffee.

'Guess we'll just have to wait and see,' Finn replied, finishing off his slice of toast, deciding against another one and grabbing a couple of pieces of fruit instead and a fresh cup of coffee. 'Are you ready to go?'

'Yup.' Montana knocked back her own coffee. 'Let's do this.' It was then she finally noticed the state of Finn's right eye. 'Jesus, Finn. What the hell happened?'

'Someone took a dislike to me outside the pub last night,' Finn replied. As Montana started to berate him, he held up his hands. 'Before you get started, no, I didn't do anything to provoke him, and no, I wasn't drinking.'

'Well, let's hope that Carol can fix you up enough for

Kathryn's liking,' Montana said. 'Or we'll end up shooting around that side of your face until the bruising goes down.'

Finn grinned. 'Do you think you can still fake falling in love with me, even with a black eye?'

Montana shook her head. 'I've seen you look worse.' But, with typical diplomacy, she didn't elaborate. Finn knew all too well that she was right, and he was grateful that their friendship had endured, despite all of the things that could have ruined it.

They strolled the short distance to the second unit, which was a small village in itself made up of trailers, all situated on the gravel car park of Roseford Hall. It was far enough away from the house not to interfere with the production, but close enough that anyone connected to the film who was staying in the village could easily walk between the two, even in this weather.

As it turned out, Kathryn the director, resourceful as ever, had worked out a way around the unexpected snowfall and decided to film a couple of kiss scenes between Finn and Montana, using the backdrop of the actual snow. 'Why waste an opportunity?' Kathryn grinned when she briefed Montana and Finn and then spoke to the rest of the crew. 'We can do some close-up shots of the two of you under the lamp post that'll only need a few of the extras who managed to get here last night as background, and when the snow clears, we can reschedule the market scenes. And,' she trailed off and scrutinised Finn, 'we can do mostly left profile shots, if make-up can't quite make that black eye disappear.'

Finn sighed in relief. He knew Kathryn was probably going to bawl him out later for getting into a scrape, but for the moment, it seemed he was off the hook.

'Well, I'm glad we're not going to lose a day, for either my eye or the weather,' Finn said as he and Montana sat patiently waiting for the make-up crew to work their magic. They were both in costume now; Finn in a pair of thick beige cords and the tweed jacket he'd come to associate most strongly with his character, Jack Salmon, and a blue button-down shirt. Carol was just dampening down his hair to get it into Jack Salmon's style and he was looking over the lines he would have to say to Montana's character under the lamp post.

'I hope we're not out there too long,' Montana said. 'The damp's going to make my hair frizz.'

'That's my job to worry about,' said Carol. 'You just do your thing and let me do mine!' She turned back to Finn. 'Hair's the last thing on my mind, anyway. We've got to get the attention away from that eye of yours.' She looked squarely at Finn, who, used to the scrutiny of make-up artists, looked calmly back. Then, she got to work with a base layer of green concealer, which she applied under both eyes, and after that, covered it with one that matched his skin tone. By the time she was finished, apart from a slight swelling that was noticeable in profile on his right side, all evidence of the shiner had been hidden.

'Now don't you go touching it,' Carol warned. 'The last thing I need to be doing is holding up production in the freezing cold just to fix your face. And the damp'll play havoc with the coverage.'

'I won't,' Finn replied. He found Carol's tone, somewhat like his mother when he'd come back from ice hockey training with a bruise or a bang, quite comforting, despite her firmness.

A little later, Finn and Montana were standing by the black

metal Victorian-style lamp post at the edge of Roseford market square. Around them were four members of the camera crew, including the clapper loader, who was writing the scene number on the board. A track had been set up by the grip and the camera was in the process of being mounted, having been protected from the cold until the very last moment. The sound operator had attached microphones to Montana and Finn, and Carol's assistant, Laney, had come out, wrapped in a thick jacket, ready to do any last-minute touch-ups for the cameras. The road had been closed, and the businesses fronting onto the market square had been asked to lock their doors and keep their lights on just in case they got into shot, although since the sequence was going to be pretty tight, that shouldn't be an issue.

Finn glanced over to Roseford Café, which, thankfully, was a little further down the road and so had not been asked to close. He found himself wondering what Lucy was up to and kept flicking his gaze between the café and the director as she briefed them on last-minute details about the scene. He owed Lucy a decent evening after the way she'd patched him up last night. He'd been looking forward to their date, but now he felt even more nervous about getting it right. This didn't go unnoticed by Kathryn, who snapped him out of his inattention with a brisk, 'Are you with me, Finn?'

'Uh, yeah. Sorry. I'm listening.'

Montana gave him a knowing look from the depths of the hood of her own thick jacket, which she was only going to remove at the very last minute. When they'd been in a relationship, many years before, Finn had always drawn a joking parallel between Montana's loathing of the cold and the behaviour of his cousin Alex's Weimaraner dog, who flatly refused to put a paw out of the door when it snowed, which, in Vancouver, where Alex had a cider farm, was quite often. The fact that Montana had agreed to shoot this movie at this time of year in the UK was testament to how much affection she still held for him.

'Okay,' Kathryn said. 'Let's go for a rehearsal.'

Finn and Montana, because of their long history of working together, needed minimal briefing when it came to a kiss under a lamp post. They, and the crew, huddled in thick jackets and woolly hats, were particularly pleased about this as all of them were keen to get out of the cold and damp as soon as possible. The sky above was a lowering grey, presaging more snow to come.

'Whose idea was it to film in England in the winter?' Montana muttered as they took their positions beside the lamp post. Tall stage lights had been set up around them to improve a dull winter's day, and the lamplight would be added in post-production.

'It's a good job I like you,' she added to Finn as she gave him a game smile. 'I wouldn't be doing this for anyone else.'

'I know.' Finn returned her smile. A movement in the corner of his eye momentarily distracted his attention. Lucy, drawn to the flurry of activity in the market square, had paused by the bay window of her café and was looking on with great interest.

'You're doing it again,' Montana chided. 'If I really was your love interest, I'd be seriously offended!'

'Sorry,' Finn replied in an undertone as Kathryn approached. She'd been distracted by a last-minute question from the grip, about how far to track into the shot.

'Okay,' Kathryn said as she joined them. 'So, Montana, if

you could deliver your first line, then pause and look across the market square as if you are seeing the place for the first time. Finn, you can then give your first line, then I want you to move in, cup Montana's face and as the camera leans in, that's when the kiss happens.'

Both leads nodded and Kathryn turned back to her crew. 'Okay, let's go for a rehearsal.' She took a step back to be out of the camera's range, called action and paused.

'Could it really be true?' Montana said, a breathless note in her voice as befitting her character, Ashley. Eyes widening, she turned to look across the market square where, in a complementary shot to be done with extras and store holders when the weather improved, it would look to be a hive of activity.

'Ashley, it *is* true,' Finn, as Jack, replied. Pausing for just a beat, he raised his left hand to Montana's cheek, stroked her face slowly and in perfect sync, they turned towards one another, lips meeting in a gentle, exquisitely timed kiss.

'Okay,' Kathryn said as they broke apart. 'That's good. Finn, can you just shift a little to your right next time as you're slightly masking the shot.'

They went again, and Kathryn nodded her approval. 'We'll go for a take now.' She glanced at the third assistant director, who was briefing the ten or so extras who would be milling around, just in shot behind Finn and Montana. The depth of field in the angle of the camera would mean that they would look like blurred silhouettes in the background, but the effect would be that of a bustling market scene. 'Picture's up,' Kathryn called, which signalled to everyone on set that the next call of 'action' would not be a rehearsal and that they were about to record.

'Roll sound, roll camera.'

The sound director called back, 'Speed.'

Mateo, also bundled up against the cold, gave Finn, Montana and Kathryn a brief thumbs up and then confirmed. 'Rolling.'

The clapperboard operator came briefly into shot with the board and then Mateo nodded again.

'Action!' Kathryn focused intently on Finn and Montana as the extras at the back of shot began to mill around. In that split second, Finn, having experienced working with Montana on many occasions, saw the veil of her character come down as she took a deep breath and Ashley, future countess, took the foreground.

'Could it really be true?' she breathed and her eyes widened once more. As directed, she turned to look across the market square, just as before.

'Ashley, it *is* true,' Finn replied and once again, a lift of the hand, a stroke of the face, a gentle kiss timed perfectly for the camera, not masking Montana this time in the slightest, took place under the Victorian lamp post.

'And cut!' Kathryn called, after a long pause to capture the full moment.

The clapperboard operator interjected 'Tail slate!' then snapped the sticks and moved out of shot once more.

'Okay, everybody, well done. Let's reset and just pull in a little more to avoid that patch of grey sky getting too far into shot.'

Montana rubbed her hands together. 'You still kiss like a pro,' she teased Finn.

'You're not so bad yourself,' he replied. 'Although you'd better get some ChapStick on those lips. I think the cold is starting to get to them.'

'Is not!'

'Is too!'

'Okay, children,' Kathryn said. 'Squabble amongst your-selves later. Let's go again.'

As the crew reset, the make-up artist dashed forward to tone down the flush in Montana's cheeks from the cold, and wardrobe straightened Finn's shirt collar. Both stars, used to this kind of last-minute attention, waited patiently. Finn's eyes once again drifted to the window of Lucy's café, but she'd moved away and he could no longer see her. Ridiculously, he was pleased she wasn't standing there. Despite the fact that this was a job, and Montana was a good friend, he suddenly felt a little weird about kissing her. He'd never felt like that before with a screen partner when he'd had a girlfriend, and he wondered why he did now, when he barely knew Lucy.

'Picture's up!' came Kathryn's call once more, and Finn and Montana prepared to repeat the scene. The repetition on film sets was something that was familiar to them both, and they were well used to having to go over scenes again and again. The camera's proximity was also something they were accus-tomed to, and after a few more takes, they broke so that Kathryn could look over the raw footage with the first assistant director.

'Take a break, everyone,' she instructed. 'And grab some-thing warm to drink if you need it. Finn, Montana, good work. Don't go far. We might need you back.'

Finn nodded and shrugged back into the thick parka jacket the unit had provided for him. It had been a chilly morning, but some good work had been done. Now, if he could just catch Lucy at the café to do a last confirmation of their plans for tonight, everything would be great.

21

'Luce! Don't look now, but Finn is coming this way,' Serena hissed. She had popped in for a coffee break and brought her laptop with her to catch up on a few emails. She turned towards Lucy, who was behind the counter, sorting out a mid-morning order of freshly baked scones, Somerset clotted cream and locally sourced raspberry jam.

'Oh, crikey! I thought he'd be too busy to come in here,' Lucy said. She'd been engrossed in watching the process of *A Countess for Christmas* being made, and when Finn and Montana had kissed, even though an enormous camera on the dolly track had virtually obscured them from public gaze, Lucy had felt the weirdest combination of excitement and jealousy. She knew that she was right to feel the first, and that the second was pretty much unjustifiable. This was Finn's job and the reason he was in Roseford.

'Well, he's heading in.' Serena waved her coffee cup in Lucy's direction. 'I'll have another one when you're ready,' she said, obviously settling in for what she thought was going to be a good show.

'Coming right up,' Lucy muttered. She wondered if Finn had seen her staring from the window and started to feel embarrassed that she'd been paying so much attention. Although, she reasoned, it wasn't every day a film crew gathered in the centre of her home village. She busied herself with Serena's fresh coffee, and tried not to jump when the bell rang over the front door and from the corner of her eye, she caught sight of Finn, still in costume, wandering through the door. He greeted Serena, who smiled back at him.

'Hi,' he said to Lucy as he approached the counter. 'How are you?'

Lucy couldn't resist a smile at the fact that his hair had been given a side parting in the style of Jack Salmon, his character. It made him look slightly less 'Finn'. He was still wearing the large puffa jacket over his costume, but the sudden warmth of the café had brought a flush to his cheeks and he fumbled with the zip of the coat, undoing it just a little as he stood at the counter.

'All good here, thanks,' Lucy replied. 'A bit quiet because the road's been closed, but I'm sure business'll pick up later.' She looked more closely at him. 'How's your eye? I can barely see a mark!'

Finn looked apologetic. 'I hope you haven't lost too much trade because of us.'

'It'll be fine,' Lucy replied. 'The snow will be keeping people away anyway while it's still so thick on the ground. Being in the valley, people tend to give us a wide berth in bad weather.' She looked at him again. 'I can't believe how well that bruise has been hidden.'

'It's amazing what a make-up artist can do under pressure!' Finn joked. Lucy couldn't help but notice that he looked around the café as he said it, though. She wondered if he was checking to see who might be listening. Eavesdroppers must be a professional hazard, she thought, deciding not to mention Finn's eye any more.

She glanced over at Serena, who was trying to look as though she wasn't listening to every single word Finn and Lucy were saying. Her laptop was open, and she was, to all intents and purposes, answering emails, but Lucy knew her ears would be on elastic.

Finn suddenly looked endearingly nervous, and Lucy's heart did a little twist in her chest. It was surreal, seeing him in costume, standing there in her café; even more than having him there in his own clothes.

'So,' Finn said finally. 'Are you still okay to meet for a drink later?'

Lucy rather got the impression that the question was just an excuse to make conversation, since they'd pretty much sorted the details last night, but her hands started to tremble and she placed the jug of steaming milk down on the coffee machine for a moment just to regain some equilibrium. 'Yes,' she said, after a moment's pause. 'I'd love to.'

Serena, who'd glided up to the counter to pick up her second coffee, interjected. 'And yes, Lucy, of course I'll babysit for you.' She grinned. 'Nice to see you again, Finn.'

'You too, Serena.' Finn glanced her way and smiled.

'Thanks, hon,' Lucy replied. 'That's a very kind offer, but Mum's picking up Megan tonight so you can stay off duty.'

'If you're sure,' Serena replied. 'I mean, your mum's coming from Taunton. If the roads aren't open again, she's going to struggle to get through.'

'That's true,' Lucy said, cursing herself for so readily accepting her mum's offer. Perhaps she should call her and cancel? The main roads might be open again by the afternoon, but the one down to Roseford wasn't the best. Besides, Lucy got the feeling her best friend rather wanted to be a fly on the wall when she and Finn got back from their date.

'I'm always happy to look after that adorable little munchkin!' Serena continued. She turned back to Finn. 'I'm not just saying that. Megan really is a sweetheart.'

'I'm sure she is.' Finn smiled back at Serena. Then, turning his attention back to Lucy, he continued. 'I have no idea what there is to do in this place when we're snowed in, so would it be okay with you to meet in the bar of the Treloar Arms?'

Lucy nodded. 'That's probably the safest option anyway, in the snow. Even if the main roads are back open by tonight, it's bound to be icy. I'm guessing that the insurance the film company has on you probably doesn't take a broken ankle into account!'

Finn laughed. 'We're on such a tight schedule, we'd probably have to write it into the script!'

God, Lucy thought. His smile really was to die for.

'I'll see you about eight?' she re-confirmed.

'Sounds great.'

Finn paused as his phone beeped. 'Sorry,' he said as he grabbed it from his back pocket and read the message. 'Looks like Kathryn, our director, has had another bright idea about how best to use this unexpected weather. I'd better go. See you later?'

Lucy nodded. 'See you later.'

Finn looked as though he wanted to say something more, but with Serena standing next to him at the counter, he seemed to think better of it. Nodding at Lucy, he turned and headed back out of the café. As the door closed behind him with another chime of the bell, Serena raised both eyebrows at Lucy.

'Not a word,' Lucy said, a warning note in her voice. 'It's a drink. Nothing more. He is who he is and I am who I am, and as far as I'm concerned, that's all there is to it.'

'You can't blame a girl for dreaming when her best mate gets asked out by a movie star,' Serena replied. She gave a sigh. 'If only I could be so lucky.'

Lucy passed Serena her new latte. 'You never know,' she said softly. 'Christmas is when magic is meant to happen. Perhaps we'll both end up falling in love this year. Or maybe just kissing someone lovely under the mistletoe.'

'Now who's fantasising?' Serena said, and Lucy noticed the sadness in her voice. 'It's not exactly as if the woman of my dreams is going to come strolling through tiny little Roseford and sweep me off my feet, is it? It's no fun being the only gay in the village.' Seeming to realise she was sounding maudlin, Serena gave Lucy a quick grin. 'Can I still make reference to *Little Britain*?'

'I'm sure that's not true any more, reference or no reference,' Lucy said consolingly. She passed Serena a scone. 'And aren't there better prospects in Bristol, anyway?'

'Yeah,' Serena said. 'Which makes me wonder why I'm spending so much time hanging out in the old hometown with you, really!' Never downcast for long, Serena's mood was already changing. 'And with Montana de Santo actually living here for a bit, at least I really can dream!'

'That's my girl!' Lucy laughed. 'Now, shouldn't you be getting back to work before someone realises you've been offline trying to matchmake your mates?'

'Absolutely,' Serena said as she turned back to the table and her laptop. 'In fact, can you stick this in a takeaway cup? I've got a meeting at twelve and I really should be back in the office at Mum's, rather than hanging out in your lovely café. Gorgeous as this place is, I don't think it'll strike as professional a note as Mum's rows and rows of political theory textbooks behind the desk!'

'See you later,' Lucy said. As she watched Serena leave, she felt a wave of sympathy for her friend. As picture-perfect as life in Roseford seemed, less palatable issues were always at play in rural communities. Ingrained attitudes ran deep, and Serena hadn't always been so confident at expressing herself. So many younger people had left Roseford in search of work, or love, or both, that the village, even with the new opportunities that the British Heritage Fund had brought, was at real risk of becoming an unattainable place to live for them. As house prices spiralled, and jobs became more and more scarce, Roseford was reliant on tourists and projects like *A Countess for Christmas* to keep it afloat.

Lucy was lucky; buying the café had offered her stability and an income. Others hadn't been so fortunate, and many of her school friends had moved far away from their families to find work and couldn't afford to come home. Some had been locked into low-paying jobs and forced to live at home with their parents, and others were renting places in the village that were too expensive to buy on a 'normal' working wage. Jake, the guy who'd punched Finn in the eye last night, was a case in point. Places like Roseford were bathed in a warm glow when the movie cameras used them as a backdrop, but the reality was rather different. When the lights went off, and the cameras stopped rolling, the problems would still be there. Jake's prospects were pretty dire in the village, and he fell into the rural poverty trap that politicians were so hot on talking about but rarely did anything to solve. As Lucy wiped down the counter, she felt unsettled by her train of thought. Whatever it was she had with Finn might be doomed to go the same way when *A Countess for Christmas* wrapped.

22

'Honestly, Serena, it's fine – you don't have to hang around and keep an eye on me,' Lucy said, as the hands of the kitchen clock edged towards eight. 'I'll be off in a minute.' Lucy, concerned that her mum would get stranded in the snow, had called her and told her not to come over, so Serena was now going to look after Megan while Lucy met Finn at the pub.

'I've got to make sure that you look respectable for your first date in ages,' Serena replied. 'Besides, I've got all night to watch movies and eat chocolate. Five more minutes won't matter.'

'Yeah, yeah.' Lucy rolled her eyes. She ran a brush through her shoulder-length blonde hair, wiped a smudge of mascara from her cheekbone and then shrugged into her warmest winter coat. Even though the pub was only a hundred yards from where she lived, the night was still bitterly cold. She'd felt the chill as she'd locked the café for the night, and now that darkness had descended, it was only going to get colder. In concession to this, she'd also put on her sturdy winter ankle boots with a chunky sole and a pair of skinny jeans. A T-shirt and a blue sweater completed the look.

Pushing Serena back into the living room, Lucy's palms started to sweat. She was so out of practice with dating! But it was only a drink at the pub, and she was sure Finn wasn't going to do anything to disgrace himself in front of Roseford's inhabitants. No matter that most of the people involved in the production would have had to sign NDAs, she had an instinct, from the way he'd behaved at the café that morning, that Finn wasn't going to want to draw any attention to himself either.

Realising that she was dithering, and that it had just gone five to eight, Lucy grabbed her handbag and her red cashmere scarf from the coat hooks in the hallway, dropped the latch on her front door and stepped out into the chilly evening air.

The snow had become encrusted with a layer of ice, which added sparkle but also an element of danger. Lucy smiled, though, to see the snowman that had been erected to one side of the market square, built from the huge pile that had been swept away to enable Finn and Montana to shoot their scene that morning. A little grubby around the edges, the snowman still had a certain charm. She carefully walked down the pavement, which had also been cleared but upon which the ice was starting to settle again, and took several deep breaths, which plumed out in front of her in the still winter air.

It didn't take long to reach the pub, and as she pushed open the heavy oak door and walked into the bar, she noticed quite a few locals had decided to take solace in the Treloar Arms tonight. She smiled at a couple of people she knew. The heavy snow had brought out a kind of camaraderie and the buzz of conversation created a friendly atmosphere in the pub.

She could also see, sitting at tables scattered around the

room, many people she didn't recognise who must be connected to the film. Clearly, those who were staying in the village had decided that the pub was the best bet tonight, too.

It took her a moment to spot Finn, who was sitting on a bar stool near the back of the pub and in conversation with Dave the landlord. In front of him, he had a cup of coffee. As she drew closer, Lucy felt a flutter of pleasure as Finn rose from his bar stool when he spotted her.

'Lucy, hi,' he said, before he leaned forward and kissed her cheek. The warmth of his lips on her face, chilled from the short walk, felt wonderful. She lingered for a moment, appreciating the scent and sensation of him, before she remembered where she was and pulled back again.

'Hi,' she responded.

As they exchanged pleasantries, Finn gestured to a table in the corner by the roaring open fire. 'Dave reserved that one for us,' he said. 'What can I get you to drink?'

'A glass of dry white wine, please,' Lucy replied.

'Coming right up,' Dave replied. 'And what can I get you, Finn?'

'A pint of Carter's Zero cider, please, Dave.' Finn pulled out his phone and paid for the drinks.

'I'll bring 'em over to you,' Dave said. 'Take a seat.'

'Thank you,' Lucy and Finn both said in unison, laughing as they did so, which seemed to break the ice.

'Are you starting early again tomorrow?' Lucy asked, gesturing to the cider as Dave brought them their drinks.

Finn took a long, appreciative pull on his pint and shook his head. 'Nope, but I gave up alcohol a few years back.'

'Oh god, sorry!' Lucy stammered. 'You don't drink any more, do you?' She remembered reading about Finn's struggles with alcohol and other substances in a trashy magazine, and while she knew that the 'facts' were likely to have been exaggerated for the story, she hoped she hadn't offended him by commenting on his choice of drink.

'It's fine,' he said. 'I have no problems with being around alcohol, or people who drink. It was a decision I took before things could really escalate for me, and I'm completely at peace with it.'

Lucy sipped her wine. She was touched that Finn, who had earned the right to act like a difficult star, was trying so hard to make her feel comfortable. All the same, she thought, perhaps she'd go for something different if they made it to a second round.

'Wasn't that a tricky decision, though, doing what you do?' she asked. 'I can imagine that there are plenty of times you'd need a social lubricant, or a bit of Dutch courage.'

Finn laughed. 'Maybe ten years ago that was true, and I've certainly had a few moments when a shot of something to calm my nerves was very welcome, but it only keeps you going for so long. In the end, it seemed better to rely on my own head, rather than try to cope with something from a bottle.'

'I wish I'd managed to tell myself that on a few occasions!' Lucy said. 'Not so much these days, with Megan in the equation, but there were plenty of times in my teens when a bottle of Carter's Cider seemed to be the answer.'

'Oh, the underage cider-drinking behind the football pitches?' Finn's attempt at a Somerset accent was lamentable, but the twinkle in his eye told Lucy he knew it.

'I hope you've got an accent coach if that's the best you can do,' Lucy kept giggling. 'Keanu Reeves in *Dracula* was more convincing than that!'

Finn pretended to look downcast but couldn't resist a grin. 'Thankfully, I get to keep my own accent in this one. Although I can't quite remember what the reason was for a Canadian guy being in charge of an English stately home, but I'm sure the writers worked it out somehow.'

'This is a FilmFlix Christmas movie,' Lucy replied. 'I think your target audience will forgive the odd nonsensical plot hole.'

Finn pretended to wince. 'Don't let the director hear you say that!'

At that moment, a pair of smiling warm brown eyes, attached to one of the most attractive men Lucy had ever seen, paused at the table on his way to the bar. She vaguely recognised him from her visit to the set with the soup kettles, but couldn't quite place what he'd been doing when she'd seen him.

'Good evening, miss,' the man said. 'Why is a gorgeous girl like you hanging out with a washed-up old reprobate like Finn Sanderson?' His eyes twinkled mischievously, and from the tone of his voice, Lucy immediately realised that he must be a good friend of Finn's.

Finn swivelled in his seat and looked up at the man. 'Lucy Cameron, this is Mateo Torres. Lucy owns the café on the main street and saved our bacon on the first day of the shoot with her amazing vegetable soup and sandwiches.' Turning back to Lucy, he added, 'This charming fella is Mateo, chief camera operator on the movie and someone I've had the misfortune to know and work with for more than a decade.'

Lucy was somewhat surprised to find her right hand being taken and kissed by the newcomer to the table, whose long-lashed, deep brown eyes regarded her with a studied intensity, obviously meant to wind up his good friend Finn.

'It's a pleasure to meet you, Lucy,' Mateo replied in an American accent with just a trace of his native Guatemala still remaining. 'If you tire of the film star, the camera unit is definitely the place to be for a good time.'

'I'll bear that in mind if the company gets boring,' Lucy said but her smile back at Finn communicated how light-hearted her statement was. That being said, with flecks of grey in his wavy dark hair, a beautifully cut black T-shirt and jeans and that mischievous look in his eyes, Lucy knew without too much investigation that Mateo was used to women melting at his every utterance.

'I shall leave you in peace,' Mateo said, releasing Lucy's hand. 'It was lovely to meet you, Lucy.'

'Lovely to meet you, too, Mateo,' Lucy replied. Throwing a careless grin at Finn over his shoulder, Mateo ambled off to the bar.

'He seems nice,' Lucy said.

Finn nodded. 'He's one of the reasons I agreed to do this film. He's the best in the business, and a really good guy.'

'Does he hit on every woman he meets, or was that special treatment because I was with you?'

Finn grinned. 'A bit of both. He sees himself as a charmer, but underneath all of the chat, he's a loyal friend, and a hopeless romantic. But don't let him hear me say that.'

'It must be important to have good friends, doing what you do,' Lucy replied, taking another sip of her wine. 'I can imagine it must be pretty isolating otherwise.'

'You're right,' Finn said. 'It's essential to have people around you can trust. And,' he paused mischievously, 'who can make you look good when you're a couple of years off forty and playing a character who's meant to be a decade younger!'

'I'd have thought you'd be used to that by now,' Lucy observed. 'After all, you did exactly that in *High School Dreams*.'

'True,' Finn conceded. 'But doing that in your twenties is one thing... ten years on, it feels like harder work. Although having Montana alongside me helps a lot. She's been a good friend, too, over the years.'

'But weren't the two of you...' Lucy paused, unsure if she really wanted to know the answer to what she was about to ask. 'You know...' She trailed off again.

Finn grinned. 'A long time ago, Lucy. It wasn't ever going to be forever.'

'A showmance, then? Like Tom Hiddleston and Taylor Swift allegedly were a few years back?'

'Not exactly,' Finn conceded. 'We loved each other. Still do, as friends, but it was never going to last, despite what the media wanted.' He looked down into his pint, and then back up at Lucy, and he had such a tender, open look in his eyes that Lucy felt her pulse jump, and she drew in a quick breath, trying to steady it. 'Things change, and you look back sometimes and just feel grateful to be alive.'

'I know what you mean,' Lucy said quietly. 'My daughter Megan wasn't exactly planned, and at one point, I thought I'd never get over what happened between her father and me, but time, and good friends, can get you through pretty much anything, I've found.'

'Does Megan see her dad?'

Lucy nodded. 'Yes. She spends some of the school holidays and a few weekends a year with him. He's based in California now, so it's not always easy, but Rob and I have come to a good understanding over time. Much like you and Montana, we're friends now. It wasn't easy, but it's best for Megan, and definitely better for us.' She paused. 'I think you worked with him a few years back. Rob Hunter?'

'Oh, yeah.' Finn smiled in recognition of the name. 'He's a great director and a decent man. I learned a lot from him.'

'He said similar about you, when I spoke to him the other night,' Lucy replied. She decided not to mention the photograph of herself and Finn on the café doorstep that Rob had sent her. She didn't want to think about anything like that right now. Besides, if Finn hadn't mentioned it, perhaps he didn't see it as a problem.

'Having good people around can make all the difference in the film world,' Finn replied. And, almost as an afterthought, he added, 'And in life, too.'

'Despite everything, Rob and I are there for each other, and for Megan,' Lucy said. 'We kind of had to be, and we're still friends. It makes things a lot easier.'

'That's nice to know,' Finn replied. He paused and looked down into his pint glass, as if he was dithering whether or not to tell her something. Then, obviously making a decision, he looked back up at her. 'Mateo and Montana more or less saved my life,' he continued. 'I was on the verge of something terrible, but they got me through it, in their own ways. That's why I wanted to do this project with them. It might just seem like some cheesy Christmas movie, but being able to work with them again was a fabulous chance to create something wonderful. I really think we can do that.'

Lucy felt ashamed that she'd teased Finn about the film, and it must have shown in her face because he quickly continued. 'Don't get me wrong. I know it's not *Breakfast at Tiffany's*, but movies like this make people happy, lift them when they've had a terrible day, and hopefully leave them with a smile. To me, there's no better job than that.'

He shook his head. 'But I'm getting a bit philosophical for a first date, aren't I?'

'Is that what this is?' Lucy said softly.

'If you want it to be,' Finn replied. 'I know I'd like it to be.'

Their eyes met, and, as their drinks were finished, it seemed a good idea to move things on.

'So, why don't I show you around this little old village,' Lucy said, 'if you're up for it?'

'I'd like that,' Finn replied. 'It would be nice to have more of a tour now we've got the time.'

Lucy stood up and excused herself to the loo. A walk seemed like a good idea. She found herself wanting to know more and more about Finn Sanderson, and, despite the cold outside, she was looking forward to the walk.

23

Exiting the Treloar Arms, the cold air made Lucy's nose tingle as she huddled into her thick winter coat and ducked her face down into her scarf. She shivered and shrugged deeper into her coat. After the warmth of the open fire in the pub, the night felt even colder.

'What are you thinking?' Finn asked, obviously noticing how quiet she'd gone.

'Oh, just that you seem remarkably well adapted to this bloody cold night!' Lucy laughed.

Finn raised an eyebrow. 'It's cold, is it?'

Lucy laughed and slapped his arm playfully. 'For me, it is.'

Finn paused, then offered her his hand. 'You didn't bring your gloves with you tonight, I see. It must be my duty to keep at least one of your hands warm.'

Lucy paused for a split second, which Finn immediately noticed.

'Is this okay?' he asked her gently, still holding out his hand.

Lucy nodded. 'Yeah. It's just... aren't you worried about being seen?'

Finn smiled down at her. 'Can you see anyone out here in the cold? I think we're pretty much alone, unless that snowman's got a smart phone!'

Lucy was reminded again about the snap that Rob had sent her, but she didn't want to spoil the moment and the temptation to hold Finn's hand was too much. She just wanted to live the fairy tale for a little while. Making up her mind, she took his hand and she was glad of it as they negotiated their way down the icy pavement and took a slow wander around the market square. They both laughed when they drew closer to the snowman, to which someone had added a scarf, a carrot nose and a flat cap while they'd been in the pub. The streetlights bathed the snow in a warm light, and as they walked around the village, laughing, talking and getting to know one another, Lucy felt as though she was finally getting behind Finn's careful façade.

'So your mum's family originated from Roseford, then?' she asked as Finn gradually opened up and told her the story. 'That's quite a coincidence.'

'It's another reason I wanted to come here,' Finn said, pausing by the war memorial and looking at the names. 'Mom's grandfather and his brother both served in the Somerset Fusiliers in the Great War. Neither came home.' He pointed to the names, one after the other, inset into the plaque. 'They served with Simon Treloar's great-grandfather, who did come home. It was the Treloar family who paid for this memorial to be erected.'

Lucy nodded. 'I remember Simon telling me about it during the school holidays one year. He joked that it was the only piece of family history unsold when things started going tits up financially.'

'Must be hard for him,' Finn mused. 'Being a witness to his family history but not being in charge of it any more.'

'He bears it well,' Lucy said. 'But I think it gets lonely. He hasn't found the one person to share his life with yet. If there is such a thing as the one, that is.' She shook her head. 'I used to believe in that stuff – soulmates, written in the stars, all that.'

'And now?'

'Now I'm not so sure.' Lucy smiled. 'Growing up, becoming a parent... it kind of grounds you.' She looked at him from under her lashes. 'You and Montana spoiled a generation of teenage girls, you know. We all wanted that happy ending, that walk off into the sunset with the perfect person. You made things seem so easy.'

Finn gave a short, ambiguous laugh. 'If only it were that simple. Things are never quite what they seem, despite what you might have read and watched.'

Lucy smiled. 'Then let's make the most of things, since we're out here.' They'd moved away from the war memorial and were now standing under the very streetlight that had been surrounded by the film crew that morning. The snow created a muffled hush across the square and, just for that moment, Lucy felt insulated from the outside world and its influences.

'It might be cold, but it's a really beautiful night,' she said softly. 'And I'm having a really good time.' She smiled up at Finn again.

'Me too,' Finn replied. He brushed a strand of Lucy's hair back from her face and tucked it behind her ear. She shivered. His hands were cooler now, since they'd been out in the cold winter air, but the sensation of his fingers on her face brought about a different kind of tremor.

There was a long, aching pause as they stood together under the streetlight. It was not lost on Lucy that Finn had been here once before today, surrounded by lights, cameras, crew and extras milling about. The illusion of romance had been created on film with artifice, direction and careful planning. This time, they were the only people in the square, anyone with any sense taking shelter from the cold in their homes or in the pub. Now, as Lucy and Finn stood together in the same place, the intimacy was natural, easy.

Finn's eyes locked with hers, and she saw them grow wider. His hand was still on her face, and his lips parted, as did hers, in anticipation of what was about to happen. She drew closer to him and her right hand rested gently on the soft woollen jumper he was wearing.

'What are we doing?' she said, a trifle breathlessly as the moment caught up with her. 'I barely know you.'

'It doesn't feel like that,' Finn said softly. And in that moment, it was decided. Lucy leaned up on tiptoes, moved her hand to the back of Finn's neck, and brought her lips to his. The kiss was sweet, and tentative, and his mouth tasted of the cider he'd been drinking in the pub. Under the streetlight in the chill of the evening, it felt as if they were the only two people alive in this festive, snowy landscape.

As the kiss deepened, Lucy felt Finn wrap his arms around her, pulling her closer until she could feel the warmth of his body pressed against hers. Despite the layers of clothing, they seemed to fit perfectly and as she tentatively explored his mouth with hers, and ran a hand through his hair, and her knees grew weak, she forgot all about the cold.

Breaking apart at last, feeling breathless from the kiss and the icy weather, Lucy could feel her knees still trembling and thought, irrationally, that there was no way she was going to make it back to her front door without help. The kiss had been everything she'd ever imagined it would be, and also nothing like it. Finn the film star had been eclipsed by Finn the man, and she felt as though she desperately wanted to get to know him, the person beneath the public veneer.

Seeming to read her mind, Finn pulled her close and she rested her face against his jumper for a long, delicious moment. 'Wow!' he murmured into her hair. 'That was the most amazing kiss I've ever had.'

Reality asserted itself with a bump. Lucy pulled back from him. 'And I know you've had few,' she said softly, sadly.

Finn's brow furrowed, and a look of hurt crossed his face before he could hide it. 'I meant it, Lucy. This feels different.' He shook his head. 'I'm sorry. I mean, why should you believe me, right? As far as you know, this is all just an act.'

'No,' Lucy replied. 'That's not what I meant. I'm the one who's sorry. It's just taking me a while to get my head around all this. I mean, I never in a million years imagined that I'd be here, kissing you, in the centre of my hometown, and in the snow as well!' She gave a nervous laugh. 'And now I've spoiled it by saying the wrong thing.'

'You said what was on your mind,' Finn said. 'And I understand why you might be cautious.'

'Forget it.' Lucy forced a smile. 'It was a kiss. I'm overthinking things as usual. There's just this added... layer... with what you do for a living that I can't get past just yet. I guess I don't just want to be another conquest, that's all.'

'Is that why you think I kissed you?' Finn asked. He shook

his head. 'Lucy... I don't go around kissing women for the hell of it. And I don't want you to be just another conquest, as you put it.' They moved apart slightly, and Lucy felt the chill as Finn's body heat no longer warmed her.

'I know you might find this hard to believe, but being here in Roseford, meeting you and Megan, finding out about my mom's family... things feel like they're falling into place. It all feels... *right*.' He paused next to her on the pavement, his breath misting in the cold night air. Turning round to face her, he took her hand.

'I know you're nervous about getting involved with me, and believe me, I understand why. For all you know, I'm just spinning you a line to have someone to be with while I'm filming.'

Lucy shook her head. 'I might be a bit cautious, but I don't think that, Finn, really.' She reached forward and took his hand in hers, squeezing it gently. 'I admit to having been a bit star-struck when we first met, but I feel like I'm really getting to know you, and I know you're a good man, with a decent heart. I'm thankful for that. It's just...' She trailed off, trying to find the best way to put into words what was really holding her back.

'What?' Finn tugged her hand and brought Lucy a little closer to him again. In the lamplight, his eyes were flecked with amber, and the softness in them made Lucy's pulse speed up again. She could smell his expensive cologne, and the broad outline of his chest in that gorgeous cream woolly jumper was irresistible. She had to fight every urge she had not to wrap herself up in his arms again and feel protected and safe. But she had to tell him the truth, before things went any further.

'I don't want to be dragged into the limelight, if you and I are starting something,' she said quietly. 'I can't let that happen, for my sake and my daughter's.'

Finn smiled down at her. 'I get it. I do. And I promise, I'll do my best to keep you out of that side of things. After all, Adam Driver can walk around his hometown without getting hassled, most of the time. And Keanu Reeves does an even better job. This deal we make with the press... it's a two-way thing. You don't have to be a part of that.'

Lucy sighed. 'It would be so easy to believe you. And, Finn, I do want to. But I know what will happen when this movie comes out. Your face, and Montana's, will be everywhere. People will be asking you about the two of you getting back together, when the wedding'll be, all that kind of stuff. I'll have to grin and bear it, and then face endless comparisons with her, and the past being raked up... I can't cope with that.'

'Don't you think you might be overthinking things a little?' Finn shook his head. 'The movie's not out for a year. Who knows what could have happened by then?'

'So you're not serious, then,' Lucy retorted.

'It's not that,' Finn said patiently. 'I just don't want you taking one little fact, like me liking you, and extrapolating everything for the next twelve months. I know you're cautious, but please, Lucy, strike a balance between *it's just a holiday fling* and *I'm going to spend the rest of my life with this person*. Can you try to find the middle ground?'

Lucy laughed. 'I've never really been good at finding the happy medium.'

'Then let's see if we can do that together,' Finn said softly. He raised his other hand to her cheek, leaned forward and kissed her gently again. His mouth was warm, and Lucy, despite everything she'd just said, found herself responding to

Finn's kiss with alacrity once more. Her lips parted, and she slid her free hand around the back of his neck, pulling him closer until she was up on her tiptoes and snuggled against his jumper once again. For just a moment, she forgot that she'd asked for discretion, and didn't care who happened to pass by. She felt safe, desired, and at home in his arms.

As they broke apart again, she was reassured to see that Finn had a flush to his cheeks and a sparkle in his eyes. She'd always wondered whether, if kissing was part of what you did for a living, when it came to doing it for real, were the reactions still there? Judging from the way Finn's eyes had grown wide, and his breathing had shortened, she assumed that, yes, they very much were.

Finn still had an arm around her, and just for a moment, Lucy settled against him, luxuriating in the softness of his jumper and the warmth emanating from his body. If she never got to be this close to him again, she'd be more than happy with this memory. Although, strangely, as she looked back up at him, he seemed less like her teen idol and much more like a man she could fall in love with. Shushing that thought quickly, she tried to stay in the moment.

But it was easier said than done, as she felt her phone vibrate in her back pocket.

'Sorry,' she murmured as she broke apart from him. 'I'd better see who it is. Serena's babysitting Megan tonight but I still feel like I'm on call.'

'No problem.' Finn gave her such a sweet, untroubled smile that she was inclined to chuck the phone in the gutter.

As Lucy glanced at the screen, she didn't recognise the number. Ending the call, she slipped it back into her pocket.

'Anything important?' Finn asked.

Lucy shook her head. 'Nope.' She paused. 'Where were we?'

Finn's smile grew wider as he pulled her towards him again. 'Right about here,' he murmured as their lips met once more.

As Lucy closed her eyes in delight, neither she nor Finn noticed the shadowy figure with the camera phone snapping shots at them from a dark corner of the market square.

24

_____

Lucy had floated back to her front door. She felt alive, tingly and somehow insulated from the cold after Finn's kisses. She kissed him goodbye again on her doorstep and watched him loping carefully back to the Treloar Arms, being mindful of the ice.

She'd quite happily have invited him in for a cup of coffee, but couldn't face Serena cross-questioning them, so decided against it. So, after bidding goodbye to Serena, who, thankfully, was shattered and had an early start, so couldn't hang around, she closed the door and made herself a very sensible cup of tea to take to bed with her. She even resisted the urge to reply to Serena who had, when she'd got back to her mum's, texted, demanding the details. She would have to wait until the morning.

Saturday dawned with a bright shaft of sunlight beaming through the gap in Lucy's bedroom curtains. She felt pleased she'd only had the one glass of wine, so she'd slept well and didn't wake with a dry mouth or a pounding head. She had a busy day at the café; Saturday, even in the off-season, brought many visitors to Roseford and it looked as though the early-morning sunlight had begun to melt much of the snow. Lucy employed a woman, Rachel, to cover Saturdays, but Rachel had requested today off to do some Christmas shopping in Bristol, so Lucy herself was covering the café today. Now the roads were back open, Lucy's mother was coming over to keep an eye on Megan. After that, Lucy was looking forward to a night of pizza and Christmas movies with her daughter, which she would definitely need after a Saturday at work.

As she was having breakfast, and preparing for a busy day, her phone pinged and she smiled to see that it was a message from Finn. They'd swapped numbers on the doorstep last night, and he was texting to thank her for a lovely evening. His slightly formal tone made her smile even wider. *Bless him*, she thought. *You can take the boy out of Canada...* She texted him back, thanking him, but didn't suggest another date just yet. She had a busy few days and didn't want to rush into anything, especially considering that she had no idea what Finn's filming schedule might entail.

Once her mother had arrived, Lucy opened the café, noting with interest that people were already starting to arrive in the village. In the weeks before Christmas, Roseford was getting its fair share of visitors looking for that elusive perfect present for a loved one. Although there were big towns nearby, such as Taunton and Bristol, some people liked to come out to Roseford to peruse the charming independent shops and find something really lovely for that special person in their life. Lucy, when she got a moment, loved to watch the passers-by wandering up and down Roseford's main street, popping in and out of places: the artisan chocolate maker, the gallery which exhibited local artists, the florist and, of course, the shop belonging to the British Heritage Fund which sold everything from flasks to fridge magnets branded with the Roseford Hall logo.

Visitors often came into the café, laden down with their packages, for a reviving cup of tea or coffee and she, most of the time, managed to upsell a slice of cake or some scones to go with their drinks. During a lull in the lunchtime rush, Lucy was tickled to notice Mateo Torres, the chief camera operator she'd met last night, meandering in and out of the local shops, looking as though he was searching for the perfect gift for someone. She wondered if, underneath all that charm, there was a special person in his life whom he was trying to impress.

As Mateo passed the café window, he waved at her and smiled that irresistible smile and she waved back. She believed Finn when he said that Mateo was a good friend and she wondered what the story was between them. Finn had alluded to Mateo being there for him at a dark time. She hadn't wanted to push Finn last night – it *was* their first date, after all – but she was still curious. Hopefully he'd open up to her in time.

Snapping back into reality, Lucy headed behind the counter again, checking in with her customers to see if they required a top-up or an extra slice of the exquisite coffee and walnut cake, freshly baked yesterday and iced this morning, that seemed to be selling extremely well with the Saturday crowd. Once she was satisfied that all her customers were happy, she allowed herself a moment to sit on the stool behind the counter and reflect on what the next few days and weeks would bring.

She was going to be spending Christmas with Megan and her mother. Then, on Boxing Day, Megan's father Rob was going to come down and collect Megan so that she could spend a few days with him, his partner Tina, his other daughter, and his mother, who lived over in Henley-on-Thames. They'd worked all this out some months ago and Lucy knew how excited Megan was that her dad was coming over for a decent chunk of the Christmas holidays.

She then wondered, her thoughts never far from Finn since the date last night, what his Christmas plans would be. Would he be flying home to spend it with friends or family, or would he be staying here in Roseford? Her stomach fluttered as she considered whether or not to ask him. Did she know him well enough to ask about his plans? What if he was going to be alone at Christmas? It was still early days and Finn, of course, wasn't going to be around for much longer after the holiday anyway. The Roseford section of the film was only going to take a few more weeks.

It was strange how accustomed she had got to knowing that he was in the village, though. Even with the intrusion of the film crew, she'd got used to the disruption and she knew that once things quietened down again and the production left, it would feel a whole lot duller around the place. Taking another order from some more Christmas shoppers, she wondered if life in Roseford would ever feel the same again.

25

Saturday was a rest day for cast and crew, and so Finn enjoyed a leisurely morning. Dave the landlord's breakfasts were entirely too tempting to eat every day, and Finn had already realised that, if he was going to keep fitting into his character Jack Salmon's wardrobe, he needed to either cut them down to once a week or start ramping up his exercise regime. The trouble was, the snow, although thawing, made the terrain around Roseford really treacherous to run on, and the aromas of sausages, bacon and fresh toast drifting up from the kitchen were sapping his resolve.

Determined not to give into temptation, he hastily ate a bowl of cereal and a couple of pieces of fruit, and then decided, if he couldn't go for a run, to take a walk around the grounds of Roseford Hall. Despite the fact he'd been filming in the place for three weeks now, he still hadn't had the chance to spend any time seeing anything that wasn't in the eyeline of the camera. Today, now that the sun was shining and the snow was thawing, he hoped he'd get to see a little more.

Finn was, inevitably, fascinated by the idea of living in this real-life slice of English history, and, at a loose end as he walked, he soon found himself seeking out the current Lord Treloar for a chat. Simon, who was occupied with the many winter jobs that being an estate manager (if no longer the actual owner) entailed, was only too happy to stop what he was doing and talk to Finn.

'This place is incredible, man,' Finn said as they walked the grounds. 'I wish I could stay here for longer.'

'It's a real bugger to heat in the winter,' Simon said wryly. Finn noticed he had that ever-so-English way of turning a compliment into self-deprecation, and he smiled inwardly. Being Canadian, he was prone to the same thing, and having an English mother, he'd been accustomed to her doing it, too.

The two men had developed a bit of a friendship during the time Finn had been filming at Roseford Hall, their paths having crossed a fair bit one way and another since the Christmas Countdown Night. As a consequence, Simon started to unbutton a little as they walked.

'It's not that I mind having the production here,' he said. 'And your crew have been very sensitive to the needs of the family, and the British Heritage Fund. It's just that we were rather looking forward to having a bit of time to ourselves to get back in touch with the place as a family.' He shook his head. 'Don't get me wrong, I've made peace with no longer being in control here, but it would be nice, sometimes, to remember how it was when it was just me, Ma, Sarah and her girls. Now it's like everyone wants a piece of Roseford Hall.'

Finn smiled sympathetically. 'I can't imagine what that feels like.'

Simon laughed in reply. 'Sarah filled me in on what things

must have been like for you at the height of your fame. I don't know how you stuck it out.'

Pausing to admire the manicured tail of a yew peacock that had been clipped expertly by the head gardener, Finn shook his head. 'I didn't know any better. I mean, I was offered the whole world on a plate, and all I had to do was sing and act. And for a while, it was great. But it gets old real fast when you can't step out of your front door without having a camera shoved in your face.'

'I know it's not quite the same thing,' Simon replied, 'but living here, seeing the transition from family home to tourist attraction, is similar. Nothing you do is your own any more. I can't spend time in my own house, the place where I grew up, without being reminded that it's public property now. That, in a sense, so am I. A gilded cage, I suppose.'

'But a beautiful one,' Finn replied. 'It makes me feel... different... being here. At peace, somehow. I haven't felt that in a long time.'

'I'm glad Roseford is having that effect on you,' Simon said. 'And don't get me wrong, I do still love it here. I just can't help wishing we still owned it.'

'But so many people get to love the Hall now,' Finn said. 'It's become part of a good memory for them. You've made folks happy by sharing your home.'

Simon snorted. 'Didn't have much choice, really. It was share it or sell it.' He shook his head. 'Don't mind me. I'm just being maudlin.' Changing the subject swiftly, he continued. 'Are you away for Christmas? I suppose you've got some amazing Christmas Day organised?'

Finn shook his head. 'Wasn't planning on it. Montana's flying home for a few days, but I figured I'd stick around. Relax a bit in my room, watch the Queen's speech, that sort of British thing my mom talks about.'

'Well, you're welcome to come over for a mince pie if you're at a loose end,' Simon said. 'I'm going to Sarah's for Christmas dinner, but give me a call if you want some company.'

'Thanks.' Finn smiled. 'I might just take you up on that.' He liked Simon's easy, welcoming nature, and he knew he'd enjoy spending some more time with him.

At that moment, Finn's mobile pinged. It was Kathryn. Just because they weren't filming didn't mean communications stopped, and Finn noticed that she'd attached some notes to her email, which he really should look over before shooting resumed tomorrow. 'I'd better go,' he said. 'See you later, Simon.'

Simon raised a hand in parting as Finn turned and headed back to the Treloar Arms. He'd try to keep in touch with Simon when filming this movie was over, he thought. Friend-ships were formed so easily on film sets, and then abandoned just as easily, but he'd really make the effort this time.

26

Filming was in full swing for the next couple of weeks, and Lucy wasn't surprised that the only communication she had from Finn was increasingly apologetic texts, and the occasional flying visit to the café. It was frustrating, after such a lovely first date, but she understood. After all, time was tight to shoot the Roseford scenes of *A Countess for Christmas* before the action moved briefly to London, and then back to the US. The whole film would take about eight weeks to shoot.

On the Tuesday before Christmas, Lucy received a text from Finn just as she was closing up the café for the afternoon. Despite the festive season, it had been a quiet day, and so she was taking advantage of this to shut a little early and spend some time with Megan. Megan had finished school for the holidays, and while the little girl was perfectly happy to curl up on one of the sofas in the corner of the café with a book, some colouring or her tablet, occasionally helping Lucy to wipe tables and bring slices of cake to customers, Lucy wanted to do some more fun and interesting things with her daughter before the Christmas period really got into swing. She was just looking into last-minute tickets for a pantomime in nearby Taunton when the text flashed up on her screen. The message, while friendly, was decidedly cryptic.

This might sound strange, but what shoe size is Megan? And what's your size? X

Intrigued, Lucy texted back. A little while later, Finn texted her again.

Can you both meet me in an hour in the field beyond the ha-ha at Roseford Hall? Wear warm clothes! X

Now even more curious, Lucy agreed. What was Finn planning? A winter picnic? A stroll around the grounds? But then why would he need her and Megan's shoe sizes? Deciding not to think too much more about it, she flipped the sign on the café's door to closed and then went to round up Megan, who was glued to the latest episode of *Fuller House* on her tablet. The innocent portrayal of family life, loving despite its challenges, appealed to the little girl, and she grumbled good-naturedly as Lucy explained that they were going out.

'Can I wear my new princess dress that Nana bought me for my birthday?' Megan asked.

'Only if you put thick leggings under it and a jumper over it,' Lucy said. 'Finn, he's a new, er, friend of mine, asked us to dress warmly.'

Megan looked up from the tablet. 'Where are we going?'

'I'm not sure yet. We're meeting him at the Hall.'

Megan slid off the sofa and scuttled to the back door of the café, which led through to an adjoining door to Lucy's small terraced house.

They got themselves ready and then made the short walk to Roseford Hall. Lucy was glad of the thick jumper and winter coat she was wearing, and that she'd insisted on Megan putting on her warmest coat, too. The snow had long vanished, but it was still very cold. Walking through the gate of the Hall, she smiled at Geoff, the security guard who was on the gate again, and who must, surely, be knocking off for the day soon.

'Where are we going, Mummy?' Megan asked.

'Just over the main garden and down to the field at the back.' Lucy knew the place well, having spent many happy summers as a child chasing through the grounds with her friends. When the house had still been in the hands of the Treloar family, the gates had often been left open, and the local teenagers had taken full advantage of the quiet nooks and tree-covered crannies that the then rather unkempt gardens had offered them. Many a first kiss, a first drink and a first cigarette had taken place in the Roseford Hall gardens over the years. Simon's mother had tolerated it all with good grace, declaring that she was 'fine with you using the grounds, so long as you don't leave your rubbish behind'.

The field at the end of the main garden at the front of the house stretched to the horizon. It was set at a lower level to the garden, separated by a ha-ha, a sunken stone wall, built into the bank at the bottom of the garden, which then sloped upwards to suggest an unbroken sweep of grassland. Ordinarily, this would stretch to the horizon, offering a pleasing green view into the distance, but as Lucy and Megan headed down the garden, something rather more unusual came into sight.

Lucy blinked in the fading light; the sun was setting over the back of the garden, casting the grounds and the trees in a rosy, warm glow, but there was no denying what was in front of her. It was as if someone had conjured up a frozen pond in the middle of the field. She drew closer and carefully led Megan down the stone steps of the ha-ha, and as she did so, she caught sight of a tall, almost lanky figure standing by the side of the pond. Finn.

'Hey,' she said as they approached him. 'I'm pretty sure this pond wasn't here the last time I checked! Are your lot responsible?'

Finn turned and smiled at the sight of the two of them. His face was cast in the pinkish glow of the setting sun, and Lucy's stomach did a little flutter.

'Hey, Megan,' Finn said, as the girl grinned up at him. 'How are you doing?'

'Fine, thank you,' Megan replied politely, still smiling. 'What are we going to do?'

'Wait and see,' Finn said mischievously. He looked at Lucy before continuing. 'They installed this for a couple of scenes this week,' Finn replied. 'I figured it would be fun for us to try out.'

'What? Walk around it?' Lucy asked.

Finn gave her a wry look. 'Not exactly.' He bent down and picked up two pairs of ice skates, one large, one small, which he slung over one arm, then held out two pairs of hot pink leg warmers. So *that* was why he'd texted her about her shoe size! 'How do you feel about it?'

'You want us to skate?' Lucy looked doubtfully from Finn's hands out at the ice rink that had, from a distance, appeared to be a frozen pond.

'Well, since it's here, I figured we should make the most of it,' Finn replied. 'They're taking it away at the end of the week, and Montana and I have shot the scenes we needed to. Seems a waste not to take advantage.'

They were gazing out on a large expanse of ice, shaped into an oval. The edges had been artfully concealed to make it look like a pond that had frozen over, complete with a couple of fibreglass ducks at the far edge, and a smattering of potted fir trees, pots similarly disguised, to add to the winter theme. The scene had been another group shot, where professional ice skaters had been hired as extras to create the atmosphere, and he and Montana, as Jack and Ashley, had stumbled around the ice, growing ever closer in the winter wonderland of *A Countess for Christmas*.

'The funniest thing is that Montana can't skate a step—' Finn grinned '—so I was doing a lot of the long shots with the pro skater they hired as her double.'

Lucy, looking at the expanse of ice in front of them, which didn't even have a crash barrier for her to fall into, had never identified more strongly with Montana de Santo.

'Are you sure about this?' she asked. She clutched Megan's hand and dithered at the side of the ice rink.

'Absolutely,' Finn replied, giving her a naughty grin. 'I'm fully insured by the film, and I promise you that I'm not gonna let anything happen to either of you.'

'You've never seen me ice skate,' Lucy muttered. 'Montana's got nothing on me.' But she knew from the expression on Megan's face that she was fighting a losing battle. The little girl was virtually jumping on the spot with excitement at the prospect of skating on a rink that they would have to themselves. So, screwing her courage to the sticking place, Lucy pulled on the leg warmers and ice skates that Finn had sourced for her and then helped Megan on with hers.

'Your skates look different,' she observed as Finn, who was already on the ice, skated assuredly around, knees bent on a low parallel to the rink, arms at his sides.

'They're hockey skates,' Finn said. 'I asked the unit to get me some for the scene, rather than figure skates, as I'm more used to them. Growing up in Vancouver, learning to play ice hockey was a rite of passage.' Finn's skates were indeed slightly different to the more traditional figure skates that she and Megan were wearing. They had flatter-looking blades, without a toe pick at the front, and the boot parts looked more like trainers.

'So I take it you've done this a few times before, then?' Lucy asked as he continued to fool around on the ice, executing sharp and wide turns, changing direction to skate backwards and even doing the odd spin.

'Just a few,' Finn replied as he got closer to the edge again. 'I played for the local team, and did a couple of tryouts for the state. Got close to turning pro, but didn't quite cut it.'

Lucy tried not to be impressed, but Finn on the ice was definitely a sight for sore eyes. She just hoped other parts of her wouldn't be sore by the time this was over.

The white boots with the curved blades were everything Lucy could imagine when it came to ice princess fantasies, but she was a little too old now to feel completely comfortable, walking around on what were essentially thick carving knives.

Megan was squeaking with excitement as Lucy tightly laced the small white ice skates, and Lucy knew immediately that she was going to love every minute of this experience as much as she, herself, was going to be terrified. When did she get so scared? she thought. Was it motherhood that had made her afraid, or was it just what happened when you got older?

A welcome distraction was provided by Finn coming to a snow plough stop in front of where they were. A shower of ice sprayed up around him, and he grinned.

'Good trick,' Lucy smirked. 'Is that your best move?'

'Baby, you ain't seen nothing yet,' Finn drawled in his best southern American accent, somewhere between Matthew McConaughey and Owen Wilson. He held out a hand to Megan, who, after a glance at her mother, took it enthusiastically. 'Let's show your mother how we do it.'

For a split second, Lucy worried for her daughter, but Finn was so assured on the ice, and so patient with Megan, that soon she just contented herself with watching them. He took Megan's hands in his, and gently pulled her around the ice rink, instructing her in a low undertone as he did so, skating backwards so she could move forwards, until, after a couple of circuits of the rink, Megan felt confident enough to let go of one of his hands and glide along by his side. Lucy smiled as Megan gave a cry of delight and, imbued with confidence after Finn's patient tutelage and encouragement, she let go of his hand and promptly fell straight onto her bottom.

Lucy's heart gave a little flip, until she realised that Megan was, of course, absolutely fine. Finn took both of her hands and pulled her gently to her feet before lifting her up into his arms, holding her tightly and doing a circle of the rink with Megan on his hip. Panting slightly as he came back to where Lucy was standing at the edge of the ice rink, he gently lowered Megan to her feet and then glanced at Lucy, as if seeking her approval.

'Let's go again!' Megan squealed, grabbing on to Finn's right arm with both of her hands.

'How about we take your mom with us this time?' Finn said. His eyes met Lucy's, and transferring Megan to his left hand, which she continued to grip firmly, he held out his right for Lucy to take. 'What do you think, Mom?' His eyes twinkled with the ghost of a challenge, and despite her nerves and hesitation, Lucy found herself stepping onto the ice rink until she was clinging on to Finn's hand for dear life.

'I don't know about this,' she said, as she felt the unnerving sensation of all of her weight being transferred onto the skate blades beneath her feet. 'I haven't done this since I was a teenager, and it didn't go well then.'

'I won't let you fall,' Finn said gently. 'I promise.'

With Megan still holding on to his left hand, and Lucy gripping equally tightly to his right, Finn pushed off with his right foot and both mother and daughter found themselves in motion beside him. It was a good job Finn was so steady on his feet as Lucy was definitely having a bit of a Bambi moment. Caught up in Finn's rhythm, she was still gripping his right hand tightly but he was steady as a rock on the ice, even with Megan pulling on his left hand, so when he gave her instructions, she followed them immediately.

'Okay, just push off with your dominant foot and then again with your other foot. It's honestly less difficult if you go a little faster.'

'That's easy for you to say,' Lucy quavered as she stared down at her feet. Surprisingly, though, she found he was right and a little momentum went a long way to righting her wobbles. She started to glide in a wide circle over the ice, and even managed to look up at Finn once or twice, rather than keeping her gaze at her feet. Filled with a sudden burst of confidence, she pushed her foot forward, lost her balance and went down.

'Are you okay, Mummy?' Megan asked, concern combining rapidly with giggles when Lucy tried to scramble back to her feet.

Finn turned to Megan. They'd managed to halt themselves immediately when Lucy had let go of his hand and, ensuring that Megan was completely still before he let go of her, he then turned back to where Lucy's jeans were rapidly getting damp where she sat on the ice.

'Need a hand?' Finn grinned down at her.

'I need a cushion tied to my bum!' Lucy laughed. 'I think I'm going to end up with some serious bruises at this rate.'

'If that's all you end up with, it's a blessing,' Finn said as he helped her up. 'I've broken my ankle, my collar bone and dislocated my right shoulder twice.'

'You're telling me that now?' Lucy said. 'I think I'm better off sitting this one out!'

Finn, glancing to one side to make sure Megan was still stable and upright, drew Lucy to him for a brief moment. She tried not to wobble at the sense of motion under her skate blades. 'Ice hockey's a dangerous game,' he murmured. 'This is a little different.' He released her, and then reached out a hand for Megan to take. They set off again, Megan growing in confidence with every push, and even Lucy forgetting her fear for a few moments when she focused on the warmth of Finn's hand in hers.

A couple more circuits of the frozen pond later, Lucy was no longer feeling the cold. She felt the sweat on her brow and wiped a stray strand of hair off her face with her free hand.

She was still clutching Finn's hand with her other one, but she had to admit she was feeling slightly more secure than she had been at the start.

As they drew back to where they'd started, Lucy noticed a figure standing there, watching. Her heart quickened again as she realised that it was Montana, who was smiling broadly at the sight of them. Finn, who couldn't wave because both of his hands were occupied taking Lucy and Megan around the rink, nodded his head at his co-star and then gradually slowed to a sedate stop where she was standing.

'Hey,' he joked as the three of them joined Montana at the side of the rink. 'I thought you'd seen enough of this thing to last you a lifetime.'

'Dave said he'd spotted you leaving the Treloar Arms with your skates slung over your shoulder, so I thought I'd come and see how you were getting on.' She smiled at Megan and Lucy. 'How are you guys doing?'

Lucy, still panting slightly, replied that she thought she was getting the hang of it. Megan promptly burst her bubble by explaining exactly how many times Lucy had fallen over since her skating session had started.

'Sounds like you could do with a little more practice!' Montana grinned. 'Why don't I keep an eye on Megan while the two of you have another little spin?'

'I think spinning's a bit out of my league!' Lucy joked. 'I can barely stand up out there without Finn's help.'

'That sounds like a good excuse to hold hands!' Montana said, shooting Finn and Lucy a knowing look. 'Come on, squirt.' She gestured to the wooden bench that was set a little way off to the right-hand side of the rink. 'I've brought a cup of hot chocolate with me that I probably shouldn't drink. Why don't you come and help me with it?'

Megan nodded enthusiastically, and Montana swept her off to the bench.

'Well, shall we?' Finn's eyes sparkled mischievously in the fading winter light. 'It's getting a little dark to be out here much longer, so we might as well make the most of it.'

'Okay,' Lucy said, feeling butterflies in her stomach that weren't just to do with the prospect of falling over on the ice again. She shivered as Finn took her hand and gently pulled her onto the icy surface, but she once again felt reassured at how steady and at home he was on skates.

'Uh, we'll be better balanced if I put my arm around you,' Finn said. 'Is that all right?'

Lucy, unable to speak for a second, partially from fear but also from the prospect of being closer to Finn, nodded. She felt his right arm wrap around her waist, his hand coming to rest on her hip, and drew in a quick breath.

'Are you sure you're okay?' Finn asked.

Lucy glanced to where Montana and Megan were sitting, side by side on the bench. Megan was taking sips from the huge takeaway cup of hot chocolate that Montana had brought with her and, content that her daughter was being well looked after, Lucy relaxed a little. 'I'm fine,' she said softly, taking a risk and looking away from her feet to gaze into his eyes. 'Actually,' she added, 'I'm better than fine.'

Finn's smile made something inside her melt as he replied. 'I'm glad to hear that. Are you ready?'

'For what?'

And before she could ask any further, Finn had pushed forward, keeping Lucy in a steady grip, so that she was pulled into his momentum and found herself moving faster across the ice than they had with Megan. She gasped, half in fear, half in exhilaration as the cool night air hit her face and her feet moved to catch up with Finn's. Feeling his assured movements, she relaxed into the rhythm, pushing each foot forward in time with his until she felt more at home with the motion.

After a couple of circuits, Finn glanced down at her. 'Do you trust me?' he asked.

Lucy paused. 'I'm not sure. You're not going to swing me around your head, are you?'

Finn laughed as they continued their leisurely circuit. 'I was a hockey player, not an ice dancer.'

'Then I trust you.'

'Okay. I'm going to move you in front of me, facing me. When you're facing me, put both hands on my waist.' Before she could think better of it, Finn had drawn her closer, until he was skating backwards and she was moving forwards directly in front of him. She placed her hands where Finn directed, feeling the firmness of his waist under her palms. He paused for a moment to gain his balance, and she saw him take a deep breath. Then, he put both hands around Lucy's waist and lifted her about a foot off the ground, arcing into a small spin as he did so. Lucy squeezed her hands tighter at Finn's waist as she experienced the unnerving feeling of the centrifugal force bearing her around, her feet splaying slightly beneath her as her body drew closer to Finn's. Two more turns and he returned her to the surface of the ice, holding her tightly until their movement stopped and they were standing close together, bodies touching from chest to knee.

'If you'd told me you were going to do that, I'd never have

let you!' Lucy said, slightly breathless from the exertion of holding herself in position.

'Why do you think I didn't?' Finn grinned down at her.

'I thought you were just an ice hockey player,' Lucy teased. 'I can't imagine a move like that is part of the game!'

'You'd be surprised.' Finn raised an eyebrow and Lucy burst out laughing. 'No, seriously,' he continued. 'We had to learn balance and precision.'

'And I bet you had an ice-skating girlfriend when you were in high school, too, right?' Lucy smiled.

Finn looked sheepish. 'Maybe.'

They stood together on the ice for a long moment, and Lucy felt an overwhelming urge to kiss him. But they were out in the open, in front of Finn's co-star, and her daughter, so she resisted. Finn was the first to break the rather loaded silence.

'We should really get going before we lose all the light,' he said.

'Yes,' Lucy replied. 'I'm not sure I'm up for skating in the dark. Sounds like a step too far!'

'Let's get you safely back onto dry land, then,' Finn replied before gently guiding Lucy towards the rink's edge once more.

Megan had other ideas. 'Can we go round one more time, now, Finn?' she asked, turning wide blue eyes on Finn as he and Lucy reached her and Montana.

Finn shook his head. 'How can I refuse when you've asked me so nicely? Just one more go, then.' Seeking Lucy's approval with a glance, which she quickly gave him with a nod, he reached out his hand, took Megan's and they were off back around the rink.

'I have to say, being a California girl, that when they told me I was going to be ice-skating, I was absolutely terrified,'

Montana remarked as both she and Lucy watched Finn and Megan.

'I wasn't much better out there,' Lucy replied. 'I'm not quite sure when I got so nervous about everything!'

Montana, after another moment of watching Finn and Megan, and seemingly making sure that they were out of earshot, turned towards Lucy.

'Be careful with him,' she said softly. 'He's not given his heart away in a long time and he's a whole lot more fragile than he looks.'

Lucy felt jolted. 'I'm not sure what you mean, Montana. It's such early days – I have no idea what's going to happen from one day to the next.'

Montana regarded her levelly, and Lucy felt a fleeting moment of the unreality of the situation once again. She'd almost stopped feeling it with Finn, but with Montana, she felt like a satellite orbiting a star; it never really went away.

'Finn might come across as a big strong Canadian boy, lifting you on the ice like that and being the definition of calm, but he's still vulnerable,' Montana said carefully. 'It wasn't that long ago that he was on the verge of making a huge mess of his body and his life. If things get serious between you, you're going to have to realise exactly what you're taking on. He's not half as calm and confident as he looks out there and as he has been through this film. It's taken him a lot of therapy and a lot of self-control to get this far. I feel it's only fair you should know that.'

'Are you warning me off, Montana?' Lucy couldn't help the defensive tone that slipped into her voice as she asked the question.

'Absolutely not.' Montana gave her a gentle smile. 'I'd

never interfere in Finn's life like that; he's the best friend I've ever had, and I would never want to lose him, or see him hurt.' She glanced back out at the ice again. They both heard Megan shriek in excitement as Finn lifted her up in his arms and spun her around on the spot, as he had with Lucy just moments earlier. Lucy told herself not to worry, that he knew what he was doing and he was stable on the ice. After all, he'd lifted her without so much as breaking a sweat. The question was, was he as stable in other areas of his life?

As if anticipating her quandary, Montana put a hand on Lucy's forearm. 'Finn is one of the kindest, gentlest, most genuine people I have ever met and, considering the business in which we both work, that's really saying something. But he's also battled his fair share of demons in the past and some of those rise to the surface from time to time.' She squeezed Lucy's arm gently. 'I'm not saying that to warn you off, or to scare you, Lucy. He has immense self-control and puts everyone he loves first, but it would be wrong of me, seeing what I'm seeing in front of me, the way he is with both you and Megan, if I didn't at least try to put you in the picture a little bit about what that means.'

'And what does it mean?' Lucy's heart began to hammer. She'd heard the rumours and read the media reports about Finn's 'troubled' years, but to hear it straight from someone who, presumably, had been there at the time, was another thing entirely. 'What are you trying to tell me, Montana?'

At that moment, Finn skated carefully back to where they were standing. Both he and Megan had a flush to their cheeks, and a sparkle in their eyes, and it was clear that they'd had a brilliant time.

'Can we go again tomorrow, Finn?' Megan asked as she

stepped off the rink, grabbing Lucy's hand to steady herself as she hit the frosty grass.

'I'm not sure how long the ice rink's here for,' Finn replied, smiling down at the little girl. 'But if it's okay with your mom, I'm sure we can get another round in before they take it down.'

Standing there, next to the movie set ice rink, with two of the biggest teen stars of her lifetime, and her own excited young daughter, Lucy suddenly keenly felt the unreality of this situation. A creeping unease slithered over her as Finn and Montana continued to talk while she and Megan removed their ice skates. Was she really equipped to deal with the implications of a relationship with Finn, and all that entailed? And what was the truth that Montana was trying to warn her about?

27

Lucy didn't have a lot of time to mull over Montana's warning between that night and preparing for Christmas Day. Because the café was going to be open until 3 p.m. on Christmas Eve, she was up against it in terms of present wrapping, cooking and other kinds of Christmas prep. Her mother, as she had done pretty much every year since Lucy was born, was taking care of most of the festive cooking, which was always a huge relief to Lucy who, up to her eyes in Christmas pudding cupcakes and red velvet gateaux, didn't really fancy cooking something gargantuan for Christmas Day.

It was at times like this, however, that she really felt the absence of a long-term partner. Although she and Rob had got themselves to an amicable place over the years since Megan's birth, she still wished she had someone to snuggle up with at night, to help wrap the presents that she had bought Megan and to laugh as she crunched the carrot that Megan insisted on leaving out for Father Christmas's reindeer. But she was philosophical; it was, for most of the year, better that the two of them had parted: they'd have never made each other happy in the long term, and Lucy relished her independence. The café gave her a steady income, her mother was a constant tower of strength and she felt well rooted in the village. When she was younger, she'd been desperate to get away, but now she realised how lucky she was to live in Roseford and to earn a reasonable living by herself; so many of her friends had had to leave to find employment in other places.

Shutting up the café on Christmas Eve, she wondered, not for the first time, what Finn was up to. She knew that he was spending Christmas in Roseford, but he'd been very clear that he wasn't going to put any pressure on her about seeing her over the festive days. She'd invited him round for a drink on Christmas Day, but he'd politely declined. He was, he said, looking forward to the chance just to chill out, watch some television and be on his own for a bit. The nature of the film set meant he never really was truly alone and Lucy, who could have been offended by his desire to be solitary at this time of year, realised that she did in fact understand where he was coming from. As a working single mother of a young child, time alone was precious, and she valued it when she could grab it, too.

They had, however, arranged another date on Boxing Day evening, at which point Megan would have been picked up by Rob, who was taking her to see his parents for the rest of the festive period and dropping her back on 2 January. The prospect of being completely child-free on Boxing Day and meeting Finn made Lucy raise the inevitable question in her mind: would they go to the next level? The chemistry between herself and Finn felt electric and she knew from the way he kissed her goodbye after the ice-skating escapade that he felt the same way.

Despite Montana's well-intentioned warning, Lucy wanted to get to know Finn better. Maybe it was the fact that he would be leaving in January, but with the house to herself, and no work the next day, was it inevitable that Finn would end up staying? Was she ready for that?

Pushing these thoughts to the back of her mind, Lucy headed back through the adjoining door from the café to her house, and straight upstairs to the spare bedroom. Serena had offered to take Megan out for a couple of hours, so that Lucy could get the presents wrapped without fear of being discovered by her daughter, and Lucy knew she had to get cracking.

Fortunately, she'd wrapped most of the bigger items, and there were only a few last-minute purchases left. She'd have to employ her ninja skills later, as all parents did on Christmas Eve, to deliver Megan's stocking fillers, but once the last things were wrapped, she could finally relax and enjoy Christmas Eve.

She blushed when she pulled the last gift from its bag. Not willing to allow Finn to have no presents to open at Christmas, she'd bought him a fridge magnet from the British Heritage Fund's gift shop. It was a photo of Roseford Hall in the summer, and she hoped it would remind him of his time here. It was silly, inconsequential, but she couldn't resist. She wrapped it carefully and then added it to the pile in the cardboard box that she was going to stash in the wardrobe until later that night.

Just as she was closing the wardrobe door, the doorbell rang. Scooting downstairs, she pulled open the front door, expecting it to be Serena and Megan back from their trip to

Taunton. Standing there, however, looking utterly gorgeous, was Finn.

'I know I said I wanted to be on my own for Christmas Day,' he said without preamble, 'but I couldn't resist calling in one last time.' He blushed slightly. 'I hope that's okay.'

'Of course it is.' Lucy smiled. 'It's always lovely to see you.' Her heart was hammering nineteen to the dozen as she regarded him. 'Was there something that you wanted?'

'Only this.'

And before Lucy could respond, Finn had pulled her towards him and wrapped his arms around her, bringing his lips down to hers in a sweet, warm, lingering kiss that promised so much more than what he could give her on the doorstep. Lucy responded with enthusiasm until, quite a few moments later, they were both breathless and flushed.

28

Christmas Day for Finn had been many things over the years. During the heady days of *High School Dreams*, he'd spent a fair few Christmases in hotel rooms with other cast members when home was too far away to commute back to just for the holidays. The shooting schedule for such a popular show had been punishing at times and his fellow cast members and some of the crew had become like a second family as they all worked hard to produce the twenty-two episodes per season that the studio and the distributors demanded. While for the most part, work was creative and rewarding, there were plenty of nights when he'd returned to his hotel room alone, exhausted and in dire need of some kind of pick me up. This had eventually led to some bad habits, which included a brush with class A drugs and entirely too much alcohol.

One Christmas Eve in particular, when most of the cast had actually managed to make it home to their families for a few days, Finn had found himself alone in a hotel room with a bottle of Scotch and a gram of cocaine. After the initial high, he'd passed out for sixteen hours, only waking when room service had come with a three-course Christmas dinner that Montana had ordered by phone for him from her parents' house in California. That was the year she invited him back to meet her family, a few months after they'd started sleeping together and were 'officially' a couple. But Finn couldn't face the prospect of a cosy family Christmas, and so he'd declined. Somewhere, as well, a small part of him did not want to take his habits over the threshold of Montana's family home: if she was aware that his occasional dabbles were getting out of control, she'd never told him until she and Mateo had intervened some months later.

These days, spending Christmas alone held no fear for Finn. He'd left the alcohol and the substances far behind him, and having spent four weeks in the almost constant company of the actors and the film crew, he was looking forward to Christmas Day alone. There was a part of him, however, that wanted to spend it with Lucy, but he knew Christmas was sacrosanct and he didn't want to crash her family celebrations. However, he couldn't help missing her on Christmas morning.

The kiss they had shared on Christmas Eve was deep, passionate and full of promise of more sensual things to come and while he would never in a million years push her into something she didn't want, Finn definitely got the feeling that Lucy was on the same page as he was. Perhaps it was the season, or perhaps it was because in a couple of weeks' time he would be leaving to complete the shoot of *A Countess for Christmas* in London and then the final scenes in California, but the pressure of time and the chemistry between them made him desperately hope she wanted to take things to the next level as well.

After a leisurely breakfast in the bar of the pub, during which he confirmed to Dave that he'd be back down for Christmas lunch, Finn returned to his room, and, with the shooting script for the next few days' scenes in front of him, tried to learn his lines. But for some reason, they just weren't going in as they usually did. He kept getting distracted by thoughts of Lucy, and curiosity about what she was doing, how her Christmas Day was going. Whether she was thinking about him...

Two hours of staring mindlessly at the script was enough, and Finn decided he needed to take a walk to clear his head. As he left the Treloar Arms, he deliberately headed in the opposite direction to Lucy's house. He'd promised to stay away and give her the space she needed on Christmas Day, and if he passed her front door, he'd be too tempted to knock and take her in his arms again. He steeled himself to walk back towards Roseford Hall. Perhaps a mooch around the extensive grounds and some fresh air would help those lines go in a little better when he returned to his hotel room.

The snow, which had made a brief reappearance a day earlier, had virtually disappeared now, scuppering any thoughts of a white Christmas in Roseford. As Finn slipped through the public footpath gate that skirted the grounds of Roseford Hall, he noticed Bert and Ernie, the Roseford Hall peacocks, strutting about in the front garden. They'd been notoriously elusive while the house was being used for the shoot, but obviously now things were a little quieter, they'd decided to emerge and inspect their territory. As their strange, unearthly cries echoed through the cold winter air, Finn marvelled at how quiet the estate seemed, now everyone had gone home for Christmas. There was a slow, rolling mist settling in over the field where the ice rink had been, which obscured the woodland beyond and seemed to muffle any sounds except the rowdy peacocks.

Walking across the ornamental hedge garden and on through the eighteenth-century manicured front lawns, Finn's eyes scanned the horizon, looking out for anyone who might also be on a pre-lunch stroll. But the mist and the still biting cold seemed to have kept everyone close to home, and he didn't see anyone. As he reached the end of the garden and stepped down the steps of the ha-ha, he remembered how much fun it had been to skate with Lucy and Megan, and smiled. He needed to see her again; he was *aching* to see her again, and he couldn't wait until tomorrow evening when he would.

Just as he was luxuriating in festive thoughts, which were certainly helping to keep out the cold, he was startled to see a huge, treacle sponge-coloured retriever come bounding out of the mist across the field towards him. It stopped within ten feet of him, tongue lolling from its amiable mouth, wagging its tail and looking back into the mist, presumably for its owner.

'Holmes! Holmes, come! Bloody dog. I'll have your guts for garters.'

Finn grinned as he recognised the voice. Dogs were prohibited off lead in the grounds of Roseford Hall but, he supposed, an exception could be made for the lord of the manor's dog.

'He's here,' Finn called out, as the briskly striding form of Simon Treloar emerged from the mist. Dressed in a flat cap, a battered waxed jacket, light blue jeans and muddy green wellies, he looked every inch the country squire. Finn regarded him in amusement; FilmFlix's idea of what Jack

Salmon, the fictional custodian of the manor house in *A Countess for Christmas* should look like was more new-money, and far more smartly dressed: rather more Jack Wills than John Barbour, if you will. He wondered if he should have a word with Kathryn and get Jack's wardrobe tweaked a little to reflect reality. But then realism wasn't exactly the point of the movie, he thought wryly. Everything, from the frozen pond to the American countess to the imagined romance between his character and Montana's was knowingly inauthentic, in the cosiest possible way.

Simon reached Holmes and shook his collar. 'You are not to go running off like that. Bloody puppy.' He clipped the lead onto the dog and straightened up. 'Hi, Finn. Merry Christmas.'

'And to you,' Finn replied. 'How is your family celebration going?'

Simon rolled his eyes. 'Why do you think I volunteered to walk the dog?'

'That well, huh?'

'Let's just say that Ma's never really got over not being in charge of the festivities, and she and my sister Sarah are vying for supremacy over presents, timings, and who cooks the best Brussels sprouts. Between them and my nieces, who are hyped up on sugar from the treats in their Christmas stockings and desperate to open their presents, I decided I was better off out of there.'

'Sounds, uh, stressful,' Finn replied.

Simon grinned. 'Just your average Treloar family Christmas, I'm afraid. It's the one day of the year I'm kind of glad I'm single; at least I can escape for a while.'

'But you'd miss it if you weren't involved,' Finn observed. He fell into step beside Simon as he began to walk the length of the ha-ha. Simon kept glancing at the stone wall, presumably checking for loose rocks or anything else that was amiss. Even though he was no longer the official guardian of the Hall, old habits died hard.

'Oh, of course,' Simon agreed. 'And it's Sarah's first year in the cottage since the renovations were finished, so it's nice to see her and the girls settling in. It's just that me and Holmes here, being the only males present, are a little outnumbered.'

'Sounds like a few Christmases back home,' Finn replied. 'When my mom's family hosted Christmas, my cousin Alex and I were the only boys among eight girl cousins at the dinner table. I like to think it gave me a decent understanding of women, but my track record suggests otherwise.' He laughed.

'So you didn't fancy flying back home for a few days' holiday, then?' Simon asked.

Finn shook his head. 'Wouldn't have been worth it. I've got today and tomorrow off, and I'm shooting a couple of solo scenes before Montana gets back at the end of the week. By the time I'd gotten off the plane in Vancouver, I'd have had to jump right back on it again.'

'And there I was, thinking fame was all supersonic jets and first-class living!' Simon laughed. 'Shows what I know.'

'Been there, done that, happier to take things at a slower pace these days,' Finn replied. 'So it's lunch at the pub and an early night for me.'

'Lunch on your own?' Simon said. 'That won't do. Not on Christmas Day. Why don't you come back with me? Sarah and Ma are cooking enough food to feed the entire film crew, and I'm sure she'd be over the moon to meet you.'

Finn shook his head. 'That's kind of you, man, but I've

already booked a table at the Treloar Arms. Wouldn't want to piss Dave off by not turning up.'

'Call him from Sarah's place,' Simon replied. 'He won't mind. He charges enough for Christmas dinner; he won't miss one less plate.'

Finn, who suddenly really didn't feel like spending the rest of the day on his own, found himself agreeing, and before he knew it, he and Simon were heading back to Sarah's newly renovated cottage on the edge of the Roseford estate, Holmes padding obediently at their heels.

As they approached Sarah's charming pale-gold cottage, Finn leaned down and ruffled Holmes's neck. 'Is he yours?'

Simon shook his head. 'No, he was an early Christmas present for my nieces. They've had him about three months now, but the training, as you saw, is a little hit and miss.'

'I'd love a dog, but I never know how long I'm going to be in one place at the moment, so it's not exactly practical.'

Simon regarded him shrewdly. 'Do you think that'll always be the case? A nomad's life? Living out of suitcases from project to project?'

Finn felt surprised by the intimacy of the question, but he liked Simon's politely direct curiosity. It didn't feel intrusive. He felt that Simon might understand a little about being semi-public property, given his place in Roseford's community. 'Before this project, I've been based mainly in New York, doing small films, a couple of fringe theatre productions, keeping things ticking over. After this... I guess it might mean going back to California, if the right opportunity comes knocking, but I'm not sure if that's what I want. I'd quite like to settle somewhere. It's not as if I need the money. Not right now, at least.'

'Well, here's to doing what makes you happy,' Simon replied. 'And in the meantime, if you could be my ally against this house full of women, I'd appreciate it! And...' He paused mischievously. 'It'll be worth it for the look on my sister's face when she sees who I've brought home for dinner!'

Finn grinned. Somehow, he knew that Simon wouldn't have dared voice that sentiment out loud if any of the said women were in earshot. 'It would be my pleasure,' he said, following Simon in through the back door of the house.

29

Sitting back in his dining chair, Finn felt more stuffed than he had in a long time, and rather tired. Simon, at the head of the table, threw him a grin.

'Has Sarah's Christmas dinner defeated you?' he asked as he glanced at Finn's plate, which held the remnants of a roast potato and some bread sauce.

Finn nodded. 'That was incredible,' he said, turning to Sarah, who, once she'd got over her shock at seeing him in her living room, had been a welcoming and gracious host.

'Thanks,' Sarah replied. 'As Simon said, we couldn't have you spending Christmas Day by yourself.' She stood up to start gathering up the finished dinner plates and Finn stood quickly, seizing the nearest serving bowl of vegetables and the plate that had held the carved turkey meat.

'No, please do sit down,' Sarah said.

'I was taught to be a helpful guest,' Finn replied, smiling at her. 'Just tell me where you'd like these put.'

'Oh, just throw them on the side in the kitchen. Simon and the girls can help wash up.'

Finn did as he was told, and almost collided with Simon coming the other way.

'Careful, that's family china we're almost smashing,' Simon teased.

Finn laughed. 'Better give it to you, then. Coordination's not exactly my strong point!'

Later, when the dishes had been done and Simon had shown Finn to the living room, Finn settled into one of the cosy armchairs and had to fight the urge not to doze off in front of the roaring open fire. As Sarah's daughters played with Holmes, who, having had a nap under the long dining table during lunch, was now raring to go again, Finn felt content, and surprisingly at ease with this family he'd only just met. He couldn't help smiling inwardly when Sarah kept glancing over at him, as if she couldn't quite believe he was sitting in her living room, but a couple of glasses of wine had taken the edge off her incredulity, and she was starting to relax now that dinner was over.

'Can I get you anything else, Finn?' Sarah asked, topping up her wine glass.

'No, thank you, I'm great,' Finn replied. 'Although I'm in serious danger of falling asleep here and drooling onto your cushions!'

Sarah laughed. 'They've had worse.'

A companionable silence descended until Fleur, Sarah's twelve-year-old daughter, asked if anyone fancied a game of Monopoly. This was greeted by groans from all the adults except Finn. Simon protested that he really didn't have seventeen hours to play a whole game, or the patience to deal with the inevitable tantrums when someone lost, to which Fleur replied that he'd just have to learn to keep his temper under control. Eventually, realising that he wasn't getting out of it, Simon helped Fleur set up the board, and the game commenced.

'Welcome to the seventh circle of Christmas hell,' Simon muttered in an undertone to Finn, who grinned back at him, then looked at the board.

'I've played the Canadian version,' he replied. 'And I have to say, it didn't go well. I seem to remember my sister flipping the board on quite a few occasions when she went bankrupt.'

'Expect no less tonight,' Sarah replied. 'Fleur, for all of her outward sangfroid, is a competitive little thing, and so's Elspeth. They could end up coming to blows, if it's anything like last year!'

A pleasant, if rather rambunctious game ensued, and after they'd been at it for an hour and a half, it was clear that Elspeth had a great future ahead of her as a property mogul. By the time Finn had paid the rent on her collection of dark green and indigo properties, he'd remortgaged everything he owned and still had come up a couple of hundred quid short.

'Well, that's me done,' he conceded with a grin as he handed over the last of his meagre resources to Elspeth. Glancing at the clock on the wall of the living room, he was stunned to see that it was nearly six o'clock. Night had fallen softly around the cottage on the edge of the Roseford estate, and Finn hoped he'd be able to find his way back to the pub in the dark.

Simon, who was also shortly to be at the mercy of his younger niece's shrewd gameplay, put his cards lightly down on his side of the board. 'I think that's enough corporate high jinks for one night,' he said. 'I'm going to leave the rest of you to fight it out without me.' Standing up, amidst protests from his nieces, he kissed his mother and sister goodbye, ruffled Holmes's head and then turned to Finn.

'Don't leave this den of iniquity on my account,' he said. 'But if you want some company on the walk back to the Treloar Arms, I can make sure you don't fall in any of the dips in the fields!'

Finn laughed. 'Well, when you put it that way...' He pulled himself out of the armchair and stretched his arms up. He was tickled when he touched the low-beamed ceiling of the living room with his fingertips.

After thanking Sarah and Margaret, Simon and Sarah's mother, for the wonderful lunch, bidding goodbye to Elspeth and Fleur and the overexcited Holmes, Finn shrugged his jacket back on and stepped back out into the chilly night with Simon.

'That was great,' he said as they made their way back across the parkland of Roseford Hall. The moonlight shone brightly overhead, and made the going a lot easier. 'I didn't realise how much I wanted a family Christmas until you offered me one.'

'Glad you enjoyed it,' Simon said, pulling his flat cap down more tightly against the cold. 'I suppose I'm grateful that we all still get on so well, and are happy to spend an afternoon in each other's company. I know many people aren't so lucky this time of year.' He glanced at Finn. 'Did you say a lot of the crew had pushed off, too?'

'Yup,' Finn replied. 'Most of them are Brits, so they didn't have massive commutes back home, apart from Mateo and Nicole, of course, who're both based in New York when they're not on a shoot, and Kathryn, our director, who are all staying here for the holiday. It makes sense to get a local crew in where we can; cuts costs and makes things run more smoothly.'

'You sound as though you're just as taken with life behind the camera as in front of it,' Simon observed as they drew closer to the village. 'Any chance of you switching sides at any point in your career?'

Finn grimaced. 'I'd love to, but I'm not sure anyone would hire me. Actors who think they can direct don't always go down so well.'

'Oh, I don't know. Look at Branagh, De Niro and even Stallone – they didn't do a bad job of it.' Simon shook his head, and Finn smiled inwardly at the man's self-effacing nature. The apologetic 'But then what do I know?' he added just confirmed that impression.

'No, you're right,' Finn replied. 'I guess it's just out of my comfort zone right now. But who knows? Perhaps it's something for the future. At least I wouldn't need to keep turning down great food if I switched to directing. I'll have to live on watermelon for a week after Sarah's amazing Christmas dinner!'

Simon looked shocked. 'It can't be that bad, surely?'

Finn laughed out loud at his aghast expression. 'The camera really does add ten pounds, you know. Montana was always better at self-discipline than I was. I never quite escaped my tendencies to eat like a Labrador in my downtime.'

'You grew up in Canada,' Simon observed. 'You must have needed some stodge to keep out the winter cold!'

'That doesn't really cut it in California!' Finn returned, smiling ruefully.

They were at the main gates now, and Simon produced the

key to the padlock that had been chaining them shut. 'Sounds like the best reason to get behind the camera to me.'

Finn wandered back through the main gate and heard the click as Simon locked up again. 'Thanks again for this afternoon,' he said, and raised a hand in farewell.

'Any time,' Simon replied, turning back to the Hall. 'Take care, Finn.'

'You too.' As he strolled back to his room in the pub, he wondered, for the umpteenth time, what Lucy's Christmas Day had looked like. Glancing at his watch, he realised he was calculating the hours until he could see her again and felt seriously jolted. The afternoon with Simon and his family had been really pleasant; so much so, that for the first time, almost ever, on a shoot, he'd felt completely at home. He knew it was probably just the Christmas 'feels' creeping up on him, but he couldn't help wondering if he'd be far happier if he settled somewhere like this; somewhere quiet, beautiful, and less pressured. Where he could make a home, make friends, make a *life*. Where it didn't matter if he had a double helping of dessert, and he could map out his own time, instead of being told where to stand and what to say for a career. He smiled to himself; the day had made him sentimental. He was only a few years off forty, acting in a Christmas movie and awash with stirrings of attraction for someone whom he'd only just met. If that wasn't a recipe for schmaltz, then what was?

30

'Hey, Lucy.' Rob's ready smile and transatlantic twang never failed to make her smile in return. 'How are you?'

'I'm good, thanks,' Lucy replied, opening the door to her former partner on Boxing Day, 'if still a little stuffed from Mum's epic Christmas dinner yesterday!' She opened the door a little wider and Rob stepped over the threshold. 'Megan won't be a sec – she forgot to pack Magic Ted, so she's just gone to get him off her bed.'

'Can't have her fretting about Magic Ted.' Rob kept smiling. 'God, I've missed her. I'm so looking forward to taking her to Mum's. Mum's dying to see her, too.'

Lucy knew how much Megan loved her other grandmother, too. 'How's Tina?' she said. Tina and Rob had met a couple of years after she and Rob had split, and it had been such a *coup de foudre* that Lucy hadn't been able to summon the will to be jealous, although she did feel a little put out that she hadn't been as similarly smitten in the following years.

Until now, she thought, unguardedly, as Finn crossed her mind again.

'Good, thanks,' Rob said. 'She wanted to come today, but Mum's got her helping out with the Boxing Day buffet, for when we get home. I was quite glad to escape. They both send oodles of love, though.'

Yet again, Lucy felt a sense of relief that, despite falling pregnant just before her finals, neither she nor Rob had felt any desire to settle down together. They'd known, somehow, that they'd just make each other miserable in the long term, even then, and although they both loved Megan, and loved each other as friends, co-parenting suited them so much better than actually living together.

'So are you in the country for long this time?' Lucy asked.

'About four weeks,' Rob replied. 'I've been called in to consult on a project at Pinewood starting mid-January, so I'll be staying with Mum for the duration.'

'I bet she's pleased,' Lucy said.

'And it means that, if you're all right with it, I can spend a bit more time with Megan.'

Lucy, despite her affection for Rob, felt a flash of irritation that he was only dropping this in now, instead of when they'd arranged Christmas a few months ago. 'I'm sure she'd like that,' she said guardedly. 'Let me know what you've got in mind. She's back at school on 6 January, so you'll have to work around that.'

'Can't she miss a day or two?' Rob asked. 'I mean, she's not got exams or anything.'

'We'll see,' Lucy said. In all honesty, she knew she'd agree eventually, but she didn't want to seem like too much of a pushover.

'Luce...' Rob said, in the ensuing silence. He fiddled with the fob in his car key, and then, realising what he was doing, hurriedly put the keys back in his jacket pocket.

'Yeah?'

'Don't take this the wrong way, but I've been hearing things lately.'

'About?' Lucy, sensing that she knew where this was going, but curious anyway, waited for Rob to broach the subject.

'Look, I know it's none of my business, but people talk in the film industry. I know you know about that picture a few weeks back, but I heard the other day that you and Finn Sanderson have been, you know... seeing more of each other. Is that true?'

Lucy tried to affect an air of indifference, despite the fact that she could feel her colour rising at the mention of Finn's name. 'He's working on the film being shot at Roseford Hall, yes. And he's come into the café from time to time. We had a drink together.' She was damned if she was going to stand in her own hallway giving Rob the finer details of her love life. Especially when she wasn't really sure what those details were, herself.

Rob rubbed the back of his head, obviously nervous about what he was going to say next. 'Just be careful, Luce. When you and I met, you were very clear that you wouldn't be dragged into the spotlight. And I only wanted to work behind the camera. Being a friend, or even a casual acquaintance to someone like Finn... it could put you in a place you don't want to be. And Megan.'

Someone like Finn. Lucy felt a flicker of unease as she thought back to Montana's conversation by the side of the ice rink a few nights ago. She still wasn't completely clear about what she'd been alluding to, and hadn't had the chance to ask Finn about it.

'Don't worry, Rob,' Lucy said, as calmly as she could. 'I'd never put Megan in a difficult place. You know that.'

'I know you wouldn't intentionally,' Rob replied. 'But Finn used to be the world's sweetheart. Legions of women, and almost as many men, all wanted to be with him or wanted to see him marry, what was her name, Montana de Santo. Now he's got this new film coming out, after a few years away from the spotlight, he's going to be public property again.' He smiled at her, half apologetically, half in mitigation. 'I know you, Luce. You'll give your heart, and then get it broken.'

'Like I did with you, you mean?' Lucy retorted. Then she shook her head. 'Sorry. Totally different situation. I get that, really.'

Rob moved towards her. 'I hate that I hurt you, but can you honestly say you and I would have been any happier together? We both know we'd never have gone the distance.'

Lucy smiled, despite herself. 'I know. And I also know you're only trying to look out for me. But I'm a big girl now, Rob. Older and wiser. I know what I'm doing.'

Rob moved in for a quick hug. 'I understand. But I also understand this business, and when *High School Dreams* was at its peak, there wasn't the rabid social media that there is now. I just don't want you falling prey to a band of trolls who want to ruin your life because you're going out with someone they perceive as theirs.'

'I'll be careful,' Lucy said, but a small voice in her mind was already whispering that perhaps Rob was right; perhaps she didn't know what she was getting into.

At that point, with impeccable timing as ever, Megan came

bounding down the stairs and jumped into Rob's arms. 'Daddy!' she screamed, throwing her arms around his neck.

'Hey, gorgeous,' Rob said, and Lucy smiled fondly as Rob buried his face in Megan's long dark hair. 'All ready to go and see Grandma Mary?'

'Yay!'

'Be good, darling,' Lucy said, giving her daughter a hug once Rob had returned her to her feet.

'I will.'

'I'll call you when we get to Mum's,' Rob said.

'Make sure you do,' Lucy replied. 'Have a great time.'

'We will.'

Smiling as she waved them goodbye from the doorstep, Lucy couldn't help thinking back to what Rob had said about Finn upsetting the balance in her life. Perhaps, she thought reluctantly, Rob was right. Was she *really* prepared for a relationship with a global movie star, and all that entailed?

As if on cue, two minutes later, her phone pinged with a message from Finn:

Can't wait to see you. Been counting the hours since Christmas Eve! Xx

Oh god. This is actually happening. Lucy's hands started to tremble. What was she thinking? She still wasn't completely sure what she wanted this evening to be. The last time she'd been in this position, it had ended up being a disaster of epic proportions after rekindling a romance with an ex which really had not deserved to be rekindled. And now, she was about to spend some time alone with Finn, who was hands down the best kisser she'd ever known, and run the risk of falling hard for exactly the wrong guy. She was three breaths away from cancelling, and simply making do with a binge watch of *High School Dreams* and a box of Quality Street, when her phone pinged again.

DO NOT overthink tonight, girl. I know you're going to freak out unless I tell you not to. S xx

Bless Serena, Lucy thought; somehow, her best friend had a sixth sense for when Lucy needed reassurance. And she definitely needed it now.

To take her mind off the rapidly approaching evening, Lucy ran a hot bath, poured a glass of Christmas fizz and tried not to analyse the fact that she'd just shaved her legs for the first time since the summer. *Doesn't mean anything*, she thought. But she knew it did.

Oh god.

Finn had been out with some of the most beautiful women in the world, not to mention Montana de Santo, with whom he'd definitely been more than friends; how could she not be a total let-down in comparison, if she decided to take her clothes off? She was pushing thirty, had plucked out a grey hair from her parting only yesterday, and definitely had been eating too many of her own scones lately to feel completely comfortable with showing her body to him. This was a terrible idea.

But was it? Really? Finn was going to be leaving in a week or two, once the shoot had wrapped, and she'd be on her own again, just her and Megan: business as usual. She'd be left with either wonderful memories of a brief, blissful romance, or embarrassing recollections of a disastrous night; but, either way, at least there'd be no risk of running into Finn and having to relive them. Even if she might turn on the television and see him on screen from time to time.

Feeling somewhat soothed by this line of thought, Lucy slipped into the only pair of reasonably sexy knickers she owned, which, thankfully, didn't seem to be affected by the glut of mince pies she'd consumed, put on the matching bra and then hurriedly threw on a dark purple dress which fell to just above her knees. It was both sexy and comforting, with a high neckline and a fabric which outlined her curves without sticking to them. A silver necklace completed the look, and she dithered about whether or not to put shoes on, since they hadn't planned to leave the house, and it might be weird to be walking around her own home in the heels that went best with this dress. In the end, she left them off.

Finn had insisted that she didn't have to cook for him tonight, either, and that he'd take care of the food, so she wouldn't be rushing around the kitchen, trying to impress him with her culinary skills. Having been enjoying the blessed relief of the café being shut for the past couple of days, and not having to cook or be on her feet all day, she felt very pleased about this. She did wonder, though, what Finn had in mind for food; she'd read enough about celebrity diets to be a touch wary, even if it was Boxing Day and perhaps he could take a night off.

As she was contemplating all this, while brushing her teeth, and trying to take her mind off what else could be on the menu this evening, the doorbell rang. She nearly dropped her toothbrush in the sink at the sound, which jangled her nerves.

'Take a deep breath, and chill the hell out,' she told her reflection. This evening shouldn't be making her so nervous.

Finn was a good man; she knew that already. Did it really matter what happened next?

Passing Megan's room as she headed down the stairs, Lucy closed the door on the reminder that she had other responsibilities. Megan was having a whale of a time with Rob and his family; she could go off duty for a little while. Tonight was about her and Finn, and perhaps reminding herself what intimacy with another human being could be like. Shushing the thought that it had been so bloody long since she'd had any form of intimacy, she padded down the stairs and to the front door. One last deep breath and she was ready to face him.

Immediately she opened the door, her breath shortened once again. 'Hi,' she said, cursing the slight squeak in her voice. No one had a right to look that handsome, even a world-famous star. But, she realised immediately, it was because he didn't look like the coiffed onscreen idol; he looked like the man she'd got to know over the past four weeks, not the star.

That wasn't to say he wasn't immaculately dressed, of course. A crisp white button-down shirt, open at the neck and covered by a navy-blue crewneck sweater led down to mid-washed blue jeans and his usual boots. A navy-blue woollen coat completed the look, against the biting cold. The different shades suited him, and Lucy said so.

'Thanks.' Finn smiled as he walked through the door. 'That's a great dress, too.'

Lucy smiled and thanked him. Finn paused in the hallway to unlace his boots, and then tucked them away on the bottom rung of the shoe stand just inside the front door. In his socked feet, he was still tall, but, having left her own shoes off, Lucy felt a little better. She wasn't short by any means, but Finn's height would dwarf almost anyone.

As he straightened back up, Lucy could see that the bruising under his black eye had very nearly vanished. She was standing close to him in the narrow hallway, and her left hand reached out tentatively to brush underneath his eye. 'It looks so much better,' she said, running her thumb over what was left of the bruise and then over his cheek and down his neck. 'I guess make-up aren't quite so pissed off with you, now.'

Finn smiled, and caught her hand with his, bringing it to his lips before pulling Lucy closer for a kiss on her mouth. As they broke apart again, he replied, 'If it hadn't been for your prompt attention, it would have been a whole lot worse.'

As they leaned in to kiss once more, Lucy's stomach gave an almighty rumble. She laughed in embarrassment. 'Sorry,' she murmured. 'It's been a long time since lunch.' It was then that she realised that Finn didn't seem to have anything with him; not a carrier bag, not a bottle of wine, nothing. 'Er... you *did* say you were sorting dinner, didn't you? I didn't imagine that?'

'Right, right,' Finn said. He looked suddenly, endearingly sheepish. 'I, uh, left everything outside on the doorstep.' He looked down at her, and she was sure she wasn't imagining a slight blush colouring his cheeks. 'I just wanted to kiss you first. Is that really lame?'

'Not at all,' Lucy laughed, and then her stomach rumbled again. 'But at the risk of sounding obsessed, I get hangry!'

'Duly noted.' Finn smiled down at her. 'Fortunately, this won't take long to prepare.' Disentangling himself from her, he went back to the door and grabbed the bags he'd left outside. Curious, Lucy tried to look at them as he brought them in, but he hid them behind his back. 'Be patient!'

He wandered through to the kitchen, Lucy following in his wake. 'I'm not a patient woman when I'm hungry.'

Dumping the bags on the kitchen counter, Finn opened one and pulled out a bottle that looked a lot like gin. 'How about a glass of this to help take your mind off it, then?'

Lucy furrowed her brow. 'I'm not really spirits drinker,' she said. 'And gin tends to make me a bit sad.'

Finn passed her the bottle. 'Then you don't need to worry. Dave the pub landlord suggested I get a bottle of this for tonight, but I've also brought a bottle of champagne if you'd rather have something with alcohol.'

Lucy peered at the label on the beautifully simple clear glass bottle. 'Pentire Adrift, botanical non-alcoholic spirits,' she read. The bottle listed its ingredients as sage and rock samphire, among other things. 'This sounds interesting, and good.' She paused. 'And it means I'm less likely to embarrass myself.'

'I don't mean to impose my sobriety on you, though,' Finn continued, suddenly looking adorably uncertain. 'If you'd rather have the champagne...'

Lucy shook her head. 'You're sweet,' she said, putting the bottle down on the kitchen table and moving closer to where Finn stood. 'But, to be honest, I've had enough booze over Christmas; it would be good to try something a little different.' She put her arms around his neck and gave him a long, lingering kiss.

As she broke apart from him and grabbed a couple of tall glasses from her cupboard, she commented on how at peace he seemed about things.

'Not always,' Finn said. 'It took me a long time to get things rationalised and into perspective, but these days I don't have the pressures I used to.'

'And how does that make you feel?' Lucy asked, sipping her drink. To go with the Pentire, Finn had bought some decent tonic water and Lucy sliced up a lemon and found some ice to complete it. 'Do you miss all of that screaming girl adulation?'

'You sound like my therapist!' Finn grinned, taking a quick sip of his own glass. 'But no. Not any more. Maybe at one point I did.'

'And when this film comes out?' Lucy asked. 'Are you prepared for things to kick off again?'

'I don't want to think about that right now,' Finn said, putting down his glass on the kitchen counter and moving towards Lucy, a warmth and a light in his eyes. 'I just want it to be you and me tonight.'

Lucy laughed. 'That's such a clichéd line!'

Finn grinned back. 'What can I say? Sometimes they rub off on me.' But the kiss he then shared with her was anything but clichéd. His mouth, slightly cooler from the drink, tasted delicious and promised much more as the kiss deepened.

Eventually, they broke apart again, both of them a little breathless.

'I thought you said you were hungry?' Finn smiled down at her.

With difficulty, Lucy tore her eyes away from Finn's mouth, or she knew she'd forget her hunger in a heartbeat. 'I am,' she admitted.

'Then let me get on with this,' he teased, but then looked a little shifty. 'That is, uh, if you can show me how to turn the oven on.'

'Sure,' Lucy replied. 'Do I get a hint about what you're going to make me?'

Finn's expression grew shiftier. 'I said I'd bring dinner,' he replied. 'I didn't say anything about making it!'

Lucy shook her head. 'What do you mean?'

Ruefully, Finn delved into the other shopping bag and pulled out a couple of stuffed crust pizzas, which had been carefully wrapped in Treloar Arms paper bags. 'I cajoled Dave into letting me buy these from the kitchen,' he said. 'I've been known to burn water, and I didn't want to take any chances!'

Lucy burst out laughing. 'I'm sure I once read an article about you and Montana and your "perfect night in" cooking choices!'

Finn joined in with Lucy's laughter. 'Neither of us had ever been near a kitchen when that interview was done. The magazine catered it all.'

'You mean it was – gasp – *fake news*?' Lucy kept giggling. 'Who'd've thunk it? Will you be all right heating up the pub's pizzas?'

'I'll manage,' Finn said wryly. 'And I'm sure you'll be able to help if I get out of my depth!'

As Finn sorted out the pizzas, and Lucy grabbed a couple of plates, they kept chatting. This was nice, she reflected. So nice, it almost felt normal. For a little while, she could just about forget that she was sitting in her kitchen with a very famous actor. It felt as though Finn was meant to be there. Almost.

31

After they'd had their fill of the pizza, Lucy led Finn to the living room and settled herself on the sofa with a topped-up glass of Pentire. She thought that she'd need a 'real' drink to feel relaxed, but was surprised to find she was feeling chilled out in Finn's company, even without the relaxation of booze. The drink itself was refreshing and aromatic, and she'd almost forgotten it wasn't alcoholic. Perhaps she'd suggest Finn took the champagne back to the pub for a refund – after all, at Treloar Arms prices, it would've cost a fortune.

As she was musing on this, Finn had also sat down, and she fiddled with her phone to put one of her Spotify playlists on. She'd carefully removed any that included songs from Finn's past life in *High School Dreams*, fearing that she couldn't face the embarrassment if anything came on where he actually sang. The soothing sounds of the last album from James Bay drifted from her Echo as she settled back against the cushions of the sofa, feeling satisfied from dinner.

Finn leaned against the back of the sofa, shuffling slightly in his seat until his head met the cushions. Being long-bodied as well as long-legged, he'd make even the biggest furniture look like it belonged in a kids' playhouse, Lucy observed with amusement. Usually, people on the television seemed shorter in real life; not so with Finn.

'This is nice,' he said softly. 'I can't remember the last time I felt so relaxed.' He turned his head towards her, and Lucy could see the way his brown eyes had softened in the low light of the living room. He looked happy, and calm, and Lucy felt pleased and flattered that he should be so obviously at ease with her.

'I'm glad,' she replied. 'I know this sounds mad, but it feels like I've known you a lot longer than a few weeks.'

Finn raised an eyebrow. 'Well, you did watch me a lot on TV, from what Serena said!'

Lucy laughed, and slapped him playfully on the forearm. 'That's not what I meant and you know it! I just... I feel like we're, you know, friends now.'

Finn turned towards her on the sofa. 'I know what you mean,' he said softly. 'When I came to Roseford, I thought it'd be just another job. I'd try to keep myself out of the way when I wasn't working, and I'd be able to learn a bit about my mom's family. I never imagined I'd let myself get close to someone. Someone like you.'

'Someone like me?' Lucy felt a little offended, although she wasn't quite sure why. 'What do you mean, someone like me?'

Finn shook his head quickly, obviously sensing he'd not put things quite right. 'Don't get me wrong, please, Lucy,' he said. 'I mean, someone who's so sure of herself, so settled, who knows what she wants for her and her daughter. Someone *real*.'

'Real?'

'I've spent most of my career around worlds created by writers and directors, who tell me where to stand, what to say, what to sing... this movie's more of the same. But to meet you, to spend time with you and Megan... it's a reminder of a life I always wanted.' He took her hand hurriedly. 'Don't worry, I'm not getting heavy. I'm just trying to say, in the worst way possible, that I'm loving being here with you. It feels, oh, I don't know... right.'

Lucy smiled, knowing that Finn was tying himself up in knots. It was as if he felt a bit lost without a script in front of him. She was beginning, more and more, to see him as himself, and not the characters he played, and moments like this reminded her that he was just an ordinary man underneath all of the glitz and glamour of his job.

'I'm loving being with you, too,' she said softly, shimmying closer to him on the sofa. 'I think I'm more or less over the "I can't believe Finn Sanderson's in front of me" stage, and I'm really enjoying getting to know you. The *real* you.' She leaned into him and gave him another kiss, which he responded to with enthusiasm, wrapping his arms around her until they were a tangled mass of sprawling limbs and breathlessness on her sofa.

As Lucy came up for air, she locked eyes with Finn, who, mindful that he might be squashing her, had propped himself up on his elbows above her. 'Are you okay?' she asked gently.

Finn nodded and smiled broadly. 'I am very, very okay. Are you?'

Lucy smiled back. 'Oh, definitely.' She sighed. 'There's just one problem.'

'What's that?'

Running a hand over Finn's cheek, she leaned upwards and gave him a brief, passionate kiss. 'I don't want to stop. I want to take this further. A lot further.'

Cocking an eyebrow at her, Finn laughed. 'And that's a problem?'

Lucy considered this for a moment. 'Only if we're not on the same page.'

A long, loaded pause descended between them. As Lucy watched, a mixture of expressions flitted over Finn's face. Then, shaking his head, he righted himself on the sofa, put his elbows on his knees and let out a long breath.

'What's wrong?' Lucy, immediately on the alert, sat up quickly. Her knees were parallel to Finn's on the sofa, and she resisted the urge to press too closely. 'Am I going too fast for you?'

Finn turned and looked at her, and she saw the level of uncertainty in his eyes. 'No, no,' he said softly. 'I just... I need to make sure... that this—' He gestured down at himself. 'That *I'm* the person you actually want.'

The confusion surged through Lucy's mind. Of course he was what she wanted! She'd made it very plain only moments ago that she was ready to take things to the next level. Was Finn getting cold feet?

'Did I do something wrong?' she asked carefully. 'I thought... I mean, we *seemed* to be thinking the same thing.'

Finn shook his head. 'Oh god, Lucy, we are. I really, really want to be with you tonight.' He looked at her, his eyes suddenly more vulnerable and open than she'd seen them before. 'But there's just one thing I need to know first.'

Sitting on that sofa, Lucy's heart began to race. Finn's anxious face searched hers, and she reached out a hand to grasp one of his, where it lay on his knees. 'Of course,' she said softly. 'You can ask me anything, Finn.'

As the pause between them grew longer, Lucy held her breath. What was it that Finn needed to ask her? And would it change the course of the evening? She waited, heart racing, to find out.

Finn, obviously feeling the need to get a little space, stood up abruptly from the sofa. He looked back down at her where she was still seated, and reached out a hand, which she swiftly took, allowing him to pull her to her feet.

'Talk to me, Finn,' she said gently. 'I'm listening.'

Finn gave her a small, sad smile. 'I guess... and I know this is going to sound stupid, but I just need to know it's me you want.'

Lucy looked back at him, confused. 'Of course it's you. Have you not worked that out by now?'

'It's not quite that simple, sometimes.' Finn dropped his hand from hers and ran it up her arm to rest on her shoulder. 'I don't do... *this*... very often. And I've been burned before by women who say they want the real me, but then end up sharing things, personal things, with the world. And yeah, that was when I was younger, and more stupid, and in a few cases I probably deserved it, but it makes you cautious.'

'I understand,' Lucy replied. 'And I promise you, Finn, I don't expect anything of you. I'm not in it for fame, or money. God, the thought of being on Instagram for anything other than the café terrifies me. I want you. The person. Finn Sanderson, the slightly awkward tall bloke in my living room. Is that okay with you?'

Finn smiled down at her, but just as quickly, his expression became serious. 'I mean it, Lucy,' he said gently. 'I'm not into one-night stands, and I'm not that man on the screen.' He looked endearingly unsure of himself. 'I'm just me. Some guy who got a lucky break. If you want to sleep with the movie star, then I'm afraid you've picked the wrong person. All I am, really, is who you see in front of you. I can't cook, I don't drink and I'm a really crappy dancer.'

'Finn,' Lucy said softly. 'I don't want to sleep with the movie star. I want to spend the night with you. The real you. The one who brought me pizza from the pub and introduced me to Pentire, and who I'm starting to feel like I'm finally getting to know.'

'This is real, Lucy. Right here. Right now. Just you and me. No cameras, no fancy music, no lights. Just us.' Finn's voice was trembling slightly as he looked down at her, and she swallowed in anticipation of his next move. She felt her fingertips tingling, itching to touch and be touched, wanting to explore every inch of him.

'I know,' Lucy said softly. 'And I want to spend the night with you.' It was odd, she thought, how she'd been the one agonising about her mince pie muffin top and her lack of glamour earlier on, and now Finn had confessed to being equally, if not more cautious about taking that next step with her. How stupid those fears felt!

Needing no further invitation, Finn dipped his head and brought his mouth to hers in a hot, firm kiss that in moments had her senses on full alert and her whole body, not just her fingertips, tingling. She slid a hand upwards into his hair, realising with relish that he'd left out the product he normally used to keep it tidy, and enjoying its softness against her palm. As she ran that same hand down his neck, stroking his nape gently, she heard him groan.

'That feels so good,' he murmured as he kissed her. Lucy had to concur when his right hand brushed through her hair and settled on the back of her neck, too. His touch was warm, and even warmer thoughts filled her head about where else she'd like him to touch her.

Soon, it was clear from her own shaky legs that she couldn't keep standing up. Being held in Finn's arms, feeling his body pressing against her as they kissed, had left her in very little doubt where this was going to go. And much as she relished being spontaneous, she was fully aware that the curtains were still slightly open in her living room. The last thing she wanted, especially after the conversation they'd just had, was for some passer-by on a Boxing Day evening stroll to catch her kissing anyone, let alone Finn Sanderson.

'Do you, er, want to take this somewhere a bit more comfortable?' she murmured. 'I mean... that's where we're headed, right?' Suddenly, she felt embarrassed about asking the question.

'I would love to,' Finn replied, eyes fixed on hers. 'If you're sure that's what you want? No pressure, Lucy.'

Lucy nodded. 'No pressure. I just want... oh god, Finn... I just really, really want...'

Needing no further encouragement, Finn swept her up in a hug that left her in no doubt that he wanted it, too. As they swiftly climbed the stairs to her bedroom, Lucy shook her head. This whole situation still had such a sense of unreality to it.

As Lucy pushed open the door to her bedroom, her hand firmly clasping Finn's, she was pleased that the central heating had warmed the room through. Always a little chilly upstairs, the old terraced cottages could be arctic, but tonight the room felt comfortable.

'Well, here we are,' Lucy laughed nervously. Needing to break the tension, she walked over to the window and drew the curtains on the crisp, clear night overhead. The moon peered over the hill, shining brightly enough to cast its light even when the curtains shut it out, and a hard frost lay crisp and iridescent on the hillside and the roofs of the houses opposite. It was the stuff of Christmas cards, or cheesy Christmas movies, and Lucy felt caught up in it all.

She turned away from the window when she sensed Finn behind her, and wrapped her arms around his neck, pulling his head down to hers and capturing his mouth in a passionate but languorous kiss. The kiss grew deeper, more urgent, and soon Lucy was leading Finn towards her antique brass bed, needing to feel the warmth of his hands on her skin, and his body pressed against her more intimately.

'Lucy...' Finn murmured as they sank down onto her duvet. 'Are you sure you're ready for this?'

'Stop asking me if I'm sure,' Lucy replied, smiling into the kiss. 'I'm more than ready, if you are?'

In response, Finn broke away from her, grinned and slipped his jumper over his head, throwing it to the floor by the bed. 'Absolutely,' he added.

In a few moments, Finn's shirt had gone the way of the jumper, and Lucy shivered when his hands began to run over the soft jersey of her dress, brushing over her breasts and down her waist before he pulled her on top of him. She was still fully clothed, but the sensation of lying on top of a half-naked Finn and feeling his very definite arousal through his jeans had her wanting to lose her clothes as swiftly as possible.

Rolling off him so she could switch the small bedside lamp on, wanting to see a much as she could feel, she took the opportunity to slide off her tights and pull her dress over her head. A rogue thought, despite their discussion downstairs, comparing herself *yet again* to all of those gorgeous co-stars, slipped into her head, and her shoulders slumped a little, while she also tried to suck in her stomach. *Too many mince pies*, she thought, not for the first time this Christmas.

'Hey,' Finn said softly, rolling onto his side to face her as she lay back down on the bed beside him. 'Are you okay?'

Lucy smiled. 'I'm fine,' she replied. 'Just, you know, trying not to overthink this.'

Finn shook his head and stroked his fingertips over her face and down the side of her neck, over the curve of her breast and down her waist. 'You look so beautiful,' he murmured, kissing her neck so softly that she felt the goose-flesh ripple across her body and a slow, rolling tingle intensifying in the places she most wanted to be touched. 'Does this help to take your mind off things?'

Lucy's laugh turned into a sigh as his mouth met hers again. 'That definitely helps,' she breathed, as his warm hands slid over her now partially clothed body. The sensation was exquisite, and she sighed as the tension began to drain out of her, to be replaced by something more exciting.

Their kisses grew more intense, and Finn was soon wriggling out of his jeans and kicking off his socks, after Lucy's slightly shaky hands had unbuckled his dark brown leather belt. The sight of him, clad only in his light blue cotton boxer shorts, the length of his legs reaching down to the bottom of the brass bedstead and his intoxicating aroma was doing ridiculously erotic things to Lucy's insides. She moved nearer, sliding a leg in between his thighs and pressing herself as close as she could to him, feeling his warmth as he pressed back, and in no doubt, as if she ever had been, about how much he wanted her.

The room wasn't quite warm enough to stay above the duvet for long, though, so they both worked their way underneath, gently discarding their underwear as they did so. Finn drew in a sharp breath as their bodies touched again, and Lucy's wandering hands made contact between his legs. As they began to explore one another, reacting to every touch, it wasn't long before they were both breathing heavily, luxuriating in the culmination of the chemistry that had drawn them so powerfully to each other from the very first moment they'd met.

Lucy trailed kisses along Finn's throat as her hands explored other places, causing him to groan in pleasure. He was solid, substantial, and she wanted nothing more than to feel him inside her. His own fingers were pressing and stroking, and she knew it wouldn't be long before she tipped over her own edge, from the tingling that was spreading out from her core.

Their eyes met between kisses, and an unspoken question was answered swiftly. Reaching out to her bedside table, Lucy grabbed one of the condoms that Serena had so playfully given her a week ago and wasted no time. In a matter of a few moments more, she had shifted position, until she was looking down at a thoroughly love-flushed and soon-to-be-undone Finn Sanderson, whose half-closed eyes fluttered open as he and Lucy became exquisitely connected, and whose hips began to rock gently back and forth in response to her. His fingertips continued to stroke and caress, and the sensation of touching, and being touched, soon had her on the very edge.

As Finn's other hand gripped her hip, Lucy knew that he was holding back so that she could make the most of the precipice, and she bore down on him, the fact that he'd waited for her being the final prompt she needed to dive into the warm, caressing waters of her climax. She clenched and shuddered around him, for a moment lost to the sensations that were washing over her, throwing her head back and seizing the moment. Looking down at him, a few blissful moments later, she saw his eyes upon her, and nodded briefly, before he started to move, his hands firmly guiding her movements as he reached his own climax, thrusting up deep inside her with a long exhalation and a moan.

There was an extended moment of silence as they both came back down to earth. Lucy stayed where she was, relishing the look on Finn's face, and his heavy breathing in the aftermath. The sweat on his forehead, and his dishevelled hair did something to her heart as she looked down at him, and she realised that this was who he was, behind the headlines and away from the camera. He'd made himself vulnerable to her a few times since they'd met, and this was another way he'd put his trust in her, revealed himself to her. She felt a lump rise in her throat and she swallowed hard, wondering why she suddenly felt the urge to cry. She'd always imagined her teenage self would give her a high five in this situation, but, weirdly, she knew those feelings she'd had for the man she'd thought was Finn were gone; it was who he was now that mattered. Climbing off him carefully, she waited for him as he disposed of the condom, and then snuggled close. This really was the stuff that dreams were made of. And it had nothing to do with the movies.

32

The next morning dawned bright and sunny, and Lucy, who, with a young child, was accustomed to waking early, opened her eyes first. She was lying on her side, and the wonderful warmth of Finn's body behind her brought her to her senses in the loveliest possible way. Turning around to face him, she smiled as he stirred.

'Hey,' she said softly as he opened his own eyes. 'Fancy seeing you here.'

His low, sleepy laugh did things to her insides as he replied, 'Fancy.'

She raised a hand and brushed her palm across his cheek.

'Sleep well?'

'Uh-huh. Your house is a lot quieter than the pub. Even if my feet do dangle over the end of the bed!'

Lucy giggled. 'Sorry about that. Normal beds aren't built for people as tall as you, evidently!'

They'd crashed out earlyish last night, neither of them realising just how much they'd needed the sleep. Now, with the morning sun peering through the curtains of Lucy's bedroom window, it was definitely time to wake up.

'Tea?' Lucy asked. She suddenly felt self-conscious about getting out of bed stark naked and finding her dressing gown. It might have seemed daft, but last night her bedroom lighting had been softer and she'd felt a whole lot more confident. Instead, she leaned out of the bed and picked up Finn's white shirt, which lay crumpled where it had fallen the night before.

'That would be great,' Finn replied. He rolled over onto his back and just for a moment, Lucy settled against his chest. 'I had a great time last night,' Finn continued. 'You were... out of this world.'

'I bet you say that to all the girls!' Lucy teased, propping herself up on her elbow to look down at him.

Finn shook his head and pulled her downwards for a kiss. 'No,' he murmured. 'I really, really don't.'

A little while later, Lucy had made two china mugs of builder's tea and was unloading the dishwasher before heading back upstairs. Wearing only Finn's white shirt, which fell almost to her knees, she wondered what one served a film star for breakfast, and then shushed that thought. He was just Finn, now, and hopefully he wouldn't have any outlandish demands on that front. She took the tea, and a couple of slices of doorstep toast back to her room, where they both ended up tucking in with gusto.

'So do you have any plans for today?' Lucy asked.

Finn shook his head, his mouth still full of toast. 'I've got nothing on the schedule until tomorrow, when Kathryn wants me to shoot a couple of solo scenes. They're mainly just cover shots, although one of them does involve a couple of lines from me. Nothing too taxing, though. There won't be anything major until Montana gets back.'

He looked at her. 'How about you?'

Lucy shook her head. 'Strange as it sounds, I feel kind of weird about being at a loose end. As a parent, I often crave a bit of down time, but now Megan's gone with Rob, I'm not quite sure what to do with myself! Serena's gone back to her place for a day or two, and Mum's gone to visit my aunt in Shropshire, so I can pretty much do what I like.'

'So you're not opening the café?'

'Nope. Not until tomorrow. People don't tend to want to eat out much in the immediate aftermath of Christmas, so it's not worth the electricity bill.'

Finn raised an eyebrow. 'So I've got you all to myself for the rest of the day, then?'

Lucy felt pleasure spreading over her at his tone. 'If you want me...'

It was long after lunchtime when they finally got out of bed.

33

That same afternoon, after Finn had joined her in the shower, they both decided they were in need of fresh air before an early dinner at the Treloar Arms.

'I'd better get a change of clothes,' Finn said as he reluctantly tried to tear himself away from Lucy. 'But after that, we could go for a walk?'

'I'd like that,' Lucy murmured. It was nice, only having herself to think about, if a little odd. She decided to give Rob a call, while Finn went back to the pub to change, and see how Megan was getting on. Watching Finn chuck on last night's clothes, and pull his blue jumper back over his head, she couldn't resist standing on the bed and playfully ruffling his hair, which he'd slicked back in the shower.

'That's better,' she murmured, planting a kiss on his forehead. 'Don't be long.'

'I won't,' Finn replied, pulling her down off the bed and wrapping her in his arms for a deeper kiss. 'Just try and keep me away.'

She followed him downstairs to the front door, having hastily grabbed her dressing gown from the hook in the bathroom. It was old and a bit tatty, but thankfully freshly washed. With hair unkempt from the shower and a pink flush to her cheeks, she knew she made a bit of a sight. As she let Finn out of the front door, he lingered in the doorway, kissing her goodbye with more fervour than was strictly necessary, given he'd be back in a short while.

'Don't be long,' Lucy repeated, pulling the dressing gown more tightly around herself against the sudden cold of the afternoon air. She felt happy, insulated and lighter than she had in a long while.

'I'll be back before you know it,' Finn murmured. He kissed her one more time, and then headed off to the Treloar Arms.

Just as she was about to close the door, something caught Lucy's attention on the other side of the market square. She felt a sudden sense of unease, as a figure bundled up in a hat, gloves and a scarf pulled up over their mouth began to hurry away. Her skin started to prickle with the oddest sensation that she was being watched.

Stop it, she thought quickly. *You're just being paranoid.* Just because someone was on the square, it didn't mean they were out there watching her. All the same, she shivered, and not just because of the cold winter air. She closed her door firmly and hurried back upstairs to dry her hair and get some clothes on. Finn would be back soon, and she wanted to call Megan before he returned. Trying to put the bystander in the square out of her mind, she went to dig out her hairdryer.

34

True to his word, Finn came back in just under half an hour, wearing a blue and white striped rugby shirt under another jumper, and a slightly darker pair of jeans.

'Are you ready to blow away some cobwebs?' Lucy asked as she let him in.

'Sure,' Finn replied. 'Where are we off to?'

Lucy explained that at the other end of the village was a hill up out of the valley, which would take them past Halstead House and give them a superb view of Roseford from the top. As they walked, she explained how her friends Stella and Chris had renovated the Victorian wreck into a wonderful family home, as well as a writers' and artists' retreat. Halstead, it turned out, had almost as many family secrets as Roseford Hall, and Stella and Chris had discovered them over the time they'd been renovating the place.

'The name of the house rings a bell,' mused Finn as they walked. 'As you know, one of the reasons I took this job was because my mom's grandfather hailed from Roseford. While

I'm here, I wanted to find out a bit more about him.' Finn paused and looked back the way he and Lucy had come, up a steepish incline where sheep were grazing, and skirting around a thicket of trees that partially obscured Halstead House from sight.

'Mom passed on some letters and photographs to me when she found out I was going to be researching the family's history. Halstead House featured in at least a couple of them.'

'Why don't you get in touch with Stella while you're here?' Lucy suggested. 'I know she and Chris have got boxes of archive material from the previous owners of Halstead – they might have something that could help you find out some more information.'

'I might just do that,' Finn said. Then he paused. 'But today's not about the past. It's about here, and now, and being with you.' He shrugged. 'I've already discovered a few things. There'll be another chance to find out more.' Reaching the top of the hill, they both turned back to look down. Spread beneath them was Roseford, looking like a model village. Roseford Hall stood proud at one end of the village, and the market square and the High Street looked picture-perfect in the wintry air.

'If I lived here all the time, I'd never want to leave,' Finn mused. 'It's beautiful.'

Lucy laughed. 'I never pegged you for the settling down type. You must have seen a fair few places during your career.'

Finn nodded. 'Yeah. But maybe I'm sick of travelling. Maybe I need to put down some real roots. Roseford feels like the kind of place I could do that.'

Lucy was slightly unsettled by the intensity in Finn's eyes as he said this and was reminded of what Montana had said about Finn having been through experiences that made him vulnerable. Was the sudden desire to settle a way of scratching an itch for him, or did he really mean it? Flattered as she was, she couldn't help wondering if it was all too much, too soon. She decided to make light of it.

'Now you really do sound like something out of a Christmas movie!' she quipped, grabbing his hand and squeezing it. Then, to break the tension, 'Come on! I'll race you back down the hill.'

As she set off at a gallop, it wasn't long before Finn, with his far longer stride, caught her up and overtook her, grabbing her as he passed and bringing her down onto the frosty grass.

'I think it's time we got out of the cold, don't you?' he teased, all trace of his earlier intensity gone. Lucy, who immediately felt the damp from the grass seeping through her jeans, readily agreed.

35

After a detour back to Lucy's house, ostensibly to change her jeans, Finn and Lucy headed out for dinner at the pub. As they walked through the door, they saw Mateo and Nicole having a quiet meal together, and Finn raised a hand in greeting.

'I'm glad those two are back on friendly terms,' Finn murmured as they wended their way through the pub to a table at the back. 'Mateo's crazy about her.'

'Looks like it's a little more than "friendly terms",' Lucy observed as she glanced over at them. Mateo had reached out and taken Nicole's hand, and her eyes seemed soft in the low light of the pub.

'They had a thing, once,' Finn said. 'But he wasn't really ready to be exclusive back then. I hope she might give him another chance.'

'I guess it's difficult to form long-lasting relationships when you're only together for weeks, or a few months at a time.' Lucy felt the sharp sensation of her own metaphorical bubble bursting; she'd felt insulated, being with Finn, in these hours together, with no other responsibilities, but this wasn't reality, was it? One of the reasons she'd known that she and Rob weren't destined to be was that the nomadic lifestyle of a film director wasn't one that she could commit herself to, and now she was getting into something with Finn that could mean the same way of life. What was she doing?

Finn, immediately noticing Lucy's shift in mood, put a hand over hers. 'What's wrong?' he asked gently.

Lucy shook her head. 'I'm fine.' She felt the warmth of Finn's hand, and the sensation was comforting. He had such a way of reassuring her, of making her feel like he could protect her from anything. But still the doubt, in the back of her mind, lingered, tapping away like some overly enthusiastic wood-pecker, knocking at her brain.

Finn squeezed her hand. 'Lucy, I don't want to pry, but you look as though you're somewhere other than here at this table. Have I done something wrong?'

Lucy shook her head. 'No, no, Finn. Of course not.' She felt her breath shortening a little as she tried to put into words what was on her mind. 'It's just that this all suddenly seems so unreal again. This isn't my life. I'm usually working flat out in the café, then being a mother to Megan, or being knackered and getting an early night because both of those things, while wonderful, are just exhausting.' She looked up at Finn, whose eyes were fixed on her, taking in every word she said. 'I'm not sure where this fits in.'

'Do you remember what I said about wanting to settle down?' Finn said gently. 'Well, I meant it.' He held up his other hand as Lucy started to protest. 'I'm not proposing, or getting heavy, don't worry. And I don't know what settling down means, at the moment. But being on this shoot has made me realise that I'd like more control over the projects I do. I don't want to be in front of the camera all the time. And I'm financially stable enough not to need to be. I could stop working tomorrow, and provided I didn't go crazy with money, I'd be fine for a long time. I don't want to be running around the world from project to project any more either, Lucy.'

'But that doesn't mean you'll feel that way forever,' Lucy said. 'Rob, Megan's father, thought he could settle down, too, but opportunity came calling and he took it. I don't begrudge him that, but I knew then that I didn't want to be part of that life, following him all over the world with Megan in tow, or worse, staying behind on my own with her for months on end. I'm a homebody, at heart.' She smiled sadly.

'Rob was just starting out in his career,' Finn said reasonably. 'I'm not. It's different, Lucy. And I've been to a lot of places over the years that I definitely don't want to revisit because of it.'

Lucy drew in a short breath. 'Such as?' she said carefully. She got the feeling he wasn't talking about geography.

Finn let the pause between them deepen for a long moment. 'I'm not going to lie to you, Lucy. Nine years ago, I was in a spiral of alcohol and drug dependence that nearly ended my career, and my life. I'm very mindful of that, even now, and anyone who chooses to get involved with me needs to know the extent of it.' He paused. 'I don't regard you as just some casual fling on location, I think you can see that. But I also know I need to be really honest with you about things. Mateo and Montana were the ones who got me into rehab, and I owe them a debt of love and gratitude that I can never repay. I'm thankful every day that I'm not where I used to be. But at times, it's a struggle. That's why I choose the work I do very carefully. I can't let myself get back into old situations, old habits, and I'm lucky enough that I don't have to work on anything that I don't want to. Work helps, but it doesn't define me like it used to.'

Lucy put her other hand on top of Finn's, where it lay on the table. 'I'm so glad you told me,' she said softly. 'It means a lot.' And the things Montana had alluded to the night Finn took her ice-skating suddenly all made sense. 'And that's why I couldn't ask you to give your job up.' She shook her head. 'I'm sorry,' she said. 'It's a bit overwhelming, that's all.'

'I get that,' Finn said quietly. 'But I want you to know, Lucy, that I think you're amazing. I've loved getting to know you, and I'd like the chance to get to know you even better. I get that this might feel unconventional, unreal, even, but I promise you, I'm real, and right here.'

Lucy smiled. 'I feel the same way, too.' She suddenly yawned. 'I'm also just feeling really shattered. Life never really catches up with you until you stop, does it?'

As they ordered some dinner and a couple of drinks, Lucy tried to shrug off the unease she'd been feeling. Finn was right; he was here, he was real, and he thought she was amazing. She had to fight to keep from grinning every time she remembered he'd said that.

Much later, after a decent meal and a lot of laughter, Finn looked ruefully at his watch. 'I've got a really early call in the morning,' he said. 'Kathryn wants me on set at 5 a.m., so I guess we'd better call it a night.'

'I'm reopening the café tomorrow as well,' Lucy said, 'so I'd better get in early.'

They paused, as they both dithered. Eventually, Lucy broke

the silence. 'It's all right,' she said. 'You can go back to your own bed tonight. It's probably more practical, after all!'

Finn laughed. 'It's not that I don't want to spend another night with you, but an early call is my least favourite thing, and I'm generally better if I can just get dressed and get out.' He paused. 'But I will see you tomorrow evening?'

Lucy smiled. 'Definitely.'

As they shared another long, lingering kiss, hidden from the inside of the pub by the doorway, Lucy felt lighter, happier than she had earlier that evening. Finn was such a lovely guy; if it really did develop into something serious, surely they could make it work?

36

The phone call woke Finn from a deep, groggy sleep.

Glancing blearily at his phone, he baulked; it was 4 a.m. in the UK, which meant it was 9 p.m. in Los Angeles, where the area code suggested the call was coming from. Wondering if Montana had forgotten the time difference, he swiped the screen, trying to think of a witty response. A brisk 'hello' from the other end of the line immediately told him otherwise.

'Romy, hi,' he mumbled. 'What's up?'

'I should be asking you that exact thing,' Romy, his theatrical agent said, without preamble. 'Have you checked Twitter lately?'

'You know I don't bother with it when I'm working,' Finn replied. 'I've got better things to do.'

Romy gave a mirthless laugh. 'That's self-evident. Your "better things to do" have created quite the social media shit storm.'

'What?' Finn was suddenly wide awake. He could tell from the tone of Romy's voice that she wasn't happy, and a not-happy agent wasn't exactly the stuff that Hollywood dreams were made of.

'What's happened?'

Romy sighed. 'How many times have I told you to keep your private life private, Finn? Sleep with who you want, but be aware that the world will be looking out for every slip-up, every hint that they have a way into parts of your life they have no right to enter.'

'But I have!' Finn, sitting bolt upright in bed by now, grimaced as he saw a sliver of bright moon, still shining through a gap in the curtains, keeping an eye on developments. 'I haven't done anything wrong, Romy. I swear.'

'I didn't say you had.' Romy's voice was weary. 'But you and I both know it's not about doing things wrong. It's about what the world can see, and talk about. And I'm afraid, this evening, all they've been talking about is you and your mysterious new love.'

Finn's stomach dropped to his knees. 'What?'

'You've been papped on her doorstep, Finn. Full on candid, too. I mean, Jesus, she was in her bathrobe! Didn't you warn her?'

'I didn't think I needed to.'

Finn could visualise Romy pacing around her small office as she spoke. Even though business hours were over, Romy often worked late. The nature of the job, with clients all over the world, meant that it was inevitable. She also couldn't keep still at the best of times, and this did not seem like a great time. She continued speaking, while Finn struggled to get his thoughts in order.

'Part of the sell-in for *A Countess for Christmas* was that you and Montana had real chemistry. Audiences were yearning to see the two of you back together, both onscreen, and hoping that it might be real. You agreed to play the game, Finn, to do your part to make this movie a commercial success. And now you've been photographed leaving the house of some nobody, and, even worse, kissing her on the doorstep.'

'Lucy isn't a nobody!' Finn snapped. 'She's... very important to me.'

'Exactly how important?'

'Important.'

'Then I suggest you get your ass on Twitter and see what's being said,' Romy replied. 'And then you're going to have to find a way to sit down with Lucy and break it to her that she's being scrutinised by millions of your followers about everything from her hair to her choice of bedroom attire.'

Finn sighed. 'Can't we just pretend it isn't happening?'

Romy laughed again, but more gently this time. 'Do you really think that's fair to this Lucy of yours? You should have warned her about this before you let her kiss you goodbye in a public place.'

'I didn't realise the paparazzi reached as far as rural Somerset,' Finn muttered.

'Baby boy, have you learned nothing during your time in the sun?' Romy's voice was gentler now. 'There are cameras everywhere now. The old rules of the game don't apply any more. Anyone with a smart phone and an opinion can post it on the internet. You know that. You just slipped up.'

Finn shook his head, taken with the sudden, odd urge to cry. Romy's unexpected gentleness always did that to him. She was an old hand in the business, and she'd been his agent since the beginning. She'd seen him at his best, his worst and all stages in between, even sticking with him when he was in the strongest grip of his demons. *So much for the Keanu Reeves Paradox*, he thought. It clearly didn't apply to him.

'Okay,' he said finally, realising that Romy was waiting for a response. 'I'll get over there and talk to Lucy. Warn her to stay away from social media for a few days.'

'Be gentle with her, Finn,' Romy said. 'She's clearly a civilian and doesn't know the full implications of being seen with you.'

'She's not some backwater hick, Romy!' Finn retorted. 'She's got more of a clue about all this than you think.' Lucy had told him about her time with Rob, and what that had involved; he knew she would never have allowed herself to get thrust into the limelight if she'd been thinking straight.

'If she had, she'd never have let a picture of herself in that god-awful bathrobe be the one that gets picked up by social media,' Romy replied, but not unkindly. 'Good luck, Finn.'

As Finn said goodbye and ended the call, the sick feeling in his stomach escalated. Five minutes later, once he'd scrolled through the worst of what Twitter had to say, he actually did throw up. It was a vile barrage of abuse and jealousy, and he felt dirty, tainted by it. And if he felt like that, how would Lucy feel when she saw it?

It was a little after 4.30 when he'd pulled himself together, got dressed and stopped his hands from shaking. Lucy would still be asleep, happily oblivious to the storm that was breaking online, with the two of them at the eye of it. When would it be sensible to contact her, he wondered.

Just as he was contemplating this, the wake-up call from Kathryn came through. He needed to be on set in less than half an hour to prepare to film Jack Salmon looking at the sunrise from the terrace of Roseford Hall. Jack, at this point in the movie, was a changed man, a man who'd fallen for Ashley Marchant's American-born countess and, conflicted by his role as custodian and her new role as lady of the manor, he felt divided loyalties. He knew he had to psych himself into it, but thanked God he didn't have any actual lines to say in the scene; it was all about soulful looks out into the sunrise, with a voiceover he'd record later. He'd always been able to rise above his own emotions when the job called for it, submerge himself in the character he was called upon to play, but with the adrenaline from the shock of the Twitter trolling still running through his veins, he knew he'd have to work harder today. The FinnTana fans had really outdone themselves this time. How the hell was he going to break this to Lucy?

37

It couldn't be real. Could it?

In rising horror, a little later that morning, Lucy doom-scrolled Twitter, seeing the same image repeated again and again under the hashtag #FinnTrolla.

There were 'amusing' variations on the theme: #Bathrobe-Slut, #FinnSlumming, #FinnTanaIsOver, #FinnTanaFights-Back, #TeamFinnTana... they seemed endless. All, though, had one thing in common; the vitriol that was being directed towards her, Lucy Cameron, a café owner from Somerset.

Lucy's hands were trembling so badly, she dropped her phone on the kitchen floor. It landed with a clatter, and the screen protector cracked into a messy spider's web of shattered glass. How could she and Finn have left themselves open to this? How could she not have *known* that something like this would happen if she got involved with him? Finn was, obviously, still very much public property; at least the hundreds of Twitter users who'd commented, retweeted and even memed that awful shot of her in her dressing gown had thought so.

The first shot of them had passed virtually unnoticed, but this one had gone utterly, shamingly viral.

The thought of the endless comments made her feel sick. To be the target of such senseless bile because she'd kissed the wrong man on her doorstep was enough to make her actually want to vomit. And poor Megan! Imagine if she'd caught sight of any of the horrible words people had written? What if she'd seen Rob's Twitter feed and spotted the things being said about her mum?

A knock at the door, urgent and insistent, brought her to her senses. She'd called Serena the moment she'd realised what had happened, and Serena had promised to drop everything and come round. Hurrying to the front door, not even bothering to look in the mirror in the hallway, she pulled it open.

There, in the harsh winter sunlight, stood Finn. He was dressed in Jack Salmon's costume again, with the puffa jacket thrown over the top, hair starting to escape the side parting that had been imposed on it.

'Lucy.' His face was deathly white and the look in his eyes said it all. He'd seen what she'd seen. 'Can I come in?'

Wordlessly, Lucy opened the door wider and Finn stepped over the threshold. He walked through to her living room, where he stood, uncertainty radiating from his posture and his expression. He took a step towards her as she followed him into the small room, but she reflexively took a step back. She couldn't go there... not yet.

'Lucy, I'm so sorry.' Finn, at a loss as to what to do with his hands, had shoved them into the pockets of his thick jacket. 'I had no idea that this would happen. That they would be so... evil.'

'You warned me,' Lucy said numbly. 'That first night we went out. You warned me that something like this could happen. I just didn't realise how much it could hurt when it did.' She began a restless walk across the room, unconsciously trying to put some space between herself and Finn. She laughed weakly. 'I mean, I've had bad reviews from unhappy café customers before but at least it was the quality of my scones they were moaning about, rather than my choice of nightwear!'

'I don't know what to say,' Finn said quietly. 'I never intended for you to get dragged into the online stuff that follows me. I should have known better to think we could fly under the radar.' He reached out a tentative hand as Lucy paced past him, and she allowed herself to be stopped by him. The contact made her shiver.

Lucy turned towards him, aching to just collapse into his arms, to feel his body against hers, sheltering her. She wanted to feel as safe as she had last night, before all of this had happened. But how could he protect her against such a barrage of online hate? It was nebulous as the air, and as all-pervading as a killer mist, snaking its way through the cracks and tainting everything it touched.

'I think you should go,' she replied softly. 'I need some time to get my head around all this. What it means for me and Megan.'

'Lucy... please. Can we just talk? We can find a way through, I'm sure of it.'

Shaking her head, Lucy took a step back, and Finn dropped his hand from her arm. 'I can't do this, Finn. I can't cope with knowing that people are out there, ready to pull apart even the most insignificant things about me for fun on

Twitter. I've seen it happen too many times, when I've been scrolling through stuff. It feels different, and horrible, to be on the receiving end. I feel violated.'

'Then get angry, and stand tall!' Finn was suddenly animated. 'How do you think I've coped with it all these years? The lies, the speculation, people behind a screen dissecting every last thing I say, I do, I wear? You just switch off. You just ignore it. Fly high, not low.'

'That's easy for you to say!' Lucy retorted. 'You *chose* this life, Finn. You put yourself out there, in front of the cameras, for the world to judge. Wasn't that part of the bargain of getting to do what you love for a living? I didn't make that choice. I just fell in love with the wrong guy.'

Finn's face registered shock, and then went from pale to flushed as the reality of her words hit home. 'You're in love with me?'

Lucy laughed, suddenly feeling that flare of affection towards him again that threatened to make her resolve crumble. 'That's so like you, to focus on the positives.' She shook her head, and, at a loss as to what to do with her own hands, she, too, shoved them in her pockets. 'It doesn't matter how I feel. I can't risk being ripped apart by online crap. And—' She swallowed hard, her throat aching. 'I'm not prepared to put my daughter through it. It's like the Wild West online. You know that, and so do I.'

'Lucy, please...' Finn's voice held a tone of quiet desperation, and if she hadn't been so angry, and so determined to protect her daughter, Lucy knew she'd have weakened. Seeing him standing there, shocked and dejected, and, she knew, ashamed that he'd allowed her to be dragged into a messy situation, she felt a sudden rush of sympathy. But, determinedly, she quashed it. Finn would be all right; he was leaving Roseford in a few days, to complete filming in London and then California. She'd fade from his life, and there would be someone else to take her place. And she'd go back to the café, and her daily existence, heartsore, but still alive, and in control. The furore would die down, and things would go on.

'I think you should leave,' Lucy said, before she could change her mind. 'It's for the best.'

'Is it?' Finn said bleakly. 'You're letting them win, Lucy.'

Lucy's eyes filled with tears as she looked square at Finn, whose own eyes were shining in the harsh, unforgiving sunlight that poured in through her living room window. 'No one wins in something like this. You don't need me to explain that to you. You've been there, remember.'

Finn shook his head. 'For what it's worth... I love you too. This wasn't just a fling for me. That's not what I do.'

They stood together, both painfully uncertain of their next move. The silence spread between them for several long moments, until Finn, seemingly pulling himself back together, leaned forward and gave Lucy a gentle kiss on her cheek. She had to fight with everything she had to resist flinging her arms around him. The sense memory of how good they'd been together was threatening to ignite, and she clenched her jaw hard to avoid giving in to it.

'Goodbye, Finn,' she said softly. 'Take care.'

He looked at her one last time, and she could see exactly how frustrated and anguished he was. 'You too, Lucy,' he said softly. And with that, he walked back out into the hall, opened her front door, and left.

38

'You really told him to get out?' Serena's eyes widened as she took a fortifying sip from her glass of red wine that evening. She'd shown up shortly after Finn had left, and spent the day helping Lucy out in the café. Lucy was glad of her company; she'd felt as though, at any moment, someone was going to come through the doors and start shouting all of the dreadful things she'd read about herself online to her face, and the thought made her sick. Serena, to her credit, had confiscated Lucy's phone and wouldn't let her check it until the café had closed for the day. She'd also seen off a couple of stringers for the local papers, who were keen to get in on the story before any national interest escalated.

Lucy nodded, not trusting herself to speak. She lifted her own glass, which was filled with Pentire Adrift, and let the herbal, savoury taste be her focus for a moment. Then, putting it down, she sighed.

'What choice did I have? I was stupid to think we could pretend to be "normal" people in a normal relationship. I think I just got caught up in the fairy tale and I forgot that real life has consequences and, crucially, that we're never alone now the internet's been invented.'

Serena regarded her thoughtfully. 'Are you sure that's all it is?' She took another sip of wine. 'I mean, don't get me wrong, Luce, but apart from a couple of disastrous dates, how many *actual* relationships have you had since you and Rob went your separate ways after Megan was born? Don't you think that perhaps you're being a little hard on Finn for something that ultimately wasn't his fault?'

Lucy grimaced, and stalling for time, reached for a handful of the crisps she'd put in a bowl on the coffee table in front of them. 'I'm trying to protect myself and Megan from this online shit storm. I don't think that's being unreasonable, do you?'

Serena kept looking at her. 'I know that Megan is the most important thing in your life, and even though I can't imagine what it feels like to be a parent in this situation, that doesn't mean I can't try to understand where you're coming from about all this. But, Lucy, I haven't seen you as happy as you were with Finn in a long time. I mean, sure, the café makes you happy, Megan makes you happy, living in Roseford makes you happy. But all the time you and Finn were getting closer, you, I don't know, you just had this glow about you that I hadn't seen since those early days with Rob. Are you really going to throw that away because some bitches on the internet can't cope with the fact that their pet movie star is in a relationship with someone else? Someone who's not Montana de Santo?'

'Then what do you advise me to do?' Lucy replied hotly. 'I can't drop everything and be Finn's plus one whenever he wants me to be. I don't have the strength to face the endless

scrutiny that being his girlfriend is going to subject me to.'
Before Serena could interrupt, she continued, in full flow now.
'Finn once told me about the Keanu Reeves Paradox – that
Keanu, bless him, can wander around his hometown and be
virtually unnoticed, even though he has one of the most recog-
nisable faces on the planet. People respect him; people leave
him alone and they don't try to intrude in his private life.
Stupidly, I believed that that was going to be the case with
Finn and me. Now I know differently.'

'Okay,' Serena replied. 'So he was a little naïve about that.
And perhaps that is difficult to forgive, given the years he's
been in the business and the experiences he's had, but is that
worth throwing away what seemed to be the beginning of
something really good between you? I'm just saying that, from
the outside, it looks a little hasty. People will always take
photos, Lucy, we live in an image-obsessed world, and if
someone thinks they've got an exclusive, they're going to take
it. Being scrutinised like that on your own doorstep is horrible,
no one's disputing that, but are you sure you're targeting the
right person? You could be walking away from something,
some*one*, really, really wonderful. Do you really want to take
the risk?'

Lucy regarded her friend thoughtfully. 'And are *you* sure
that this is all about me?' She'd known Serena since they were
kids and while her best friend had always had killer instincts
when it came to Lucy's thought processes, there was something nagging at the back of Lucy's mind that made her
wonder if there was more to it than just the ending of the relationship between Finn and herself.

Serena put her glass down in front of her on the coffee
table. The silence that extended between them was long and

loaded. Lucy, often tempted to break moments like this, forced herself to sit back and wait for what she just knew was going to be some sort of revelation. Eventually, Serena met her eyes again.

'Look, Luce, I wasn't going to say anything. It's early days, and incredibly high risk, not just for me but for the other person involved. But I trust you and I trust that this will go absolutely no further than your sofa. Agreed?'

'Of course,' Lucy said. 'You don't even have to ask. Whatever you have to tell me stays between us.'

Lucy could see Serena battling, trying to convince herself to say what she was going to say, and seeing her best friend so uncertain was completely new territory. Serena had always been the confident one; the one who dragged them into the local off-licence when they were fifteen to buy the cheap cider that they then proceeded to get horribly drunk on in the dugout of the local football ground. When Lucy had been in a quandary about whether or not to keep her baby, it had been Serena who had been her confidante. And, long before that, when Serena had come out to her at age fourteen, Lucy had kept that confidence until Serena was ready to go completely public with it. Theirs was a friendship that had enjoyed the best of times and endured the worst, but now Lucy was at a loss as to what was so important that Serena was hesitating to tell her.

Serena took a deep breath.

'You're not the only one who's been tangling with a dilemma.' Her face flushed under Lucy's scrutiny.

'Oh, yes? Go on.'

Serena paused and refilled her glass from the bottle of red on the coffee table. 'I need a bit more fortification before I spill the beans,' she said, throwing a mischievous but distinctly nervous grin at Lucy.

Lucy waited patiently, knowing that Serena would tell her eventually. Once her friend had had another sip of her glass of wine, she turned back to Lucy on the sofa.

'The thing is, Luce, this film crew arriving in Roseford changed my life, too.'

'What are you trying to tell me, Serena? Are you going off to Hollywood to try your luck? When does the flight leave?'

'No, you stupid cow!' Serena laughed, the tension broken, as Lucy had intended. 'It's not just you who was swept off your feet.'

Lucy's jaw dropped. 'But you never said anything! Who is it? What's been happening while I've been under Finn Sanderson's spell?'

'Lucy, if I tell you this, you have to promise me that it goes no further. The other party involved... Well, let's just say they're not ready to go public and they probably won't be for quite a while yet.'

Okay...' Lucy replied. 'So who, and what?'

In response, Serena grabbed her phone and tapped it until her camera roll appeared on the screen. Without another word, she selected a photograph and passed the phone to Lucy. There, clear as day, was a selfie that nearly made Lucy drop her glass.

'Oh my god,' she breathed. 'But that's... That's...' After staring at the photo for a little longer, she handed the phone back.

Serena nodded.

'We hit it off on festive night, when I showed her around the shops in Roseford. She was looking for a gift for her mum for Christmas and we found the perfect pair of cashmere gloves in the gift shop. She's amazing, Luce.' Serena paused. 'She's funny, gorgeous, kind, and I've never felt this way before about anyone.'

'But she's...'

Serena nodded. 'I know. And for that very obvious reason, this is the only photograph I was allowed to snap of her and me.' Sadness crossed her face. 'It's innocent enough to be just two mates having fun, but what you don't see is that we were holding hands out of frame and we had literally just got out of bed. She flew back from California yesterday and we've been hiding out together in my flat in Bristol. It's been the best twenty-four hours of my life, Lucy.'

'Oh, Serena,' Lucy said softly. 'So you know just as well as I do the risks of having a relationship like this.'

Serena nodded. 'A little more so, I would say. Montana isn't publicly "out", and as far as I'm aware has no intention of being so, at least until this film is released, if ever.' She shook her head. 'Much like Finn, the will-they-won't-they of Finn-Tana has become a huge selling point for this movie, and whether I like it or not, she and I have to consider that in the next few months.' Serena brushed away a sudden tear from her eye and Lucy grabbed a handful from a box of tissues on the side table by the sofa and passed one over. They'd mopped each other's tears up countless times over the years, and the gesture was automatic.

'So that means you have to keep things a secret between you?' Lucy said, once Serena had wiped her eyes.

Serena nodded. 'If I want to keep seeing her, we have to keep things absolutely private for the time being. We can't afford to get snapped on a doorstep kissing. Can you imagine what would happen if we did? I mean, you and Finn, a straight couple, have been ripped apart by the FinnTana trolls. Can you think for a second what would happen if one half of that dream couple was actually revealed to be in a same-sex relationship?'

Lucy, having had a taste of the wrath of the fans over the past twenty-four hours, could well imagine, and shuddered. 'Social media is so polarising,' she said. 'Anyone with a keyboard and an opinion can say what they want.'

'Exactly,' Serena replied. 'And much as I'd love to shout out to the world that I'm dating Montana, it's the last thing I can do. At least for now.'

'And you're okay with that?' Lucy asked.

'For the moment,' Serena replied. 'If keeping quiet, and being discreet, means I get to spend time with her, talk to her on the phone, love her, then I'm good with it.'

'But doesn't that feel like she's ashamed of you?' Lucy asked. 'Ashamed of your relationship?'

'A bit,' Serena replied. 'But I have to believe that, in the long run, it'll be worth it. It won't be like this forever, Luce.' She shrugged. 'You don't quite get what it's like; for years, I had to deny who I was, who I wanted to love, because I was afraid of what my family and my friends would say.' She looked downcast again at the memory, and Lucy reached out a hand and gripped Serena's free one. 'Luce, I knew that you would accept me and my sexuality, but you know as well as I do how long it took Mum to come around. And much as she's on my side now, fighting my corner, there was a while when she kept trying to convince me that it was all a phase, that I'd get over it and marry a decent bloke.' Serena gave a short laugh. 'I still think she thinks that, from time to time.'

Lucy knew that the levity in Serena's tone belied the struggles she'd had, and her heart ached for her friend. 'But this is high risk, Serena. What if Montana never comes out? What if someone does find out, and you end up getting the grief I have, or worse?' Lucy could well imagine how some people would take the news that one half of their favourite pairing was gay. A few nasty comments on a social media site could be the least of Serena's concerns. Even in the twenty-first century, there were people who wouldn't take the news well.

Serena moved on the sofa and put her arms around Lucy in a quick hug. 'I'm stronger than you think,' she said. 'And Montana's all about "controlling the narrative". As soon as this film's out there, we're going to go public.'

'You're sure about that?' Lucy asked. She wasn't completely familiar with the machinations of Hollywood but from what she'd heard about it through Rob over the years, she knew that 'controlling the narrative' could mean any number of things, depending on who was in control. Would Montana really be free to make that decision, when the time came, and, just as importantly, would she really choose to?

'I'm as sure as I can be.' As Serena released her from the hug, Lucy saw a softness in her friend's expression that she'd never seen before. Perhaps it would be all right after all, she thought. Perhaps Serena and Montana would get the happy ending that she'd walked away from with Finn.

'I wish I could be as strong as you,' Lucy said softly, feeling suddenly tearful.

'You can,' Serena replied. 'Call him. Be brave.'

Lucy shook her head. 'I can't. I'm not that person, Serena. You know that.' She forced a smile. 'Miss Cautious, remember.'

'Even if that means losing the one person you've given your heart to in years?'

'Yes. Even then.' But as she said it, Lucy's composure crumbled. 'But it hurts, Serena. It really, really hurts.' She grabbed the remnants of the bottle of red wine and sloshed it into her glass. Just for tonight, she needed to numb the pain. But what happened tomorrow, and the next day after that? Would her heart ever be hers again?

39

Finn's car was booked for six o'clock the next morning, and the hours couldn't pass quickly enough. The charming cosiness of his room in the Treloar Arms, that had seemed so lovely at the start of the shoot, now felt thick-walled and claustrophobic. After hours of staring at the curtained top of the mahogany four-poster bed, he'd got up at two, made the first of a long line of cups of coffee from the machine in his room, and waited for the dawn.

There would be three days in London, shooting a couple of light-hearted scenes with Montana, when their characters were in pursuit of a piece of parchment that was crucial to her character's new title of countess in a vault that just happened to be buried right in the heart of the city. Then a flight out of Heathrow to a studio in a lot in Los Angeles to shoot on one of the sound stages. After that, the project would be complete. He'd fly back to New York, have a chat with Romy and then decide what the hell he did next. There was a small project that a group of students from one of the New York film schools had pitched to him several months ago that he'd thought would be a good antidote to the candy canes and schmaltz of a Christmas movie, and that, hopefully, would help to still his mind and, yes, he hoped, fix his breaking heart.

He'd never intended to fall for Lucy. He'd liked her immediately, and they'd had a wonderful time while he was in Roseford. But it had ended up being more than that; much more. Lucy had seen past the careful veneer, and he'd let her. He'd found himself loving her, and when she'd called time on their relationship last night, he'd been reeling, not to mention more than a little frustrated at her point-blank refusal to see sense.

So what if there'd been internet abuse? He'd suffered it so often himself that he barely even registered it any more. What they'd had, the gradual development of feelings between them, had been worth so much more than a few keyboard warriors bitching about a grainy photograph. Who cared what they thought? He felt a sudden, impotent rage that a bunch of anonymous Twitter users had destroyed something so wonderful. How could Lucy let them win?

Realising it was the caffeine revving up his system, Finn tried to calm himself with a few deep breaths. Lucy was entitled to her feelings, and her thoughts. Unlike him, she wasn't used to being the target of such abuse, and it had come as a dreadful shock to her, how much it actually hurt. He settled back onto his bed with a sigh and sipped the remnants of his coffee. Glancing at the clock on the bedside table, he wondered if Montana was awake yet. She was hanging around in Roseford for another day, as she had some solo scenes to shoot in the interior of the house, and then she'd be joining him in London. He suddenly needed his best friend's counsel, and, although it was only four in the morning, he decided to send her a text. If she was asleep, she'd pick it up when she woke, and if she was awake, maybe they could talk.

A couple of minutes after the message was delivered, his phone rang.

'Hey,' a sleepy voice said on the other end of the line. 'What's up?'

'Sorry,' he said. 'I didn't mean to wake you.'

'I was awake,' Montana said wryly. 'Couldn't sleep knowing you were going away later. How are you doing, baby?'

'Can I come to your room?' Finn asked. He was aware his voice had started, unaccountably, to tremble.

'I'll come to you,' Montana replied. 'Give me a minute.' She ended the call, and Finn was left staring at his phone, trying to sort his head out.

In less than a minute, there came quiet knock at his bedroom door. Finn slid off the bed and crossed the small space, not even bothering to check the spyhole before throwing it open. There stood Montana, in a pair of jogging bottoms and a T-shirt, her hair tied back in messy plait, her glasses propped up on her nose.

'How are you doing?' she repeated softly as she stepped over the threshold. 'Need to talk?'

Finn, unaware of just how much he'd been holding back until that moment, nodded. As Montana enfolded him in her arms, he found, with a mixture of shock, sadness and surprise, that he couldn't stop crying.

* * *

A little while later, after using almost the entire box of tissues on the dressing table, Finn let out a shaky laugh. 'I didn't know I needed that.'

'Honey, a good cry is sometimes all you need.' Montana rubbed his back to emphasise the point, and Finn, not for the first time, felt extremely grateful that she was such a good friend to him.

'So what am I going to do?' Finn asked. 'It's over with her, before it's even begun.'

'Look at us,' Montana sighed. 'You're heartbroken over some English girl you've only known for a few weeks, and I'm finally considering being honest with the public about who *I* love, at the worst possible time for both of our careers. Ya couldn't make it up, could ya?'

Finn gave a watery grin. 'Who'd have thought a winter shoot in a Somerset backwater would turn both of our worlds upside down?'

'In the old days, I'd have ordered us a bottle of Scotch and we'd have finished it by the time your car arrived,' Montana said. 'But we're way past that, thankfully.'

'I'm not sure Dave would take kindly to being woken up at four in the morning, either,' Finn replied. 'Even if the Scotch you ordered was his most expensive bottle.'

'Fair enough,' Montana replied. 'And that's the last thing you need.'

'Oh, I don't know,' Finn said. 'There are times when I think that being sober has made me awfully cautious. I guess I wanted to protect myself from getting hurt and falling back into the old ways so much that I stopped taking the risks I used to.'

'Which is *definitely* a good thing,' Montana said. 'No one who loves you wants to see you going to those places again.'

'I know,' Finn replied. 'And I'm grateful to you and Mateo for being there for me, looking out for me so often. I just can't help thinking it's ironic that the one time I have put my heart on the line, I mean *really* put it on the line, it was a mistake that would have set me back a long way in my recovery, if it had happened in the early days.'

'Sometimes you just have to admit that love hurts as much as it heals,' Montana said. 'I learned that with Sam, but it didn't stop me from letting myself fall in love again. And even if this thing with Serena doesn't work out, I'll be glad I tried, glad I took the risk. She's worth it.'

'Is she worth coming out to the wider world, too?'

Montana paused for a long moment. 'You know... I really think she is.'

Finn pulled her close into a hug. 'I'm glad for you,' he murmured into her ear as she wrapped her arms around him again. 'I really am. You deserve to be happy.'

'And so do you,' Montana replied. 'Perhaps, when Lucy's had some time to cool down and think about it, she'll realise that there are more important things than what some idiots are saying about her online.'

'That's easy for you to say,' Finn replied. 'You and I have had years of this. She's in shock, and she wants to protect her daughter. I can't promise her that it won't happen again, and she's frightened. I don't blame her for that. We made our choices to live in the public eye – Lucy didn't.' He felt a wave of desolation wash over him once more, and shook his head. 'I'm sorry. We've been over all this once already.'

Montana moved round on the bed and looked Finn square

in the eyes. 'We learned to live with it,' she said gently. 'That doesn't mean it doesn't hurt. Lucy's raw right now. Give it time. She said she loved you, remember? Hold onto that.'

'And in the meantime, I've got the shoot in London, and then it's back to LA. So I don't really have time to think about it.'

'Exactly,' Montana said firmly. 'Let time do its thing. And we'll do what we do best; pretend to be madly in love with each other for the cameras!'

Finn laughed, and this time he felt his spirits lift a fraction. 'I love you, Mary Ann Cooper.'

'And I love you, Finn Sanderson, but if you ever call me that in public, I'll, what is it Serena says, "knock your block off"!' Montana lay back on the bed and gestured to the pillow beside her. 'Now, by my reckoning, you can get an hour's sleep before your car gets here, so lie down here and keep me company.'

Finn did as she told him, and as he closed his eyes, he was amazed to find that he did, indeed, feel a little clearer and calmer. Montana had the knack of getting to the root of his troubles, and even after all these years, it still surprised him. Friends like her were difficult to come by, and he felt grateful every day that she was still in his life. After all, she could have abandoned him years ago. Not many people would have put up with him in the grip of his personal darkness. And, once again, she'd helped him to keep the demons at bay. A rogue thought flitted through his mind just before he dozed off that, had Lucy let him, he'd felt sure that she, too, would have been the light he needed to keep him out of the dark. But now, with an aching heart, he had to concede that he'd been wrong.

40

As the film crew packed up and left, so things started to return to normal in Roseford. Soon, Roseford Hall would be open again to the public, the spring would bring even more tourists into the village, and trade would pick up at the café once more. After an initial flurry of interest from the press, Lucy was relieved when things died down again. Now, apart from the odd rogue message on her Instagram page, the spotlight on her had dimmed, and she was grateful. When Finn had left the country, so had the focus on their relationship.

Lucy tried not to think about how things had ended with Finn, and during the day, as more and more visitors flocked to Roseford to look around the Hall and shop on the main street, it became easier to consign what they'd had to the past. Finn, obviously sensing how much it would hurt them both, hadn't tried to contact her after he'd left, and although she was fairly sure he and Simon Treloar were still in touch, and Serena kept her up to date with Montana's movements, Lucy was glad she'd made the decision.

The whole thing had seemed like a fairy tale at the time, and as the months went by and winter turned to spring, it felt almost as though it had happened to someone else, and she'd been the star of her very own romantic Christmas movie; albeit without the happy ending. Megan, after initially pestering Lucy about when they were going to see Finn again, had seemed to accept that it wouldn't be any time soon. She was soon caught up in school, and they both enjoyed seeing the hyacinths in their china pots starting to peer through the soil from where she and Lucy had put them on the windowsill of the café. Everything changes, Lucy thought. And everything eventually healed, even a broken heart.

One morning in late spring, Lucy was putting through a stock order when the café door chimed. Looking up, she saw the co-owner of Halstead House, Stella Simpson, perusing a menu. Stella often ordered cakes and cream teas from Lucy for her guests, and was here to place a bulk order for the week.

'We've got a full house,' Stella said as she gave Lucy her order, to be collected in two days' time. 'The spring's made everyone want to get creative. We're fully booked now until Easter – not that I'm complaining!'

'That's great,' Lucy said. Everyone in Roseford had been delighted when Stella and Chris had made such a success of Halstead House's retreats. For a few years before Stella had come to Roseford, Chris had been struggling to renovate the property more or less single-handed. A widowed single father, he'd become a virtual recluse since the death of his wife, but falling in love with Stella had changed everything for him. Now, the happy family atmosphere of Halstead House was often mentioned in guests' feedback, and certainly contributed to its popularity. Chris and Stella were a success story because they took a risk, and trusted each other, and it had paid off.

'Are you going to be able to get any time off over the Easter holidays?' Stella asked as Lucy totted up the bill.

'Yeah, thankfully. Megan's great about hanging out in the café, but I wanted to be able to take her away for a few days, and on some decent day trips too, so Rachel's going to look after this place for a week or so. It'll be good to get a change of scene.'

'Chris wants to take Gabe away for the Easter holiday, as well,' Stella replied. 'In the old days, when I was a journalist, I'd have been up to my ears in deadlines, but now, with the retreat, we can set our own timetable, so I'm looking forward to getting away for a bit.'

'It must have given you a real insight, working for AllFeed,' Lucy said. 'Did you ever, you know, cover stuff you didn't feel comfortable about?'

Stella regarded her levelly. 'All the time. It kind of went with the territory. But most of the time, I tried to keep things fair.' She picked up a napkin from the dispenser on the counter and toyed with it. 'Of course, not everyone has to follow a professional or ethical code. Some people can just say what they want, and they quite often do.'

'Tell me about it,' Lucy said quietly.

'Lucy.' Stella looked up from the napkin and straight into Lucy's eyes. 'You can say it's none of my business, but if you walk away from something because of the trolls online, then you've let them win. Are you sure you want to do that?'

'No one wins in a situation like this,' Lucy replied, feeling her heart beating a little faster. 'You of all people should know that. You saw enough of that kind of stuff when you were a journalist, after all.'

'But you shouldn't let other people dictate what you want for your life,' Stella said. 'Believe me, it's not worth it. So a few people might actively disagree with you, but are you really going to let them ruin what could be something wonderful?'

'I wish it was that simple, Stella, I really do, but I just don't think I have the strength to keep defending myself and protecting Megan from all of the online rubbish. I don't want to be a part of all that.'

'I'm sorry,' Stella said. 'I don't mean to stick my oar in where it's not wanted. I just know what it's like inside that world, and if you can find something good, and pure, it's worth holding onto.'

Lucy smiled. 'I'll bear that in mind.' But as Stella bade her goodbye, with the promise to return in a couple of days and pick up the order, Lucy knew that getting back in touch with Finn was still a step too far for her. Besides, she thought, Finn was bound to be working on a new project, with new people, and perhaps there was someone new in his life. She'd be just a warm memory of a cold winter's night.

As she was finishing up for the day, the café door jangled again. 'We're closing, I'm afraid,' she called out. She had her back to the door, but as she turned around, she saw that the customer was Marie, Jake Fisher's sister. Jake, who'd lamped Finn that night outside the pub.

'Hi,' she said. 'Was there something that you wanted before I close up for the day?'

Marie looked at Lucy, and Lucy noticed the dark shadows under her eyes, the nervous way her gaze kept flicking from Lucy to the window and back again, and her wringing hands.

'What's wrong, Marie?' Lucy asked gently. 'Is there something on your mind?'

'Lucy.' Marie hesitated again. 'I want to tell you something.' She glanced again towards the window, visibly afraid.

'Of course,' Lucy said. She'd have to pick Megan up from after school club in half an hour, but Marie was clearly in distress, and her heart went out to the girl. 'What is it that you want to say?'

Marie took a deep breath, and before Lucy could offer her a cup of tea for her nerves, she'd begun to blurt out her story.

'I'm so sorry. Jake made me do it. I didn't want to, but he threatened to tell Mum about the weed I smoked before I got the job at the pub, and I knew she'd go ballistic.'

'Hey, hey, slow down,' Lucy said. 'Start at the beginning.'

Marie hung her head. 'I was chambermaiding at the pub while the film crew were in the village,' she said. 'Jake asked me to keep an eye out; he wanted me to see if there was any stuff I could find out about Finn Sanderson and Montana de Santo while they were staying. Dave and the rest of the staff at the pub all had to sign a, what was it, a non-disclosure agreement? We all did, so that we didn't go blabbing to the media.'

'Okay,' Lucy said. 'So what happened?'

'Jake reckoned if we could get something on one of them, we could sell it to a newspaper, make some quick cash. The trouble was, neither of them did anything weird. I mean, they're celebrities, surely one of them had some habits, right? Anyway, Jake kept putting the screws on me, trying to get me to go through their rooms, find something we could use. But there was nothing. Both of them were just really... boring.'

Lucy suppressed a smile. For nineteen-year-old Marie, going through the belongings of two stars in their thirties must have been about as exciting as watching paint dry. If they'd been YouTube stars or Instagram influencers, perhaps she'd have been more invested.

'Go on,' she said, trying to encourage the nervous girl, who still kept looking towards the café's window.

'Well, Jake got impatient after a few days and decided to do something himself. He tried his best to get Finn to punch him, that night during the karaoke, but Finn wouldn't rise. He obviously had more sense. Instead, Jake lost it and punched Finn. He was lucky Finn didn't press charges.' Marie paused. 'He was trying to goad him into something that he could then post online, go viral, you know. He'd seen a video of another actor who'd lost it with a fan and thought he could do the same.'

'Finn wouldn't have done that,' Lucy said. 'He knows better.'

Marie nodded. 'He always thanked me for cleaning his room, and when he left, he gave me a really good tip, even though the film company were paying the bill. He seemed nice.'

'He is,' Lucy said. 'He really is.'

'Well, Jake got angry after his plan didn't work. He wanted something he could sell. So he made me follow Finn when he went to your house on Boxing Day. By that point, he had a few pictures of you in the village, but he wanted something really good. He thought he could sell it to a paper, or a news site.' Marie's voice trembled at the memory. 'He made me get up early the morning after and wait outside your house for ages, across the road where you wouldn't see me. He was convinced that if we followed you, we'd get something.'

'And you got lucky,' Lucy said. 'You managed to get that picture of me in my awful dressing gown.'

Marie nodded. 'I took a few shots, and then went home. Jake took my phone, downloaded them and sent them to a few online news sites, but they weren't interested. They didn't care if Finn Sanderson had a new girlfriend; he wasn't important enough, or the photos weren't juicy enough... I don't know.'

'So Jake decided to share them online instead?'

'Yes. He made a Twitter account using a fake name and shared them hundreds of times, using all the different hashtags. Finn and Montana's fans did the rest.'

'And I'm a star in my dodgy pink dressing gown,' Lucy said. Then she felt an insane urge to laugh. Giving in, she did, until the tears were rolling down her cheeks.

Marie looked at her as if she was, indeed, mad. 'You're not angry with me?'

Getting a grip, Lucy tried to calm herself. 'Would it make any difference now if I was?'

'Jake's going to kill me when he finds out I've told you all this,' Marie said, and she suddenly looked terrified. 'Promise you won't tell him, Lucy? He'll take it out on me and Mum.'

Lucy, appalled by the fear in Marie's eyes, reached out a hand to touch Marie's arm, and was shocked when Marie flinched away from her. 'Does Jake hurt you, Marie?'

Marie shook her head a little too quickly. 'No. Well, he hasn't for a long time. But since he lost his job, he's been desperate for money. Mum's working all hours cleaning, and he's got no qualifications, so he's stuck. He hates being dependent on us.'

'So he thought he saw his golden ticket when the film crew came to town.' Lucy filled in the gaps out loud. 'It's a shame it didn't work out for him. I bet he didn't get a penny for that shot of me.'

'And you got all of that abuse from Finn's "fans".'

'I won't say it wasn't awful,' Lucy replied, knowing that Marie deserved honesty, since she'd been so frank with her. 'But there are worse things that could have happened.'

'Please don't tell him I told you,' Marie pleaded. 'He's not a bad person; he's just frustrated.'

'He needs to stop making you afraid,' Lucy said. 'Being out of work is no excuse.'

'And please don't tell Dave. If he finds out what I did, going through guests' stuff, he'll sack me on the spot.'

'Did you take anything from the rooms?' Lucy asked.

Marie looked shocked. 'Of course not! I'm not like that.'

'Then we don't have to tell Dave, do we? You were just being extra thorough with your cleaning, right?'

Marie looked baffled, and then the penny dropped. 'Right. I'm really sorry, Lucy. Finn was lovely. Did... did the photo cause a lot of trouble between you?'

Lucy paused. Was it fair to burden poor Marie with the truth, when the girl had been so brave in owning up to her? That would be a step too far, and Lucy's conscience couldn't take it. After all, she'd only been doing it because she'd been intimidated by her brother. 'It's fine, Marie. Honestly. It wasn't nice, being all over Twitter, but it would have happened eventually, with or without your photo.'

Marie looked doubtful, but then obviously decided the easiest route was to take Lucy at face value. 'Thank you. And I am sorry. I'll never do anything like that again.'

'Your apology means a lot. Thank you.' Lucy, mindful of the time and that she had to pick up Megan, reached behind her to the counter and wrapped up the last of the day's scones in a paper bag. Thrusting them into Marie's hands, she said, 'Have these. They'll go stale overnight otherwise.'

Marie, who looked as though she needed more than a few scones to feed her up, took them gratefully. 'I'd better get going. Mum'll be home soon, and I promised I'd get some dinner on.'

'Take care, Marie,' Lucy said as the girl turned to leave. The moment Marie had closed the front door behind her, Lucy sagged back against the counter. She felt exhausted, but strangely lighter. Three months had given her a little more perspective on the Twitter unpleasantness, and she realised that, although she might have felt violated and vulnerable by the intrusion and the trolling, Marie had been under far more pressure. She felt angry at Jake, once again, for his irresponsibility. How could he have put his poor sister in such a terrible position? She had a good mind to go around there and have it out with him, but she knew that it wouldn't do any good, and could even make things worse. But what could she do to help? Marie had said that Jake lacked a focus, a goal since he'd lost his job. Was there anything she could do to improve his situation? Ever the fixer, despite such provocation, her mind started to tick.

41

The morning after the revelations from Marie, Lucy decided to take matters into her own hands. She couldn't bring herself to confront Jake directly about the misery he'd had a hand in causing, but she did want to do something to make Marie's life more bearable.

Shutting up the café, she posted a sign on the door that read 'back in 30 minutes' and headed up to Roseford Hall. She'd overheard Bill, the head gardener, complaining that he'd been left short-staffed since his last apprentice had left to go to Cannington Agricultural College full time, and she had an idea that might help both Marie and Jake. At the very least, it would, hopefully, give Jake a focus.

Calling out a cheery 'good morning' to the manager of the small tea and coffee concession inside the grounds of Roseford Hall, she went off in pursuit of the person who'd be able to help. She knew enough about Simon Treloar to know that he'd be keen to come on board, and it wasn't long before she found him in his small office at the back of the house.

As house custodian, Simon had notional oversight of all decisions made, even though the British Heritage Fund had the final say. It was a weirdly parochial arrangement, given that the Treloars were no longer in charge, and Simon seemed both contented and frustrated by it at times. Today, Lucy hoped she could persuade him to her way of thinking.

Knocking on the heavy oak door of his office, Lucy heard him call her in, and, pushing against the weight of the door, she hurried inside.

'Hi,' Simon said, looking up from the large, messy sheaf of papers on his desk. 'What can I do for you, Lucy?'

Lucy grabbed a seat on the other side of the desk and flumped into it. She'd known Simon since they were teenagers, and there was no need to stand on ceremony. She was counting on that friendship for what she had in mind.

'So, I was wondering if I could tell you something, in confidence?' Lucy said. She was amused as Simon nearly dropped his pen. Notoriously awkward around 'delicate' matters, he often seemed like he'd have been more at home with his Edwardian ancestors.

'Yes, right, absolutely,' Simon said, once he'd scrabbled for his pen and managed to cast it to one side. 'Always happy to, er, talk.'

'Don't worry,' Lucy teased. 'I'm not here to declare undying love to you, you berk!'

Simon grinned. 'I'd say that was a relief, but I'd be worried about offending you.'

'Anyway,' Lucy said hurriedly, not wanting to get sidetracked. 'I was wondering if you'd found someone to help Bill out in the grounds. I know he lost his apprentice to full-time college, and I think I might be able to help.'

'Don't you have your hands full at the café?' Simon asked. 'Unless you were planning a change of career, of course.'

Lucy shook her head. 'Not me. But I know Jake Fisher is at a loose end at the moment. He did a bit of a course at Cannington a few years ago, but never finished it. Would you be interested in hiring him temporarily? Just to see how it works out?'

'Why this sudden act of charity towards that toe rag?' Simon asked. 'Wasn't he the one who was behind that viral photo of you and Finn?' Simon trailed off, obviously worried he'd said too much.

Lucy started. 'How do you know it was him?'

Simon rolled his eyes. 'People talk around here, Lucy. Not least Jake himself in the pub. He couldn't resist spilling the beans the other night, when I happened to be in earshot. He's a nasty piece of work, and he's vile to his mother and sister, too. I'm surprised you're in here, trying to get him a job.'

'He's had a hard time since he lost his last job,' Lucy said. 'And I know I should be the last person to take his side, but I can't help wondering if he needs someone to give him a chance, and a focus. Even after everything he's done, surely he deserves that?'

'I don't know, Lucy,' Simon said warily. 'Even if I did have the final say over hiring and firing in this place, which I don't, I'm not sure I'd trust him to work here. He's got a nasty temper, and he tried to do some real damage to you, just for a quick buck. Not to mention what I've heard about the way he treats his family. I think we're better leaving well alone, there.'

'But his sister Marie's worried about him,' Lucy said. 'And I'm worried about her. She's a vulnerable girl, and Jake needs help if he's going to sort his life out. A job here, in the open, doing what he's good at, might be a good start.'

'Aren't you worried that it all looks a bit *privileged people helping out the less fortunate*?' Simon countered. 'You and I... we're lucky to be where we are. He's got every right to chuck it back in our faces.'

Lucy nodded. 'I know. And that's why I don't want to get involved. But you've still got heft here, Simon. You can influence things, can't you?'

Simon sighed. 'You're not going to give up on this, are you? Even though he had a hand in putting you out online for the world to see?'

Lucy paused before replying. 'You know as well as I do that Finn and I... we wouldn't have lasted anyway.'

'Why do you say that?'

'I don't want to be in the public eye, ever. I just want to live my life. That wouldn't have been possible, being Finn Sanderson's girlfriend. The pressure would have done for us in the end.'

'Are you quite sure about that?' Simon turned to his laptop. 'I'm probably breaking all kinds of confidences here, but he misses you.'

'How do you know?' Lucy asked, her heart doing a little flip.

'Oh, we have the odd chat,' Simon said, obviously trying to play it down.

'You're still in touch with him?' Lucy asked incredulously. She'd suspected as much, but was surprised nonetheless when Simon confirmed it.

'Weird as it sounds, we became mates while he was here. He sends me a WhatsApp or two, mainly to check in and ask how you are. He knows you didn't want the pressure of being in his life, and he respects that, but he asked me to keep an eye on you.'

Lucy was torn between pleasure and irritation. There was something a bit patronising about Finn keeping tabs on her, but it wasn't too weird, she supposed, if Simon and he had, indeed, developed a friendship. 'Tell him I said hi, the next time you text him,' she said eventually. She wanted to tell Simon to tell Finn that she missed him too, but she was worried about opening another emotional can of worms if she did so, since she'd tried so hard to squash everything down after Finn had left.

'Why don't you tell him yourself?' Simon said gently. 'I'm sure he'd love to hear from you.'

Lucy shook her head. 'Not at the moment, Simon,' she said. 'I can't think about it, about him right now. But I can try to help Jake and Marie, if you'll let me.'

'Oh, all right, then,' Simon said wearily. 'But you know there's no guarantee he'll take the job, even if the BHF and I offer it to him, right?'

'I know,' Lucy replied. 'But at least we can say we tried.' She got up from her chair and, on a whim, added. 'You and Finn got on well, then?'

Simon laughed. 'I know! It sounds as weird to me as it does to you. But he wasn't what I expected. He's a decent bloke, and if anyone could navigate you through the stormy waters of being a famous actor's, er, girlfriend, then I'm sure he could.'

'I don't think I'm ready for that,' Lucy replied. 'But... thanks, Simon.'

As she hurried back to the café, she mused on Simon's words. Had she been a little too harsh, that wintry day, when she'd called things off with Finn? Had she run scared because she feared not the spotlight or the scrutiny, but allowing herself to fall in love? Allowing herself to be coaxed from her cosy existence into emotions that she'd shut off for a long, long time? Should she have been braver, like Serena and Montana, and allowed Finn to get closer, instead of using the photographs and the trolling as a reason not to? Feeling as unsettled as she was pleased that Finn still cared, she flipped the sign on the café's door and plastered on a bright smile as the next customers entered. *Later*, she thought. But how much more time did she need?

42

Later became late summer in a heartbeat. Finn had been burying himself in work in New York, starting with the independent film with the students and culminating with a significant role in a big budget, ensemble cast superhero movie, to be screened in the latter half of the following year. It had been a last-minute offer when a bigger name had dropped out, but Finn wasn't offended; opportunities like that were tough to come by, especially if you didn't actively chase them. Romy had thought it would be good for him to boost his profile in a franchise, and although he wasn't sure where else the role would lead, he took it. Anything to wallpaper over the hurt he still felt about Lucy.

Simon Treloar had kept in touch, and reassured him that Lucy and Megan were both fine. Finn didn't feel entirely comfortable asking Simon about them, but he was too much of a gentleman to pester Lucy, and had too much pride to push it, when she'd made her position so abundantly clear. He'd resigned himself to putting their relationship in the past, but he hadn't quite been able to bring himself to start dating again. Montana had been his friend and counsellor, and Mateo was, once again, lead camera operator on the superhero movie, so he had them to lean on, if he needed them. He tried not to, though. Montana was finding it increasingly difficult to keep her relationship with Serena under wraps, and was desperate for *A Countess for Christmas* to premiere so she could move on, and, maybe, go public with Serena. Finn asked Montana a couple of times to ask Serena how Lucy was but, again, he didn't want to push it. Montana had her own life, and her own concerns, after all. They'd been at opposite ends of the country since *Countess* wrapped, and were long overdue a reunion.

One evening, just as he was finishing up an email to Romy, telling her that he'd be taking September and the first couple of weeks of October off before the premiere of *A Countess for Christmas* in mid-October, a call came through from Kathryn, the director of *Countess*.

'Finn, how are you?' she asked. 'Busy, I hope?'

'Oh, you know,' Finn replied noncommittally. He never knew if he was supposed to pretend to be up to his ears in work or not when in conversation with a director who might want to offer him another job.

'Well, I'll get straight to the point,' Kathryn continued. 'There's been a bit of a disaster on the audio front for a couple of the exterior shots. Can you get yourself into a studio to do an overdub sometime in the next week?'

Finn glanced at the paper organiser he still used to keep a note of dates and appointments. 'I've got three days next week. Where do you need me?'

Kathryn let out a relieved breath. 'There's a studio in

Brooklyn that we can use. I'll text you the details. Can we say next Wednesday?'

'Sure,' Finn replied. It would keep him out of trouble. 'Anyone else involved?'

'No, just you,' Kathryn replied. 'Montana's doing hers from California, so we'll just add yours into the mix when we get them.'

Well, Finn thought, it would keep him out of trouble for another day. And it wasn't like he'd put anything else into the diary between now and the premiere. An overdub wasn't the worst thing that could happen – he'd had to do plenty of them before. When conditions weren't right during the recording of a scene, or a line of dialogue didn't 'pop' as it should, doing them again was often part of the post-production process. It didn't always come so late in the day, with the film's release a mere eight weeks away, but then nothing about that shoot had been ordinary. Falling in love with Lucy hadn't been part of the plan either.

Suddenly frustrated, Finn's fingers walked the familiar walk to his phone, where he still had Lucy's number. Should he call her? Would she answer now the months had passed? Shaking his head, he stopped himself. What good would it do? He was over three thousand miles away in New York. Burying his emotions, once again, he waited for Kathryn's email with the script for the overdub to arrive.

An hour or so later, just as he was reading through the lines and making a couple of notes, his phone rang again.

'Hey, baby,' Montana's familiar voice said. 'Just checking in. How are you doing?'

'Not bad,' Finn replied. 'I've got the lines for the overdub.'

They chatted idly about work for a while, before the conversation took a turn.

'So, the premiere of *A Countess for Christmas* has been moved forward to the start of October,' Montana said. 'We always say Christmas is getting earlier every year, and this year it really is.'

'I hadn't heard that,' Finn said. 'Where are we doing it?'

'They want to fly us to London,' Montana said. 'You'll probably get your tickets and passes in the next few days.' She paused. 'There's a plus one option…'

Finn went very still. 'Are you thinking about asking Serena to go with you?'

Montana's sigh went on for a long time. 'I don't think that's such a good idea, do you?'

'I thought you were all about going public?' Finn replied. He knew that Montana and Serena had been managing to spend some time together over the summer.

'I don't think the premiere is the right time, with the world looking to you and I to get back together,' Montana replied. 'But we will do. Soon.'

'Well, I'm looking forward to seeing you,' Finn said. 'Whatever you and Serena decide to do.'

'Take care,' Montana said, and ended the call.

Finn shook his head. All he wanted to do was to get onto a plane, find Lucy and persuade her to see him again, but for the moment, that was off the cards. Texting Mateo, who was back in New York, he suggested they meet for dinner. He hadn't seen him since the superhero movie wrapped, and he wanted to touch base. He hoped an evening out with his friend would allow him to do that.

As they tucked into the most delectable crayfish linguine in a little Italian restaurant a few streets from Finn's apartment, Finn began to unbutton to Mateo. He'd missed his friend, and they had a lot to catch up on.

'So your English rose still won't take your calls?' Mateo asked, between mouthfuls of a delicious Pinot Grigio.

Finn shook his head. 'I haven't tried. She wanted space. I didn't want to pressure her.'

Mateo grimaced. 'You're something else, you know that?'

'What do you mean?'

'You're so afraid of rejection, like all of your kind, that you'd rather walk away from something than fight for it.'

'My kind?' Finn raised an eyebrow. 'What? Canadians?'

'Actors. You'd think you'd be used to it by now, but when it comes to giving your heart... you're a coward.'

'She told me to get out of her life,' Finn repeated patiently. 'What was I supposed to do?'

Mateo laughed gently, a low, rumbling sound that never

failed to make Finn feel more optimistic. 'You show her you're worth fighting for, *pobrecito*.'

They ate in silence for a while. Then, tired of mulling over Mateo's advice, Finn changed tack. 'How exactly did you convince Nicole to give you another chance?'

Mateo shook his head, mouth still full of crayfish. 'Ah, my boy, what can I say? The heart wants what it wants. In the end, she couldn't resist me.'

Finn raised a sceptical eyebrow. 'And the truth?'

Looking faintly sheepish, Mateo confessed. 'I begged. She felt so sorry for me, she gave me a second chance just to shut me up. The rest, as they say, is history.' He stretched arms out that were fatigued from shifting cameras around all day. 'My wandering days are over. Who knows, in a few years... a house in the country, a couple of kids...'

'I never thought I'd see the day,' Finn said. 'But I'm happy for you, Mateo, I really am.'

'You'd be happier if you called your English rose again,' Mateo observed.

'Maybe once the premiere of this godforsaken Christmas movie is over,' Finn replied. The problem was, he feared he'd just be setting himself up for another round of heartbreak if he did. Perhaps Mateo was right after all, and he was too afraid of rejection.

44

Lucy was up to her ears in tourists when Simon Treloar came through the café door. Roseford usually had a busy autumn, before things gradually tailed off into winter, except for a flurry in the weeks before Christmas, and this year was no exception. In that strange mid-autumn period that wasn't warm enough to be an Indian summer, but wasn't festive enough to be the Christmas run-up, Lucy always tried to make the café seem even more of a welcoming and inviting place. As a result, she'd placed several carved pumpkins in the windows of the café, which she and Megan had had enormous fun creating the previous weekend, brought in some fronds of beech leaves that had turned a deep russet, and adjusted her menu to include pumpkin soup and pie, and hearty, filling toasties.

'Hey,' Lucy said as Simon approached the counter. She couldn't stop; she had full tables and hungry customers, but she flashed a smile at him as she expertly operated the coffee machine, managing to fill the cup and keep eye contact at the same time. 'What can I get you?'

'I can't stop,' Simon replied, 'but I thought you might like to know that the British Heritage Fund have permanently appointed Jake Fisher as their new assistant gardener. They were pleased with his trial months, and offered him the job with a day release to Cannington College once a week to complete the course he started before.'

'Oh, Simon, that's great news!' Lucy replied. 'How did he take it?'

'You know Jake,' Simon said flatly. 'He has a habit of looking gift horses in the mouth! But I think Bill won him over in the end, promising him free rein in maintaining the orangery over the winter.'

Lucy smiled wryly. 'I guess we can't expect miracles, but hopefully that'll mean he's less likely to take his frustrations out on Marie and his mum now he's got some job security.'

'I hope so,' Simon said, a serious tone in his voice. 'If he'd done what he'd done to you to me, I'd have been far less forgiving.'

'It's Marie and her mum who need the support,' Lucy said. 'Compared to what he's put them through, a few photographs don't seem so bad, do they?'

Simon's head jerked up from the Hallowe'en menu he'd picked up and was perusing. 'He wasn't violent, though? I mean, is he safe around other people?'

Lucy shook her head. 'Marie said not, but an angry man is intimidating, regardless of whether he carries through with his threats, and she felt as though she didn't have a choice but to go along with his plan. A new focus, hopefully, and a decent permanent income could change things for them all.'

'That's fine, but the rules still apply. If he puts a foot out of line, he's out,' Simon said firmly. 'Whether that's at home or at work.' He paused. 'I did make that clear to him.'

'Sometimes people deserve a second chance,' Lucy said. 'I hope Jake's sensible enough to realise that this could be his last.'

'Time will tell,' Simon replied. He paused and perused the specials board behind the counter before adding, 'So what's a pumpkin latte, then, Lucy? Will I like it?'

Lucy laughed. 'Maybe. Want to try one?'

'You're busy enough as it is,' Simon said. 'Maybe next time.'

He bade her farewell and ambled back out of the café, greeting a couple of the locals as he went. Lucy supposed he was kind of a minor celebrity in his own right, being the current Lord Treloar, but Simon managed to live a relatively normal life, even if he did have the millstone of that title around his neck.

That train of thought nearly took her back to Finn, but she stopped it in its tracks. She had enough to think about between now and Christmas without throwing old feelings into the mix. She tried to focus on what, hopefully, was a job well done. If Jake was prepared to make a go of his new job, he would be easier for Marie and their mother to live with. She vowed to try to catch up with Marie at some point and check in. She knew miracles didn't happen overnight, but it was all right to hope, wasn't it? Goodness knows she needed something to feel optimistic about right now. The prospect of a Christmas that was such a stark contrast to the previous year's was something she couldn't bear to contemplate.

45

'Finn, Finn, look this way, Finn. How do you feel about starring in *A Countess for Christmas*? Is this the comeback that the "all-American" boy wanted?'

It was the second week of October, and Finn had been psyching himself up to face the cameras on the red carpet for days. His dinner suit was beautifully cut, he was well rested, despite the jet lag, having only flown into the UK the day before, and, to all intents, purposes and onlookers, he was ready to face the world.

Finn smiled weakly into the dozen cameras and microphones that were being thrust in his direction and gave a slight nod, even though it was the last thing he wanted to do. This *was* the business, after all. 'Sure,' he replied. 'It's, uh, great to be back.'

'And what was it like working with Montana again, ten years on from your *High School Dreams* romance? Any chance of a reunion for real?'

Finn's stomach turned uncomfortably as he took a

moment to digest the question. There was always so much at stake; one wrong answer or, at least, one that could be spun the wrong way and he could be 'cancelled' in an instant. And what was he supposed to say about Montana? What could he *possibly* say? Realising that he'd zoned out for a few seconds, he refocused his attention back on the reporter.

'Never say never,' he said weakly, hoping that this was the correct response. He and Montana had discussed things at length again a few nights ago, and they'd both decided that the industry premiere of the film was not the right time to make any startling revelations. Those would come in their own time. There was no need to set the gossip mags off just yet. After all, they had the rest of their lives to sort their love lives out to both of their satisfaction.

As if on cue, a shout went up from the photographers, and, glancing around, Finn saw Montana exiting the back seat of a black limousine gracefully, looking absolutely stunning in a slinky red dress, slashed to the thigh. As she headed in his direction and wrapped him in a warm, scented embrace, the photographers went wild.

'Montana! Montana, to me! That's great. Who are you wearing? Any chance of a kiss for our Insta feed?'

'Just go with it,' Montana whispered into Finn's ear as the cameras flashed and the crowd went wild. 'We'll be inside in a minute.'

Turning back to the assembled media, Montana gave a gracious smile, and Finn, playing along, kept his arm wrapped around her waist.

'What can I say, fellas?' Montana said, megawatt smile enough to rival the flashes going off all around them. 'It's great to be back with Finn, doing a project we love. See you guys later.' She blew a kiss to the photographers, and then, snuggling protectively into Finn's arm. 'Come on,' she said, 'let's get inside.'

Finn smiled down at her. 'You really are amazing at this, you know,' he murmured. 'I'm so glad we're doing this together.'

Montana smiled back. 'Me too, you gorgeous, silly boy. Me too.' And she leaned up and kissed him on the cheek. With that, photographers and fans alike went wild.

* * *

Back in Roseford, Lucy groaned out loud and smacked her head against the cushions of the sofa. She never imagined she'd still miss him so much, but seeing Finn and Montana, impossibly glamorous, standing on the red carpet looking every inch the perfect couple, she felt as though someone had reached into her chest, grabbed her heart and was slowly ripping it apart in front of her. She took a gulp of her large glass of Chablis and closed her eyes, willing the alcohol to soothe her. The live stream of the industry premiere of *A Countess for Christmas* was being hosted by AllFeed, the biggest online news and entertainment website, and although she'd tried and tried not to switch it on, after the first glass of wine, the temptation to see Finn, even through the pixelated lens of a live feed, was just too much.

On cue, her mobile pinged with a message from Serena:

You'd better not be watching it.

In irritation, she pinged back:

I'm not.

There was a slight pause before the response came back:

Liar. Do you want me to come over?

Lucy smiled, despite herself. Texting back that she was 'absolutely fine' and the Chablis was all the company she needed, she slumped back against the cushions, watching numbly as the live stream showed the faces of the many other people involved in the production. She smiled to see Nicole and Mateo arm in arm and the crew and supporting cast all holding court for the journalists. Then, there was a final shot of all of them, on the steps of Mountbatten Hall, before the stream faded out, and a placeholder hovered onscreen with the title of the film and its official release date on FilmFlix.

It was no good, she thought as she fumbled with the remote control, and then filled up her glass again. The only solution was to have another glass of wine.

46

Much later, after the press junket had taken their (mostly figurative) pound of flesh, and he and Montana had smiled until their faces hurt for the cameras, Finn let himself into the luxurious hotel room in the steel and glass splendour of the Radisson Blu in Greenwich, chucked the jacket of his dinner suit down on one of the king-size beds, loosened his black tie, bent briefly to take off his dress shoes and then flopped back on the other bed, totally exhausted.

Premieres always did this to him; not that he'd been the star of many in recent years. He'd had a few supporting roles, but this was the first time in a long time he'd been one of the main attractions on the red carpet. His naturally introverted nature was at odds with the demands of the public role of an actor, but he'd learned to cope. Head up, smile for the cameras, be patient with the inanest of questions and don't mess up. Easy. Not.

No one would've known just what turmoil his heart was in from the performance he had put in this evening; especially when Montana had arrived and they'd really played it up for the press. Despite his shyness when the cameras stopped rolling, though, there was a part of him that hated himself for loving the adulation and the attention. Of course, being stared at was par for the course when you were an actor, but disappearing inside someone else's character was one thing; actually enjoying the attention for just being yourself was quite another. He was reminded of times when the publicity was like oxygen and he'd taken far worse substances than oxygen to deal with it. But those were far away now: the future was what was important.

All the same, he felt a sickness when he thought of Lucy sitting at home in Roseford. Had she been watching the live feed of the premiere? Probably not. She'd made it pretty clear that she didn't see herself as having a future with him, so why would she? All the same, even after all this time, he couldn't help wondering how she would have reacted when Montana did her customary megawatt-smile-wrap-her-arms-around-her-co-star routine. He knew what a performance it was, for both of them; but to the 'real' world who lived on the dopamine hit of celebrity gossip and who still yearned to see Finn and Montana make a go of it as an actual couple, there were plenty out there online who would lap it up. He resisted the urge to go to Twitter and find out how the premiere had been received. His agent would give him the potted version over the next couple of days and he had absolutely no desire to see the rabid sycophantic comments of the FinnTanas. Especially after everything they'd said about Lucy.

Lucy...

Finn was overwhelmed with tiredness. He yearned, suddenly, for something to take the edge off; to level out his mood and get him through the night. His hand hovered over the room service menu, and he knew that, if he made one phone call, he'd have a bottle of Scotch and whatever else he wanted in his possession in minutes. Outside of the order and professionalism of a hotel, in darker alleys, there was always someone who knew someone who could get other, less legal things, too.

But was that what he *really* wanted? The instant gratification of a drink, or something else, to alter his mood and stop him from feeling the acute loss that being away from Lucy had awakened? That losing her had engendered? Would it be worth the pain, on all levels? Shaking his head wearily, he picked up the phone.

47

'Come on,' Serena said brightly, the next evening. 'I'm sick of you moping around in your house. We're going out.'

Serena had travelled down to Roseford after work that day, and was standing on Lucy's doorstep looking suspiciously well groomed for a night at the pub. Lucy noticed her smart new jacket and beautifully cut black jeans, and that she was definitely wearing more make-up than usual for someone who didn't usually bother when she worked from home.

'I can't,' Lucy said flatly. 'Rob's mum's got flu, so Megan's with me this weekend, and Mum can't babysit as she's out in Taunton on a works do, so I'm staying put.'

'No, you're not,' Marie said, from where she was standing behind Serena. 'I'm here to babysit.'

'And you know how well she's been doing at the local preschool,' Serena added.

Lucy did know that; Marie, after her confession about the photographs, had managed, with a little help from Lucy, to get a full-time job in the local day nursery, and had babysat

Megan a few times on the rare occasions when Serena had dragged her out for an evening. Megan loved her, and the feeling was mutual.

Marie rummaged in her handbag. 'I've got something for you, too,' she said. She handed Lucy a slightly crumpled envelope. 'It's, er, from Jake.'

Lucy felt a jolt of surprise. Jake hadn't said a word to her since the unpleasantness with the viral photos, and she'd given up on the prospect of an apology. But as she opened the envelope, and scanned the contents of the letter, she smiled a little. It was a brief but heartfelt 'sorry' note, and it also thanked her for the hand she'd had in getting him the job at Roseford Hall.

'Simon wasn't supposed to tell him about that,' Lucy murmured. 'But then he never could keep a secret.'

'Jake's been so much better since he started working again,' Marie said. 'And his salary means that Mum can cut down on her hours, which means she's much less tired. We finally feel like we're a bit more secure.'

'I'm so glad,' Lucy said, giving Marie a quick hug. 'Megan's in the living room. Help yourself to tea and cake if you want some.'

As Marie thanked her, Serena took charge again. 'Come on, Luce!' she ordered. 'Get your lippy on and come out for a quick drink at the Treloar Arms. It's karaoke night tonight, and we both know how much singing cheers you up.' Serena chivvied her towards the stairs.

Grumbling good-naturedly, but realising that she wasn't going to get out of it that easily, Lucy ambled upstairs and did as she was told. A night out at the pub would do her good, actually. She'd barely been anywhere except the café for weeks, and she could do with escaping the four walls of her house for an hour or two. Much as she'd enjoyed bingeing the latest reality show on FilmFlix, she quite fancied a change of scene. She was grateful, though, that *A Countess for Christmas* wasn't dropping onto the channel for another week or so. She wasn't sure she'd have been able to stop herself from the pain-pleasure of seeing Finn onscreen, after all that had happened between them. Like pressing on a bruise, she'd have been compelled to watch it, no matter how much it hurt.

'Hurry up, Luce!' Serena called from the bottom of the stairs. 'Karaoke starts at eight.'

'I'm not singing,' Lucy called back. 'I'm on the wagon as of today, and I'd need at least a bottle of wine inside me to sing in front of Dave and his staff. Not to mention Big Barry Somers and his crew.' After the heavy head that had been induced by the wine she'd sunk watching the industry's coverage of the premiere of *A Countess for Christmas* last night, she'd decided to stick to Pentire or Diet Coke for a while.

Eventually, lipstick applied and hairbrush dragged through her locks, she headed back downstairs. She hadn't bothered to change; an old grey jumper and blue jeans were smart enough for the pub. Again, she noticed how smart Serena looked as she caught sight of her in the hall.

'Yeah, I'll see you in a minute,' Serena was muttering before she ended whatever call she was on.

'Who was that?' Lucy asked as she reached her friend.

'Oh, just Mum,' Serena replied blithely. 'I forgot to ask her to make up my bed in the spare room for tonight.' She blushed, which was unusual for her, but Lucy let it slide.

'Okay, let's get this over with,' Lucy said. 'I can't believe you're dragging me out for karaoke.'

'It's the best this village can offer, you know that,' Serena replied. She seemed buzzing with excitement as they walked out of Lucy's front door and towards the pub.

'What are you so happy about?' Lucy asked.

'Oh, nothing,' Serena replied. 'Come on, you'll miss your slot.'

'My *what*?' Lucy stopped dead on the pavement. 'What do you mean my slot? I'm not singing tonight.'

'Oh, don't be such a Debbie Downer,' Serena replied. 'I nipped into the pub before I knocked on your door, and I've put us in for 8.15 singing "Bootylicious". We'll make Beyoncé proud, I'm sure!'

'No. Way.' Lucy planted her feet. 'I'm going home.' She turned back to her house, but was waylaid as Serena grabbed her arm.

'Lucy, please,' Serena said softly, and Lucy noticed her eyes were shining with sudden tears. 'I really need this tonight. Come and sing with me. Just one song.'

Lucy turned back around to face her friend and, never being able to refuse her when she became emotional, gave her a big hug. 'All right,' she said. 'But only because it's you.'

They headed the short distance to the pub and braced themselves as they heard the tuneless rendition of 'Dancing Queen' that was being belted out by a group of half-cut Sixth Form students young enough to be Abba's grandchildren.

'We'll be better than them, at least.' Serena turned and grinned at Lucy as she pushed open the door of the pub.

'Don't count on it,' Lucy muttered. She was so caught up with hanging her coat up on the rack by the door, and checking that her phone wasn't on silent, that she missed Dave's announcement detailing who was up next. As the pub went strangely silent, Lucy walked through to the main bar area, and froze.

It couldn't be.

Not here.

Not now.

He'd sworn he was never going to sing in public again.

There, sitting on a high stool, microphone in hand, right next to the karaoke machine, a nervous expression on his face, but staring directly towards her, was Finn. As the opening bars of the song rolled across the pub, Lucy's knees started to knock so badly, she was in danger of providing impromptu percussion.

'What... what's *he* doing here?' Lucy whispered to Serena, who smiled gently back at her. Lucy felt as though she was going to pass out as she clutched the dado rail on the wall next to her. Then, seeing the look on Serena's face, 'You set this up, didn't you?'

'With a little help from the love of my life,' Serena said wryly, casting her gaze off to her left, where none other than Montana de Santo was sitting with Mateo and Nicole. Montana gave Lucy a wide smile. 'Now, you'd better pay attention. He's singing in public for the first time since forever, and it's all for you.'

Lucy let Serena guide her to an empty seat, and as the intro to the song came to a close, she felt the goosebumps shimmer down her spine and over her skin. The song had always been a favourite of hers: Sting's 'If I Ever Lose My Faith in You', and Finn's voice, so familiar to her from years and years of listening to him sing on *High School Dreams*, did not disappoint. A little deeper and slightly more gravelly from lack of practice than it had been in his peak television days of stardom, it sounded more personal, and much more emotional.

Realising he had an entranced audience, but with his eyes still fixed firmly on Lucy, Finn rose from the bar stool, and began to move across the room. Lucy knew she had about two and a half minutes left to compose herself and think of something to say. *What the hell are you doing here?* seemed a good place to start.

But as Finn drew closer, and the realisation that he was conquering his fear of singing, in the most public way possible, with nowhere to hide and no auto-tune to cover his cock-ups, Lucy's irritation at being stitched up by Serena and coerced into interacting with Finn in public began to dissipate.

The middle eight of the song kicked in, and Finn was almost to her table. Lucy, who barely trusted her legs to hold her up, rose from the seat Serena had found for her, and waited for Finn to get to her. In the ensuing bars of instrumental, he reached her and, tacitly asking permission with his eyes, he took her hand. The next few lines of the song were sung in a distinctly shakier tone, but, to Finn's credit, he managed to hang in there until the end, gripping Lucy's hand for dear life as he did so.

Finally, as the closing bars sounded around the pub, Finn looked down at Lucy, and she saw the mixture of nervousness and tenderness in his eyes, and just how hard it had been for him to sing again, even if it was just karaoke in the village pub.

'You did it,' she said softly, in the beat before the applause, wild and raucous, rang around the pub.

Finn nodded. 'I had to. For you. I wanted you to see that...' He trailed off, swallowed hard, and continued. 'I wanted you to see that I'd conquer anything, even this, for you. I needed to face my fears.' He glanced away from her, and ran an impatient hand over his eyes. 'Look, Lucy, can we talk? Somewhere a little quieter?'

Lucy laughed shakily. 'I thought I had a duet to do with Serena. That's how she got me here.'

Serena, with impeccable timing as ever, glided over with Montana in tow. She turned back to look at Montana, and then lifted her right hand and kissed it. 'I think we've got the duet covered.'

'Let's get out of here,' Lucy said. 'It's not cold out there. We can walk.'

'Don't be too long,' Montana said. 'The car's coming at eleven o'clock and you've got an early flight from Heathrow.'

'You're leaving again?' Lucy gasped, suddenly aware of just how much she minded.

'I'm starting a new project the day after tomorrow in Georgia,' Finn replied. 'But I don't want to talk about that now. Come on.' Still holding her hand tightly, he pulled her gently out of the pub's front door.

48

Lucy couldn't quite believe that Finn was back in Roseford, and holding her hand.

'Am I dreaming?' she asked, as they made their way out of the pub and towards the war memorial in the centre of the village.

'If you are, then so am I,' Finn said. 'Lucy, I...'

'Finn, I...'

They both trailed off, laughing nervously.

'Please, you go first,' Finn, ever the gentleman, said after a beat or two.

Lucy drew a deep breath.

'I was going to say I was sorry,' Lucy said softly. 'I reacted badly to a scary situation. I wasn't thinking about you, I was just thinking about how hurt and embarrassed I was to be put in that position. I pulled down the shutters and went straight into self-preservation mode because I didn't know how to respond. I should have given you the chance to talk to me, to explain how we could make things better, but I didn't. And for that I apologise.'

Finn shook his head. 'I should have tried to explain to you about how things might have gone, once word got out about us. I guess I'm just so used to dealing with the social media pressure that I've become desensitised to it. I forgot how much it can hurt.'

'You mean you can eventually learn to ignore it?' Lucy said.

'Not exactly,' Finn replied. 'But it stops having such power over you. It becomes background noise, rather than the centre of everything.' He pulled her close, so that she was resting against the warmth of his dark blue and grey striped rugby shirt. She could feel his heart beating frantically as she leaned in, feeling soothed by his nearness as she had when they'd been together before.

'I can't imagine it ever not upsetting me,' Lucy murmured. 'But maybe... maybe it's worth it if...' She paused.

'If?' Finn's voice grew husky. 'If what?'

Lucy drew in a deep breath, trying to steady herself. She looked up at Finn, and once again saw the tenderness in his eyes that she'd missed so much over the months since they'd parted. 'If we can find a way to be together.'

Finn's arms tightened around her, and Lucy felt the relief washing over her, that he was back here, pressed against her. She leaned up on tiptoe, and as her mouth met his, it was a kiss so gentle, so full of wonder, that her knees nearly gave way again for the umpteenth time that night. The kiss deepened, and the only thing that made them break apart was the sound of a low whistle from behind them.

'So you two are all made up then? Well, it's about time.' Mateo's voice was warm, and distinctly amused.

Lucy and Finn broke apart, and turned to face Mateo, accompanied by Nicole, Serena and Montana, who all had knowing expressions on their faces. Serena and Montana were holding hands, and Mateo had his arm slung casually around Nicole's leather-jacketed shoulders.

'Maybe there should be a triple wedding,' Mateo joked. 'Roseford certainly came good for all of us, after all.'

Finn laughed. 'We've got a lot to work out before then.'

He looked down at Lucy for confirmation, and she smiled. 'Definitely.' She shivered in the cooling autumn air. 'And I don't know about you guys, but I could really do with a cup of tea to calm my nerves.'

Montana laughed. 'That great English solution to everything.' She glanced wryly at Serena. 'Why am I not surprised?'

Just at that moment, Simon Treloar came loping up from the direction of Roseford Hall. The look of surprise on his face was something to behold.

'Hello!' he exclaimed, bringing a lively Holmes the retriever to heel before he jumped all over the people in front of him. 'Have you come back to film the sequel already?'

Finn turned and, still keeping one arm protectively around Lucy, shook Simon's hand. 'It's good to see you again, Simon.'

'You too,' Simon replied. 'Are you staying long?'

'Unfortunately, no,' Finn replied. Then, turning almost shyly to Lucy. 'But I hope to be back soon. Very soon.'

Lucy smiled up at him. 'I'd like that,' she said softly. 'Very much.'

'Well, I hate to be the one to break up the reunion,' Montana said, as Simon departed once more, towed off by a still enthusiastic Holmes, 'but if we're going to get that cup of tea in before the car comes, we'd better go now.'

Lucy laughed. 'Fair enough. Back to mine?'

As the others headed back, on the short walk to her house, Lucy pulled Finn back to her. 'I do love you,' she said softly. 'And I'm so glad you came back.' She ran a hand up his shoulder and into his hair, bringing his face close to hers again. Their kiss was deeper than before, and Lucy relished breathing him in. And this time, she couldn't care less if she ended up on Twitter.

* * *

A couple of hours later, Finn's phone buzzed, which temporarily halted the raucous laughter in Lucy's living room.

'The car's outside,' he said quietly. Then, turning to Montana, he said, 'We should go.'

Montana, who was snuggled into the sofa with Serena, nodded. 'Guess so.'

Nicole and Mateo, who were in Roseford for a few more days on a short break between projects, announced that they were back off to their room at the Treloar Arms. After hugging everyone goodbye, they left.

Serena and Montana had vanished into the hallway to say their goodbyes, leaving Finn and Lucy in the living room.

'I wish I didn't have to go,' Finn said huskily. 'I feel like there's so much more we need to say.' He ran a hand over Lucy's cheek.

'We'll have time,' Lucy said gently. 'There's all the time in the world, now.' She reached out a hand and rested it on his cheek, and he leaned into her caress. 'Promise you'll call me when you land?'

'And every hour after that,' Finn said. He gathered her up in his arms. 'God, I'm going to miss you, Lucy Cameron.'

'Come home soon,' she murmured. She held him close as long as she could, but eventually, Montana, with her lipstick thoroughly kissed off, poked her head around the living room door.

'Time to go,' she said softly. Then, she crossed the room and gave Lucy a hug. 'I'll see you soon.'

Lucy returned the hug. 'Thank you,' she whispered. 'I'm so glad you brought him here.'

Montana laughed. 'You and me both, honey. You and me both.'

A few minutes later, Serena and Lucy stood at her front door and waved to Finn and Montana's car until it disappeared over the bridge out of the village. When it was out of sight, Lucy turned to her best friend.

'Did that *really* just happen?'

Serena gave a slightly shaky smile. 'Yup.' She reached out and squeezed Lucy's hand. 'And they'll be back before you know it.'

'Doesn't it seem a bit surreal to you?' Lucy asked as she closed the front door once more. 'That we both fell in love with two stars who spent last Christmas pretending to be in love with each other?'

'Not really,' Serena deadpanned, then grinned. 'Well, okay, maybe a bit!'

As Lucy put the kettle on for a last cup of tea, she couldn't help thinking that perhaps Christmas wishes really did come true, after all.

EPILOGUE

A FILMFLIX CHRISTMAS

'Come on, Finn, it's starting!' Megan's impatient voice emanated from the living room, and Finn turned to Lucy and grinned. 'Seems like I've been given my orders.'

'Don't give her an inch,' Lucy laughed. 'Or she'll take a mile.'

'And don't forget the popcorn,' Montana called. 'I've been cutting out carbs for days for this.'

Lucy shook her head. If anyone had told her a year ago that she'd be sitting down to watch her teen idol, the man whose posters had lined her bedroom walls, in his latest Christmas movie, with the teen idol himself, his gorgeous co-star and her best friends in the world, she'd have choked on the mouthful of mulled wine she'd just taken.

Finn smiled down at her and, before he could pass her the bowl of popcorn, he slid an arm around her waist. 'I still can't believe we're here together, after everything that's happened,' he said softly. Then a frown crossed his features. 'Are you sure you're ready for this?'

Lucy smiled up at him. 'Why wouldn't I be? You're here, right now, with me. What's onscreen is a story.' She stood on tiptoe and kissed him gently on the lips. 'This is real.'

Lucy felt herself being lifted off her feet as Finn's arms tightened around her. As they broke apart, Finn was still smiling. 'It still feels a bit surreal.'

'No kidding,' Lucy said.

The months since they'd reunited in October had been some of the most pleasantly strange of Lucy's life. After they'd agreed to give their relationship another try, Finn had spent the first month in Georgia, working on his directorial debut. It was a small production, with a relatively low budget, and he'd handpicked most of the crew to ensure he had the best support network around him. Mateo was there, of course, and Nicole had stepped in as third assistant director. Kathryn, the director on *A Countess for Christmas*, had been at the end of a phone to answer any queries, but the general feeling was that Finn's eye for detail and nose for how to tell a story onscreen had made a project that had good odds of commercial success. His intention, after all, had been to get behind the camera instead of in front of it, and he'd made a great start.

Lucy, in the meantime, had been gearing up for the Christmas season, and had managed to take on another member of staff in the café, which had enabled her and Megan to fly out to Georgia for half-term week and spend some time with Finn. Then it had been back home for the usual round of Christmas events and concerts before the school holidays rolled around once more. Now, Finn had a month off, and he'd decided to spend it with Lucy, and was putting the finishing touches on his research project about his great-grandfather, which he'd developed with both Stella

Simpson and Simon Treloar's help. There was even talk of a screenplay, although that would take some time to green light.

It wasn't going to be easy, being apart when Finn was working, but Lucy had a feeling they'd cope. She'd been pleased to see that, ever since Montana and Serena had made their debut as a couple to the social media world, the heat had been taken off Finn. Serena had been welcomed, by and large, as Montana's new partner, and the trolls had been quietened by the supportive voices.

'Guys, get your asses in here, quickly,' Montana called stridently. 'You don't want to miss a minute of this.'

'There is a pause button on the remote,' Lucy called back. 'We're just, er, sorting out the snacks.'

'Uh-huh.' Montana's face, quickly followed by Serena's, appeared around the kitchen doorframe. 'If we can keep our hands off each other for an hour and a half, I don't see why you can't.' She snaked an arm around Serena's waist and gave her a quick kiss. 'So get in here and let's do this.'

Finn laughed. 'Yes, ma'am.' Then he turned back to Lucy. 'I don't usually watch anything I'm in. This is a first for me.' He laughed nervously. 'Does that sound weird?'

'Not at all,' Lucy replied gently. She was mindful of his anxiety, and couldn't resist asking, 'Are you sure you're okay to watch it this time?'

'With you next to me, I think I'll manage,' he said softly. 'So long as I can hold your hand when it gets embarrassing.'

'That's a deal,' Lucy said. 'And I've got plenty of cushions you can hide behind, too.'

'I might just take you up on that.'

'Come *on*, Mummy!' Megan's voice reached them again.

They walked hand in hand through to the living room, and

as the sleigh bells in the opening bars of *A Countess for Christmas*'s soundtrack echoed through the surround-sound speakers, and the title appeared onscreen, Finn playfully hid behind Lucy in embarrassment.

'You can sit next to me, Finn,' Megan called, wriggling off the sofa and grabbing the bowl of popcorn from his hands as he emerged again.

Lucy smiled broadly at the sight of her daughter and Finn settling back down together, getting ready to watch the film. She'd fallen for a fairy tale last Christmas, but this year, she'd fallen in love with the real thing.

ACKNOWLEDGMENTS

I can't believe I'm doing this for the eighth time! And, as ever, there are so many people to thank. Firstly, my fab agent, Sara Keane, for the help and support with this one. Then, of course, the marvellous Boldwood team: Sarah Ritherdon, the best editor a writer could ever want, Nia Beynon, Claire Fenby, Megan Townsend, Caroline Ridding, Jenna Houston, Laura Kingston, Emily Ruston, Tara Loder, Emily Yau and the brilliant and visionary Amanda Ridout for giving my novels such a wonderful platform. That also goes for the wonderful family of Boldwood authors, who are such a supportive and friendly team.

I'd also like to give a huge shout-out to the absolutely wonderful, velvet-voiced Harriett Hare who has brought my novels to life with her fabulous audio readings, too. Harriett's voice is the perfect match for my novels, and I encourage you to go and listen to the audio versions! Also, many thanks to Sandra Ferguson and Cecily Blench for being excellent proof and copy editors respectively.

This book was such a blast to write, mainly because I wanted it to have All the Christmas, Ever, and to really tap into what makes a fun, escapist Christmas story. When it came to style models for this book, I had to look no further than the amazing Vanessa Hudgens, Rose McIver, Oscar Isaac and, with a pang in my heart, the late Cory Monteith, to fulfil my visions of Montana, Lucy, Mateo and Finn. Vanessa and Rose are, of course, stalwarts of the Christmas movie genre, and Oscar was the only person I had in mind for the charming and charismatic Mateo Torres. I can't help thinking that Cory would have made a wonderful Finn Sanderson, which is why this book is dedicated to his memory. Watching *Glee* during the writing of it has a lot to answer for (as well as giving me Finn's first name, of course!). One final mention, cast wise, to my gorgeous, lovely cousin Serena Bicknell, who let me borrow her first name for Lucy's wonderful, supportive best friend.

I'd like to give extra special thanks to Nicky Lianos for all of the insights into how a location film set works. All subsequent errors are my own! Also, a shout-out to Steph and Harry Blythe and their gorgeous dog, Watson, who provided the inspiration for the lively and lovely Holmes the retriever.

As ever, these books wouldn't get written without the support of my wonderful friends and family – Nick, Flora and Rosie all have endless patience when my head is in the clouds of a story, as does everyone who has to endure me during this time. Thank you all!

And finally, I'd like to thank you, the reader, for walking with me on another narrative adventure – my readership means so much to me, and it's always lovely to hear from you! Thanks for showing up again and allowing me to entertain you. Remember, you can sign up to my mailing list to find out about upcoming events and books, too: https://mailchi.mp//1b4d64d563ad/3n36l8i2mn.

See you next time!

MORE FROM FAY KEENAN

We hope you enjoyed reading *Winter Kisses at Roseford Café*. If you did, please leave a review.

If you'd like to gift a copy, this book is also available as an ebook, digital audio download and audiobook CD.

Sign up to Fay Keenan's mailing list for news, competitions and updates on future books.

http://bit.ly/FayKeenanNewsletter

A Place To Call Home, another heart-warming read from Fay Keenan, is available to buy now.

ABOUT THE AUTHOR

Fay Keenan is the author of the bestselling *Little Somerby* series of novels. She has led writing workshops with Bristol University and has been a visiting speaker in schools. She is a full-time teacher and lives in Somerset.

Visit Fay's website: https://faykeenan.com/

Follow Fay on social media:

facebook.com/faykeenanauthor

twitter.com/faykeenan

instagram.com/faykeenan

bookbub.com/authors/fay-keenan

Boldw**oo**d

Boldwood Books is an award-winning fiction publishing company seeking out the best stories from around the world.

Find out more at www.boldwoodbooks.com

Join our reader community for brilliant books, competitions and offers!

Follow us
@BoldwoodBooks
@BookandTonic

Sign up to our weekly deals newsletter

https://bit.ly/BoldwoodBNewsletter

Printed in Great Britain
by Amazon